His Wicked Highland Ways

by

Laura Strickland

His Wicked Highland Ways

Cover Art by *Diana Carlile*

The Wild Rose Press, Inc.
PO Box 708
Adams Basin, NY 14410-0708
Visit us at www.thewildrosepress.com

Publishing History
First Tea Rose Edition, 2015
Print ISBN 978-1-62830-888-4
Digital ISBN 978-1-62830-889-1

The man arose from the pool stark naked and dripping wet, like a god newly formed. Jeannie took another half step backward and blinked, not entirely believing the sight that met her eyes: some six foot of male, all rippling muscles, scars, and tattoos, with a curtain of sopping red-brown hair that slapped his shoulder blades, and a handsome, dangerous face. His eyes were tawny brown, almost the same color as his hair, and spiked by wet, black lashes. But after one glance, Jeannie could not make herself look there.

Instead her gaze dropped—and dropped. Sweet, merciful heaven! Was that how men came equipped? She might be a widow in name, but she had never seen her husband, Geordie, naked. Theirs had not been that kind of relationship, or that kind of marriage.

But she had an eyeful now, right enough, and for the life of her could not keep from staring. What a ridiculous, daunting, and marvelous appendage! How did men ever manage to walk around like that?

But this man did not attempt to walk. He merely stood in the shallow pool with the water lapping around his…Jeannie's strained mind supplied the word "weapon"…and gazed at her as if he found her as hard to fathom as she found him.

Praise for Laura Strickland

"The world building is phenomenal."

~Daysie W. at My Book Addiction and More

~*~

"Laura Strickland creates a world that not only draws you in, but she incorporates it…seamlessly. …the kind of book that keeps you awake well into the wee hours, and sighing with satisfaction when you've finished the very last page."

~Nicole McCaffrey, author

~*~

"As I read I became so involved with the story, I found it difficult to put down the book…. Definitely…an author to watch."

~Dandelion at Long & Short Reviews

~*~

"A fascinating historical world, and engaging characters,…brilliant lines of dialogue and a few laugh-out-loud moments, to ease the tension from the underlying violence."

~Helen at Love Romances and More

Dedication

This one's for Adrienne,
with thanks for her unflagging support
and her ever-vigilant eagle eye

Chapter One

Argyle, Scotland, August 1750

"I hear he is a terrible, wicked man," Aggie said, her voice rife with scandal, "a typical highlander, always flashing his dirk or his sword, going off his head with temper and committing vile murder, or worse."

Jeannie Robertson MacWherter, hunched over her small plot of garden beneath the surprisingly warm August sun, wiped the sweat from her brow with the back of one filthy hand and shot a look of annoyance at her companion, Aggie Moffat. Though ostensibly Jeannie's servant—and her only one—Aggie had in truth become far more since the death of Jeannie's father last year. Now Jeannie bit her tongue, pushed away her irritation, and reminded herself just how dear to her Aggie was.

"Have you been gossiping again?" she asked sternly. "You know what I told you about believing everything you hear."

Aggie looked stricken. Back in Dumfries, from whence the two women hailed, she had gathered snippets of news and wild stories the way other women might gather flowers, and treasured them as tenderly. But things were different here in Argyle. Jeannie wanted to start new, keep her nose—and that of her maid—clean.

1

"Well, but," Aggie said in earnest self-defense, her lowland brogue coloring every word, "it is just so dull here. I do vow, mistress, I will perish if something interesting does not happen soon."

Jeannie understood the sentiment. The two of them had been in residence at the small stone house in Glen Rowan since May, and life could not be more different from the bustle and clatter of Dumfries. Jeannie had been totally unprepared for the quiet, the deep, seamless dark that fell at night, and the isolation of the glen.

Only three houses occupied the small valley set like a green jewel cupped in God's hand half way between Oban and Glencoe. One belonged to the landed family Avrie, the other—near the head of the glen and currently unoccupied—to the man Aggie now decried. With so little to talk about, Jeannie could only sympathize with Aggie's exaggeration.

Still, Jeannie could not permit such chatter, especially of a stranger.

"You've been listening to the folks at Avrie House again, have you?" she accused and added, not giving Aggie a chance to answer, "Anyway, what could be worse than murder?"

Aggie took the second question as an invitation and lowered her voice to a throb. Her plain, somewhat homely face, enlivened by a pair of truly beautiful blue eyes, acquired the glow with which she always imparted what she termed news. "I am speaking of him having his way with women, of course."

Jeannie experienced a twinge of disquiet. The man in question—one Finnan MacAllister—had been a friend of her late husband, Geordie, and was arguably the last person Jeannie wished to encounter. Yet she owed her presence here at this peaceful refuge to him.

Now dismay caused her to sit back on her heels and regard Aggie fiercely. "Are you speaking of rape? Because, if you are, that is a very grave accusation to make." Not that Jeannie felt inclined to defend the man, but fair was fair, as her father had always said—at least when he was sober.

"Well," Aggie admitted with a touch of remorse, "not that, maybe, but he definitely works his wiles on them and is far too persuasive, if you know what I mean."

"I certainly do not. If you say he seduces women, we have nothing to worry about. It is surely difficult to do from a distance." To Jeannie's knowledge, Finnan MacAllister was not in residence at the big stone house, Dun Mhor, and had not been since her arrival.

Of course he did not have to be in residence to make his intentions felt. Jeannie's mind shied away from the letter even now tucked into a chest in her bedroom. She had not told Aggie about that dreadful missive, nor would she.

"They say," Aggie continued with renewed enjoyment, "he has had every woman in the glen."

"Oh, has he?" Jeannie could not keep the sarcasm from her voice. It made no great number from whom to choose—the old Dowager Avrie at Avrie House, her various servants, and presumably the wives of her landsmen. "And from whom did you get this nugget of knowledge? Dorcas, in Mistress Avrie's kitchen?"

Jeannie knew for a fact Aggie stole away and walked the short distance to Avrie House for a cup of tea whenever she could. But the Dowager Avrie's cook, whom Jeannie had met on two occasions, was clearly a harridan with a mean streak and a spiteful tongue.

Not that Jeannie thought well of Finnan MacAllister. Far from it. And he, from the tone of his letter, clearly thought very ill of her in return.

You have no right to occupy the premises at Rowan Cottage and will vacate immediately, he had written in a heavy, black, yet—for a reputed murdering savage—very respectable hand. *This missive will serve as your notice. I give you thirty days to remove yourself.*

It had been dated 15 June. It was now 16 August, and the wicked Finnan had not appeared in the glen to enforce his demand.

"Has he," Jeannie added spitefully, "had Dorcas and that awful cohort of hers, Marie?" Marie, a squat troll of a woman, had a tongue like a wasp. Jeannie had loathed her on sight.

"Well, no."

"Then he has not 'had' every woman in the glen, has he?" Jeannie challenged. "Be careful what you say, Aggie. I wish a peaceful life here, and a clean start."

Besides, everyone at Avrie House obviously detested Finnan MacAllister even more than Jeannie did herself. They might have good reason, or they might not; it was scarcely Jeannie's place to tell. The Avries had once owned this beautiful glen. It was rumored Finnan MacAllister had schemed and cheated it away from them and precipitated the death of Lady Avrie's son. But that, too, was gossip.

"Now," she urged more briskly, "help me weed this pitiful crop, or we shall have nothing to eat this winter."

Jeannie, a city lass born and bred, made no fit gardener. Everything she had planted, from parsnips to cabbage, struggled and wilted. The soil here seemed determined to thwart her every effort.

"Yes, miss," Aggie agreed. She enjoyed the garden even less than Jeannie. At least Jeannie appreciated being out in the sweet air and the views of enclosing, purple-clad hills.

Aggie bent to pull a weed, but her tongue, once unhinged, seemed to defy restraint. "They say he's slaughtered two score men or more."

That, Jeannie might be willing to believe. Her husband, Geordie, had once been Finnan MacAllister's brother-at-arms. They had served together, so Geordie confided, when they first took up their swords as mercenaries. When in his cups—which happened frequently—Geordie spoke of old battles and his friend Finnan's ferocity in a fight. None could best him, and few stood before him. Even by Geordie's account, and Geordie had virtually worshipped the man, Finnan had few scruples beyond survival.

"They say," Aggie went on with relish, "his sword is enchanted. The one time he was nearly beheaded occurred only because that blade fell from his hand."

Yes, and on that occasion Geordie had been there to save Finnan's life. Jeannie, still balanced on her heels, looked about this place she had, in only four short months, come to love—hers through a bequest made to her now-deceased husband in gratitude for that very moment.

Finnan MacAllister, so Geordie had said, never forgot his friends. Nor his enemies.

Despite the warmth of the day, a chill traced its way up Jeannie's spine. She had in all honesty not loved her husband, but he had offered her protection when she desperately needed it. Geordie MacWherter had been a drunkard, a wild Highlander, a former mercenary living a ruined life. But he'd had a gentle heart. And this refuge he had left her remained all she had in the world.

She thrust her trowel into the thin, rocky earth and rooted up a stubborn weed. Funny how weeds were all that wanted to grow here. Gorse, bracken, and heather, along with a hundred other specimens she could not name, thrived without care, while her poor vegetables struggled.

Ah, but the weeds belonged here; her transplants did not. Just as, perhaps, she did not.

"I want you to promise you will not go to Avrie House and gossip with those two vipers," she said firmly. Aggie had promised before and what good had that done? "The Dowager Avrie is very ill, and I would not have her upset by idle chatter."

"She's dying," Aggie said with no perceptible decrease in enjoyment. "Not expected to last the winter. And anyway, there's no one else with whom I can visit save the women in Avrie's kitchen. I swear, miss, I will go mad here in this Highland prison."

"Prison? How can you say so? Just look at that view."

"But these nasty, tiny flies bite all the time. The more I sweat, the more they bite. The weather is abominable—"

"Not today."

"Not today, no. But how many times have we been caught out in one of those storms that blow up without warning?"

More times than Jeannie could count. The rain

swooped in from the sea beyond the hills, and she had frequently been drenched to the skin. This was a strange, wild place, but beautiful also.

"I know it is not easy." She reached out and covered Aggie's hand with her own. "And I cannot express how grateful I am that you agreed to accompany me."

Aggie's eyes immediately filled with tears. "Where else would I be? We've been together since we were both children and your dear, sainted father was kind enough to take me in."

Jeannie's dear, sainted father, who had determinedly drunk his way through all they owned, leaving her penniless.

She squeezed Aggie's fingers warmly. "This is an adjustment for us. It's lonely, and the nights are long." Enough, sometimes, to spur a woman to madness. "But spreading gossip among our neighbors will not help."

With a rush of earnest righteousness, Aggie said, "Very well, then, I will not spread gossip. But say I may still go to Avrie House, miss."

"For heaven's sake, why?"

Aggie's cheeks grew pink, and her eyes gleamed. "Have you seen Lady Avrie's groom, miss?"

"I have not."

"Young he is, and not ill-favored." Again, Aggie lowered her voice. "And you know, miss, a girl might live in this wilderness without many things, but not the attentions of a man."

Chapter Two

Finnan MacAllister floated just below the surface of the pool, communing with a trout. The water—still cool even on this warm August day—lapped about his naked body, and his submerged ears were privy to all sorts of gurgles and ripples he told himself made up the fish's language. His hair floated out around his head in a mop of reddish brown, and his eyes, wide open, stared up through the water at the achingly blue sky.

If he kept very still, the trout in this pool would come to him and impart their knowledge, whisper it right in his ear perhaps. God knew he was in need of some wisdom. For the past ten years, ever since taking up his sword in defiance of a broken heart, his existence had gone from bad to worse. Everything he had done had come back in some way upon him.

Now that lowland bitch had set foot here in his glen. Worse, she'd taken up residence in the haven he had meant for Geordie. Ire spiked in his breast and chased away the ease his time in the water earned him. The grasping she-devil had broken his best friend's heart, and Finnan meant to exact revenge—just as soon as he discovered what would hurt her most.

The cool, silken body of a trout brushed his cheek, and he held his breath, lungs bursting. When he had been a lad in this glen, he'd been able to stay under water for the count of two hundred. These days he had lost the art, but if the trout meant to whisper to him, he would damn sure exert himself.

The trout, not just a fish but a creature of mystery and magic, carried great wisdom, according to the old tales by which Finnan lived. One way to acquire that wisdom was to kill and eat it, or threaten to eat it, for in such an instance the trout often bargained for mercy.

Finnan showed mercy to few men, but animals were different. He'd once beaten a man half to death for flogging a tired horse, and had killed a man for abusing a hound. He whispered an ancient prayer for forgiveness whenever he went hunting, and the idea of killing a trout violated all he believed.

And what did he believe? He knew what people said about him, that he had no moral sense at all. He did, but he'd acquired it the hard way, through loss and necessity.

The trout brushed his other ear, and he heard a whisper through the gurgle of the water. He would have to break the surface soon in order to breathe.

He thought, *Tell me.*

Bargain for peace.

Peace. It was the one thing he truly lacked and the most difficult to find. He now had wealth and material gain. He even had a measure of satisfaction. He'd regained this place he loved more than his own life. To his surprise, none of that had brought him happiness. And no peace.

How? he asked the trout.

When you love your enemy, peace will conquer your heart.

Ah, what drivel was this? Love his enemy? Aye, and he had expected better of the trout.

9

He broke the surface with his lips, took a big breath, and settled back again. He might not get the answers he wanted, but the water washed away his rage, if not his sins. And how bonny the day looked through the fluid screen before his eyes—that blue sky with one or two white clouds sailing, the leaves of a rowan tree that leaned over the bank. He did not want to think about anything.

Certainly not of the traitorous woman he needed to chase from his glen. Anger whipped through him once more at the thought of her. Treacherous lowland hussy—born, no doubt, to trick and deceive. How could Geordie have been taken in by her? Yet there had been a childlike quality about Geordie MacWherter beneath all his courage and bluster. Geordie had believed in love the way Finnan believed in magic. Indeed, it had been one of the things they talked about during their weary, hopeless nights or the terrifying ones before a battle.

Geordie, like Finnan himself, had been dispossessed, surviving by the sword and longing for things he could not have: a home of his own, someone who would wait for him there, a family. No doubt this lowland bitch, this Jeannie Robertson—or MacWherter, now that she'd wangled marriage to Geordie—had seen that longing in Geordie's eyes and taken advantage.

The trout brushed against his left cheek and shoulder. *Peace*, it whispered again.

Ha! There would be no peace until he paid that trollop back in full and chased her from the glen.

He thought of the letter even now tucked into his traveling pouch, the last he had ever received from Geordie.

I have done everything I can think to make her love me, but she will not. I am not sure I can go on this way, for I love her more than my own life.

The next Finnan had heard, his friend, his brother-in-arms with whom he had shared the long trail through battle and every sort of hardship, was dead—betrayed.

He broke the surface again and took another great breath, an angry one this time, before letting himself sink back.

And now she thought she could invade this place he had sweated and bled to regain, and occupy the home Finnan had saved for Geordie. Staked her claim because she was Geordie's widow. Ah, but she had no idea with whom she was dealing.

He closed his eyes, deliberately seeking a return of his elusive calm, and whispered a prayer not for mercy but success. Men about to enter battle frequently reinforced their belief in magic. Finnan had seldom failed to take up his sword without speaking a prayer or performing a small ritual. And this fight against the Widow MacWherter would be a battle of the most sacred kind.

"Favor me," he whispered to the trout and to the water.

Above him the light flickered. He opened his eyes and beheld a vision.

All blurred and ethereal it looked, seen through the medium of the water, like a reflection of light. Yet he could not mistake it for anything but the form of a woman leaning over the bank to peer at him—graceful and slender, with a bright halo of gold about her head and wide, curious blue eyes. They widened still further when she glimpsed him and realized what he was. Her lips parted like those of a child beholding a wonder.

Finnan moved in reaction, and the water around him rippled. Or was that the trout chuckling?

The woman withdrew but, he knew, not far. He could feel her there even as he cursed himself for his incaution. His weapons, like his clothes, lay on the bank. Yet she, a mere woman, could present no real danger.

Then why did his every instinct cry out in warning?

Seldom had Finnan MacAllister been caught off guard. Only look what the search for knowledge brought, he chastised himself. How had he forgotten his own rule? A man could never, never let down his defenses.

Chapter Three

The man arose from the pool stark naked and dripping wet, like a god newly formed. Jeannie took another half step backward and blinked, not entirely believing the sight that met her eyes: some six foot of male, all rippling muscles, scars, and tattoos, with a curtain of sopping red-brown hair that slapped his shoulder blades, and a handsome, dangerous face. His eyes were tawny brown, almost the same color as his hair, and spiked by wet, black lashes. But after one glance, Jeannie could not make herself look there.

Instead her gaze dropped—and dropped. Sweet, merciful heaven! Was that how men came equipped? She might be a widow in name, but she had never seen her husband, Geordie, naked. Theirs had not been that kind of relationship, or that kind of marriage.

But she had an eyeful now, right enough, and for the life of her could not keep from staring. What a ridiculous, daunting, and marvelous appendage! How did men ever manage to walk around like that?

But this man did not attempt to walk. He merely stood in the shallow pool with the water lapping around his...Jeannie's strained mind supplied the word "weapon"...and gazed at her as if he found her as hard to fathom as she found him.

Ah, and she never should have walked so far down the glen. But dearly as she loved Aggie, Jeannie sometimes needed to escape her chatter, and the beautiful day had lured her on.

Into danger, clearly. Who was he? Obviously someone of ill repute, a traveler, a dangerous outlaw, a madman. What if he decided to use that terrible weapon on her, and she on her own?

Instead he spoke the way a man might to a frightened horse. "There, now, no need to be afraid. I'll not harm you."

Jeannie took another judicious step backward. If she ran, would he be able to catch her? No doubt, given those long, muscular legs.

She shook her head, and her hair tumbled about her shoulders. Never well-disciplined, the yellow curls invariably escaped their pins, and she'd lost most of those on her walk down the glen.

He spoke again, in a voice smooth as warmed honey, lilting, and very Highland. "Where are you from, lass? You'll be a maid at Avrie House, no doubt." Deliberately he snagged his plaid, which lay on the bank, and wrapped it around his waist.

"Why were you lying in the water?" Jeannie forced her voice past suddenly stiff lips. "I thought you dead, drowned."

"Did you, now?"

Jeannie curled her lip. "Well, I do not usually go peering at naked men."

He smiled, to devastating effect. Mischief lit his face and brightened the oddly colored eyes. "So I would imagine. What is your name?"

"Neither do I go about giving my name to strangers."

"Wise lass." He stepped from the pool onto the

bank, every muscle rippling once again. By heaven, he made a splendid sight, with that mane of hair flowing over his back, broad shoulders complete with several scars, and a supple chest decorated with tattoos and a line of brown hair that led straight downward like a roadway to temptation.

Jeannie shook herself, a woman emerging from a dream.

"I will just call you 'Bonnie,' shall I?" he continued. "For bonny you certainly are."

Jeannie edged back another step. On the bank, even in his bare feet, he loomed over her. Why didn't she just run? Perhaps because she felt like a mouse before a hawk—if she ran, he would swoop in upon her, and then…

"Are you a rover?" Jeannie eyed the rest of his clothing, still on the bank: worn leather boots, a leather vest, and what looked like leggings. "A poacher?"

"Nay." He drew himself up and then made her a magnificent bow, very much like some pagan deity. "I am lord of this place."

Oh, no. Jeannie caught her breath while alarm skittered through her still more strongly. He was the wicked man, the one Aggie had been busy describing only yesterday afternoon. Yes, and wicked he did look—every inch of him.

Jeannie more than believed the stories now. Yet he had once been her husband's friend, Geordie's very closest companion. She should tell him who she was. But the words stuck in her throat. "I must go," she said instead.

"Wait." He held out a hand; Jeannie narrowed her gaze upon it in fascination. Brown from the sun, unexpectedly graceful and long-fingered, it—like the rest of him—was marked by scars, one of which bisected the tattoo of a running horse, all spiraled lines rendered in the Celtic fashion. "Do not go just yet. 'Tis not often I see a vision walking."

His gaze, marked by those absurd dark lashes, examined her in a deliberate, leisurely way, hovered over her mouth, moved to her bosom, and swept down her body in a look as tangible as a touch. Despite her native caution and despite knowing who he was, something inside Jeannie melted in that heat. Indeed, this man would have had his way with women—scores of them. Perhaps hundreds. *Wicked.*

"I am no vision," she retorted as stridently as she could. "I am…" But the words would not come. She thought again of the harsh letter hidden back home, and tried to equate its elegant script and wording with this savage. It was obvious he must have had a lawyer write it for him. Yet the signature, a bold scrawl that read *Finnan MacAllister*, had been made in the same hand.

He took a step toward her. "'Tis warm and pleasant here in the sun. And I am sure we could find a way to pass an hour or two."

An hour or two? She doubted she would survive ten minutes at his hands. Or maybe she would. Perhaps touching him would change her at some fundamental level, call up the primal woman she suddenly suspected lurked inside.

Nonsense. She had been raised a decent, moral woman in the sane if sometimes difficult world of lowland Dumfries. She needed no truck with a Highland wild man. Yet she stood, precisely like the mouse before the hawk she'd pictured, while he took another step closer.

Oh, and she could see him so much more clearly now, the individual droplets of water gathered on his skin, the sheen of hair around taut, hard nipples, the utterly fascinating array of tattoos. A woman might spend all afternoon tracing them with her fingers, one by one.

He asked softly, his voice pure music, "Will you get in trouble wi' your mistress if you are no' home soon?"

She was already in trouble, standing on quicksand that sank away beneath her feet. She shook her head.

"Well, then," he crooned, "you can stay and welcome me home. I ha' been away a while, but I have come back now with just a wee bit of business before me."

"What sort of business?" Jeannie asked. As if she did not know. Yet he thought her a simple housemaid, his for the charming and taking.

"I've a she-devil to see on her way, a right cuckoo, who has taken up residence in the wrong nest."

"Oh?"

"Aye, but she'll get her comeuppance soon enough. How long have you been at Avrie House? I will fair admit, I do not remember you. And I would remember such a face."

He took yet another step closer. Barely a whisper now separated them. He reached out with that beautiful hand toward Jeannie's cheek, and the breath froze in her lungs.

All sorts of thoughts and wanton images immediately flooded her mind. She wanted to tear that plaid from his loins. She wanted to throw herself down on the mossy bank, hike up her skirts, and offer herself to him in a primal dance attended by the warm air, the warmer sun, the earth, and the water of the pool. She wanted to taste him, starting with his lips and working her way downward. Of course, she told herself a bit wildly, she would do none of those things. But he possessed a potent—and wicked—magic.

She imagined his warm, strong fingers curling round her face and into her hair, the sensation both beguiling and possessing, but she took a decisive step back out of his reach and fixed him with a fierce stare.

"Wait." Now she spoke the word, her voice a-quiver. Hauling on every bit of courage and determination she owned, she looked up into his eyes.

She'd been mistaken—they weren't just tawny brown but flecked with gold and copper that caught the light like the peaty trout pool. All his intelligence shone there, along with that bright desire, an entirely potent combination.

She told him, "I am not who you think."

A smile lifted the corners of his mouth, revealing two dimples. "Who are you, then? A fairy woman come walking from the nearest *sidhe*? You are surely enchanting enough."

"I am the cuckoo you wish to chase from the nest."

Yes, and his wits moved very swiftly indeed. With a hiss very like that of a snake, he withdrew his hand without having touched her, and the expression in his eyes changed from teasing warmth to hard disparagement. He leaped back so quickly he tottered on the edge of the pool.

"You?" His gaze measured her in a new way, dismissing the brightness of her hair, rejecting her face

18

and form. "I should have known. Geordie said you were beautiful—and coldhearted."

"He said that of me?" Despite herself, Jeannie felt surprised.

"Aye, did you think he would not write his nearest friend, telling the events of his life?"

Jeannie thought Geordie had spent his days and nights too sore drunk to pick up a pen or put it to paper. She did not say so. Instead she voiced the obvious. "You are Finnan MacAllister."

"I am." He straightened his spine, and Jeannie experienced a sharp echo of the attraction that had so nearly undone her. "And you are the scheming trollop who broke my friend's heart."

Chapter Four

Well, so this was Jeannie Robertson—Jeannie MacWherter now, to give the she-devil her due. Geordie had married the wench fairly, even if he had lived to regret it. Finnan told himself he should have expected her to be this beautiful. Geordie was not the man to give his heart easily. Beneath all his muscle and bluster, Geordie had cherished a vision of the perfect woman, carried many years.

Finnan stood on the bank of the pool with the warm sun striking his back and regarded the woman with distaste. As young mercenaries, he and Geordie had fought their way across most of Scotland, seducing whatever women crossed their paths. But that was just coupling, an act as basic as enjoying a flagon of ale. Through it all Geordie always saved a part of himself because Geordie believed in the real thing: love.

How many nights—or days—had Finnan and Geordie, lying beneath the high, distant stars or huddled in the rain, talked about *someday?*

Someday, for Finnan, had always meant coming home and regaining possession of this sacred place, taking it from the grasping fingers of his enemies. He'd done that, and the glen possessed his heart.

For Geordie, *someday* had always centered around a woman—the perfect woman. "We'll have a home, Finn, a real home, and I won't have to go wandering any more. She won't want me to go wandering because she'll miss me so. She will be beautiful, warm, and true—and she'll love only me."

Geordie believed he had found that woman when he met Jeannie Robertson. Finnan still remembered the words scrawled on the paper in Geordie's difficult hand.

She is everything I ever imagined, everything a man could want, sweet, kind, beautiful, and with a good head on her shoulders. She looks like an angel, with golden hair and eyes so blue I cannot think straight when I gaze into them.

Aye, and she did look like an angel, Finnan admitted, glaring at her now—the treacherous wench. Treacherous she must be, for that had been only the first of Geordie's letters, penned before she took his heart into her hands and shredded it.

But how dare she appear so innocent? The curve of her cheek, which he longed to touch, was sweet and rounded as that of a child; those blue eyes looked guileless, and the same deep shade as the sky over her head. Her body, well-curved also, pulled at him from beneath her plain clothing with a promise equal parts chastity and seduction. He ached to strip that drab brown dress from her, just to see what lay beneath.

Had she, indeed, been a housemaid, he might well have had his way with her. He shuddered, an involuntary reaction.

"Did you no' receive my letter?" he demanded. "The one bidding you leave Rowan cottage?"

"I did."

"Then why are you still here?" He added viciously, "You are not wanted."

She licked her lip nervously, calling up a lie, no doubt. Against Finnan's will, his gaze followed the motion of her tongue.

"As Geordie's widow, I have a right to occupy his home."

Finnan experienced a flash of rage. "The home I kept for *him*, not you."

"As his wife…"

Finnan let her get no farther. "Aye, you made damn sure of that, did you not? Buttoned it up all legal."

"Mr. MacAllister, I am not quite sure why you have formed such a hard opinion of me."

"Geordie was my brother-in-arms. Have you any idea what that means?"

"Certainly." She raised that delectably rounded chin. "It indicates a close bond."

"Bond? We were more than bonded. We were brothers beneath the skin. I would have done anything to defend him." He added with a flash, "I would still."

"Admirable." Her chin jerked up still further. "Then where were you when he needed you in Dumfries?"

"Eh?" Did the bitch seek to chastise him? "Aye, I would have done well to be there and keep him from your grasp."

"Think what you will, Master MacAllister."

"Laird MacAllister."

"What?"

"'Tis what I am, and what you will call me. I worked hard, suffered and bled, to claim this glen, and it is mine, every leaf and stone of it."

"Oh?" Mockery invaded those seemingly sweet blue eyes. "Is it hard work, then, terrorizing a helpless old woman?"

"If you are speaking of Lady Avrie, there is naught helpless about that old *cailloch*."

"She is eighty years old."

"And she bred a nest of vipers more terrible than she. I have already dealt with her son. Her grandsons have taken fright and run away."

Jeannie Robertson—MacWherter—sneered at him. "Most honorable."

"How dare you toss that word at me?" She, who had schemed over a man's most vulnerable possession, his heart.

"I am surprised you know its meaning. We have heard of you since coming here, Laird MacAllister. It seems there is little to which you will not stoop for your own gain."

He smiled viciously. "You had better believe it. Now will you take warning and vacate Rowan Cottage?"

"I will not."

"Then run on your way, Mistress MacWherter. But I warn you—best to watch your back."

****

Jeannie, calling hard on her dignity, walked away from Finnan MacAllister, trembling in every limb and willing herself not to let him see how badly her knees wobbled beneath her. The vile bully! Did he think he could threaten and verbally bludgeon her into leaving the only home she and Aggie had?

Oh, why had she walked so far, and why lingered? Why peered into the peaty-brown pool at the place where he lay? She should have kept to her own patch of ground.

What made him want her gone from here so very badly? She pondered the question even as she trod the path home beside the sparkling burn, in the warm sunshine, past Avrie house with its grim, gray walls, buttoned tight. Why did he despise her so? Her mind worried the question the way a terrier worried a rat. He did not even know her, save as the wife of his friend.

And, for that matter, why had he not been there for Geordie, if their ties remained as close as he claimed? In Dumfries, Geordie had no one but Jeannie's father and, later, Jeannie herself. Had Laird MacAllister any idea how far his friend had fallen? Did he know how Geordie died?

Well, and he certainly did not seem the man to sit calmly and listen to her explanations. She saw again the flash of rage in those unusual eyes of his that turned them from warm to terrifying. A wild, unstable, and admittedly attractive creature he seemed—undoubtedly every bit as wicked as everyone said. Did he have the right to toss her and Aggie out of the cottage? If so, where would they go in all the wide world?

Disquiet speared through her, and her knees trembled harder. What would she tell Aggie? And how to fight this man, with all his confidence? It seemed the only thing he detested more than Jeannie might be the Avries. Could she seek to band together with them in order to defy him? But the Dowager Lady Avrie was just an old woman, and sick at that.

Yet the Avries might have the wherewithal to hire a lawyer, as Jeannie did not. She resolved to speak with Lady Avrie soon. It seemed her only option.

What had her father always said about highlanders? Angus Robertson, lowland bred and born, had decried his countrymen to the north as undisciplined. "Scratch a highlander, Daughter, and you will find a savage. They might play at being civilized, but do not ever believe it. They sit up there in those mountains and brood about old wrongs while sharpening their swords and dreaming of spilling blood. As for righteousness—their kirk is whatever land they can hold, and the only place they consider holy."

Jeannie stopped in her trek—or, were she honest, flight—and gazed about herself at the glen. Who could blame a man for believing all this beauty revealed the hand of God as truly as stone pillars and stained glass? Especially a man like Finnan MacAllister, who chose to lie naked in the water and then arose like some hero in an ancient legend.

She saw again the way he moved, and the tattoos that coursed over that body rippling with muscle. Another shiver traced its way up her spine, long and slow—this time caused not by fear but by longing.

Chapter Five

Finnan MacAllister scowled at the page that lay before him, half covered in his own bold, dark hand. The letter to his lawyer, one William Cunningham of Edinburgh, impinged the man to use every legal means at his disposal to evict the Widow MacWherter from Rowan Cottage. Finnan smiled grimly to himself. What sort of monster did that make him, seeking to dispossess a widow and desperate to defeat an aging dowager? The very monster Jeannie MacWherter thought him, no doubt.

He remembered—and not for the first time since their encounter—the way she looked at him, the fear and distrust that flooded those beautiful eyes when she guessed his identity. Oh, aye, they were glorious eyes that had lured poor Geordie to his doom.

But he, Finnan, not the man to fall victim to such charms, meant to serve her as she deserved. He frowned at the paper and clutched the pen in his hand.

Would tossing her out of Geordie's house do that? Would she not just scuttle away back to the lowlands—admittedly precisely where she belonged—to wreak her deceits on some other benighted man? How would that provide Geordie justice?

Nay, but he wanted her to suffer, needed her to feel what Geordie had felt, the disappointment and betrayal.

He wanted her to experience in full the harm she

had done.

He abandoned his letter, arose, and went to the window, where he gazed out. The fine, fair weather of the last two days had flown and rain had moved in. Lowering, gray skies met his eyes, and drops streaked the windows, unrelenting. No matter—the glen always looked beautiful to him, even with the green turf soaking and the mountains weeping down rivulets like tears. This place occupied in full his heart, as a woman might that of any other man.

The thought sparked an idea. He contemplated it, and his vision blurred so he saw his own reflection in the glass, mirrored from the light of the single candle behind him.

Who was he, then? Still the young boy who, dispossessed, had fled unbearable pain with only his father's sword and used it to make his way in the world? Was he the mercenary who took brass in return for the slitting of throats? The warrior who had stood at Culloden and survived? The madman, as they called him, willing to do what he must to hold this glen?

He had much for which to seek revenge: his father's death, the loss of his sister. But, his meeting with Jeannie fresh in mind, he longed above all to be Geordie's avenger.

So, how best to settle the deceitful Mistress MacWherter? There seemed but one way—pay her in kind.

He had little doubt of his ability to seduce any woman. Had he not done so from the borders to John O'Groats? Usually, though, he enjoyed the process. Seducing his friend's widow would be a far different proposition. Not that he might not enjoy it—in a far different way. He thought again of the curves beneath her plain brown dress, of stripping the fabric away to savor their pleasures, and to his surprise he grew aroused. Aye, well, they said revenge was a dish best served cold—or perhaps flaming hot between the sheets.

What would Geordie think of Finnan taking his woman? It was a line they had been careful never to cross. If one of them had a lass in his eye, the other stayed well clear. But this situation proved far different. This, he would do *for* Geordie. And for himself.

That thought crawled into his mind on a wave of hot blood. He imagined plunging into Jeannie MacWherter's heat, seeing her eyes go wide, those lovely lips of hers part as she begged for more. He imagined her handing him her heart on a platter, where he could make it bleed.

He grunted and turned back to the table, took up his letter, and tore it into a score of pieces. He would need no lawyer to settle Jeannie MacWherter's account.

****

"Will it never stop raining? I swear it is going to drive me mad." Aggie voiced the belief as she leaned against the window frame and peered out. Jeannie could not imagine how Aggie could see anything through the flowing curtain of water that obscured the glass. "I wish we could go home."

"It rained in Dumfries," Jeannie said with forbearance she did not really feel, and glared at the dress she sat mending. Aye, it had rained in Dumfries; she remembered splashing through cobbled streets on errands for her father before he died, or to fetch him from the tavern. At the end, the tavern had been her only destination.

"Not like this," Aggie asserted.

That was true; Jeannie had never seen rain like that in the glen, elemental torrents that chased any sane person inside.

Upon that thought, she heard a rapping and lifted her head from her sewing. "What was that?"

"A flapping board in the loft," Aggie answered, turning from the window at last. "Did I not say I heard it the other night? Either that, or a ghost." Aggie paused, eyes wide. "You do not suppose the ghost of your husband would come here?"

Jeannie almost snorted in derision, but could not quite. Something about life in this place of mist and lamenting skies encouraged a belief in the mystical.

As if to prove her words, she heard the knocking again.

"That is someone at the door." She laid her sewing aside, got up, and hurried across the combined kitchen and sitting room to the door. Rowan Cottage, though comfortable enough, felt small as a doll's house after her father's quarters in Dumfries. Confined inside, she and Aggie tended to bounce off each other and chaff unbearably. She could scarcely imagine how they would survive winter—given Finnan MacAllister let them stay that long.

She swung the door wide and lost all the breath in her lungs. Finnan MacAllister stood there precisely as if her thoughts had summoned him.

Ah, and did the man spend all his time soaking wet? She had to admit the look flattered him, and at least this time he was fully clothed in a kilt over rough leggings, a leather jacket, and his plaid up over his head against the rain. All now shed water, sopping.

From beneath the edge of the red tartan his tawny eyes gleamed and reached for hers. Alarm, primal and powerful, speared through her. She reacted immediately and attempted to shut the door in his face.

He moved before she could, splayed his fingers on the oak panel beside her head. Shocked, Jeannie stared at the long brown digits of his right hand, tattooed all round with the figures of twining snakes. Or were they dragons? Before she could decide, he spoke.

"Good day to you, Mistress MacWherter."

"It is most plainly not a good day." She struggled to shift the door, but it might have been braced by rock for all her success. Heavens, but the man possessed formidable strength!

He smiled, and wicked light invaded the tawny eyes. Jeannie promptly lost all the breath in her body once again.

"Still, Mistress MacWherter, I have walked all the way down the glen. Will you not invite me in out of the rain?"

Jeannie clung to the door latch, caught by that smile the way a salmon might be pierced by a gaff. Her heart beat hot blood into her face. As soon invite him in as a marauding wolf.

"Why did you walk all the way down the glen, Laird MacAllister?"

"To call on you, of course."

Jeannie lifted her chin. "Correct me if I am mistaken, but when we parted yesterday afternoon, it was not on terms that might encourage a social visit."

"That is precisely why I am here." He donned a look of remorse, as unconvincing as the afore-imagined wolf playing at being a lamb. "I have come to apologize, Mistress MacWherter, having realized too late how very rudely I behaved. Indeed, it tortured me all the night long."

Yes, and Jeannie had thought of him all night, as well, relived the shock of seeing him lying in the water, and recalled the sight he made emerging. She had been teased by the question of whether, before he snagged the plaid and covered himself, she had seen a tattoo even on that appendage most private to him.

"Apology accepted," she said and tried once more to shut the door.

The muscles of his arm flexed and kept it open. "Och, Mistress MacWherter, but I ha' barely begun to beg your pardon."

Why did his voice, lilting and musical, make something suggestive of that statement? Jeannie had a sudden image of him on his knees, aroused and begging.

She fought for breath. "Does this mean you will call off your demand that we vacate this house?"

"For the sake of mercy let me in from the wet, and we will discuss it."

Against every instinct, Jeannie stepped aside. She heard an abrupt movement in the doorway of the parlor—of course, Aggie had listened to all.

"Come warm yourself beside the fire," she told MacAllister.

He padded behind her, as soundless as the wolf she envisioned. Just inside the main room she met Aggie's wide eyes.

"Make us some tea, please, Aggie. And perhaps find a cloth so our guest may dry himself."

For once Aggie moved to obey without a word. MacAllister stepped further into the room, which looked smaller for his presence. It also looked bare and shabby. Jeannie had been able to bring so few things from the south. A single candle burned beside the bench where she had been sewing, the brown dress tossed down in a tumble. The fire smoldered on the hearth; the room felt dreary and chill.

Finnan MacAllister's gaze swept the place, and she wondered what he saw: a haven? A room of little comfort?

"Miss," Aggie hissed from the hearth, and thrust a cloth into her hands. Jeannie experienced yet another flashback to Dumfries. Aggie had been terrified of spiders, and after the death of Jeannie's father, before the two women were tossed from his quarters, the job of removing them had fallen to Jeannie. Aggie would sidle up to her just so and hand her the dusting cloth, careful not to get too near.

Jeannie urged herself to think of Finnan MacAllister as nothing more than a great, ugly spider with which she must deal.

Impossible. The man moved with smooth, fluid grace and, well, quite honestly, was much too handsome.

"Here, Laird MacAllister." She offered the cloth, which he ignored.

Instead, all dripping leather, wool, and hair, he stepped to the hearth, where he said, "Do you call this a fire? 'Tis a poor and pitiful excuse."

"We have had trouble coaxing the chimney to draw," Jeannie said a bit defensively. Also, it being August, she hated to waste fuel, of which she had precious little, though she would not admit that to him.

"There is naught wrong with the flue. I had this cottage gone over for Geordie's sake."

"Well"—Jeannie shifted from one foot to the other—"it will not draw."

"That is because of the rain. The wet, heavy air damps the fire down." Even as he spoke he plied the iron poker, showing skill he might employ with a sword, and the fire leaped up wild and bright. He tossed on more fuel, and Jeannie bit back a protest. Time enough to worry about future shortages after he left.

"There now." He straightened and regarded her with satisfaction. "No sense you sitting here cold in your own room."

Jeannie scowled. She found it difficult to accept this changed attitude he professed. Every instinct screamed danger, even as she offered him the cloth once more.

"As I say, Laird MacAllister, I did not expect to find you at my door."

Busy using the cloth, he did not answer. She watched him rub his face, dab at his arms and those long, muscular legs, and swab his neck. When he took the toweling to his hair, her fingers began to itch. She wondered how it would feel to plunge them into that thick, wavy mane.

"Well, but 'tis the truth I told you," he said in that lilting voice. "No sooner did we part yesterday than I began to regret my harsh attitude. And then I had my own visitor during the night."

"Visitor?" Jeannie echoed, and cocked her head. What was it to her whom he entertained?

But he leaned toward her and lowered his voice.

"Aye, Mistress MacWherter, and it was none other than the ghost of your husband."

Chapter Six

From the hearth came a crash as the maid dropped the tray and all its contents. At least, Finnan thought, one of the women in this house had bought his tale. His eyes moved to Jeannie and measured her reaction; would she swallow it also? An intelligent if deceitful woman, she might be far harder to fool than an empty-headed servant.

He heard her draw a sharp breath and saw annoyance flood her eyes. With him, or the maid? No doubt, he thought, she rode her servant hard.

But when she turned to the lass, she sounded patient and gentle. "Here, Aggie, pick that up best you may."

"But I've broken the teapot!" the maid wailed. "And it came with us all the way from Dumfries, wrapped in your petticoat."

"Nothing to be done about it now. Find two more cups."

"There are no more cups!" The maid cried, clearly overset.

"Find whatever you can and pour straight from the kettle."

Finnan heard a sob, and the girl began to gather the crockery. Jeannie, her expression indecipherable, straightened and turned back to him. "My apologies, Laird MacAllister. It seems tea will take a few moments. Will you not sit?"

There were but three seats, a narrow bench and two stools. Finnan took one of the latter, avoiding the bench that had her gown draped over it. She gathered the garment up carefully and laid it aside before seating herself in the flickering light from the candle.

Ah, and how blue her eyes looked in that golden light. He could see why poor Geordie had thought her the bonniest thing he had ever seen.

"Forgive me," he murmured. "I seem to have startled your maid."

"You make an incredible assertion, Laird MacAllister. A ghost?"

"Not just any ghost, but that of Geordie. What did he tell you of our friendship?"

She considered it and shook her head. A tendril of gold, one single curl, tumbled down beside her ear. Finnan struggled not to notice. "He spoke of the past but rarely, and only when in his cups."

Finnan frowned. Geordie had not been a drinker, at least not in the days when they traveled and fought together. Oh, aye, he would take a dram when offered—what man would not? But he had often chastised Finnan for drinking to excess.

"As I said when we met beside the pool, Geordie and I were close as brothers—closer. There is a particular bond between fighting men." That he could not expect her to understand.

"He once told me you were the best friend ever a man could have." She twined her fingers together in her lap and raised those wide, blue eyes to Finnan. "That is why I find it so difficult to understand why you should want to chase me from his home now, when I am in need. You say he wrote you letters."

Anger licked up inside Finnan at her feigned innocence. "So he did."

"Might I ask what he said of me that angered you?"

Finnan fixed her with a fierce gaze. He could not let his ire overset him, not when he played the part of the remorseful friend. He spread his hands. "You must understand we were used to confiding in one another, always. 'Twas part and parcel of the pact we made to one another, to keep in touch. He sent the letters to a mutual acquaintance in Fort William, and I collected them whenever I could." Sometimes sorely late, but he had them, every one. "Of you, he said many things. I acknowledge now I may have taken his words a-wrong—I was not aware he had turned to drink. Whisky can affect both a man's mood and his opinions."

She frowned. A second golden tendril fell, this one beside her cheek. "Still, I would know what ill he said of me."

Finnan just bet she would. Scrambling in her mind, she was, wondering how the game she played with Geordie had gone wrong. She had not guessed Geordie sent letters to anyone. Finnan had to convince her he'd been mistaken, that his anger against her had flown.

Carefully, he said, "Does it matter now? I have come here to apologize. Geordie and I were used to defending one another and guarding each other's back. And there was something in him that tended to make me feel protective." Too true, that. "We each vowed to come whenever the other called."

She gave him a cool look. "As I said, it is a pity you did not come to him in Dumfries when he stood in dire need of a friend."

"I did not know. His letters did not call on me for help." Geordie had been lost, aye, and clearly miserable, as evidenced by his presence in the lowlands, of all places. The past haunted him even as it did Finnan. But never once had he requested Finnan's presence. "He had only to call on me," he said simply, "and I would have been there."

Indeed, he had very nearly gone anyway, when Geordie wrote to say he meant to wed the woman he had met. But he had been engrossed in his own battle here, trying to regain his birthright.

"As it was," she went on, not quite calmly, "he had only my father for companion. They formed a...a curious relationship. In fact, that is how Geordie and I met."

"Aye." Geordie had described that as well. *I helped the old gentleman home on more than one occasion, where I met his daughter. A precious flower she is, blooming in this cold, gray place.* "Your father, a scholar—Angus Robertson."

She inclined her head. "A once-practical, learned man, with a scientific mind, who taught his daughter not to believe in ghosts."

"Ah, well." Finnan treated her to his best smile. "You are in the highlands now, where 'scientific' principles tend to fly out the window. There exist in this glen many things you cannot hope to comprehend— fairies, boogies, a sea horse in the burn, and the spirits of ancient warriors. This is no' the lowlands, you ken."

"Nevertheless, Laird MacAllister, until a boogie man comes walking up the glen to my door, I will not believe in spirits."

A boogie man had come walking up the glen to her door, Finnan reflected, did she but know it, one set to seduce her.

He wanted to ask how long it had taken her to persuade Geordie to kiss her, he who had believed so completely in true love. Had Geordie been lost at the first look from those blue eyes? How long would it take Finnan to persuade her to kiss him?

He fair ached for it, the touch of that soft mouth on his, ached for revenge, that was.

The maid cleared her throat and then sidled in between them, moving the way a man might in the presence of a wildcat. She carried a mug of what Finnan could only assume was tea in either hand. He longed for something stronger.

"Thank you, Aggie. Are there any scones left?"

"I will bring some." Aggie's voice made only a whisper. She placed a mug at Finnan's elbow and handed the other to her mistress before turning away to the shelves beside the fire.

"So." Finnan lowered his voice to a conspiratorial level, even though the lass could still hear every word. "You do not want to know what Geordie said to me?"

"I do not."

"Even though I walked all this way through that torrent just to tell you? And even though 'tis to your benefit?"

"I thought you walked all that way to apologize."

"That too."

"Do you often expect sane, rational women to sit and discuss the conversations of ghosts?"

"Not 'ghosts'—just the one." He took a sip of tea, which scalded his tongue.

39

"Very well, then, Laird MacAllister, I will play at your game. What did the ghost of my husband say?"

He shot her a sharp look. Did she recognize this for a game, a trap?

The maid pushed in between them again, with a plate that held three meager scones. "I am that sorry, miss. It is all we had."

"Thank you, Aggie. Leave us, please."

The girl handed her mistress the scones and fled up into the loft. Finnan eyed the plate and raised his gaze to Jeannie's face. He had to admit, nothing here seemed as he'd expected. Where was evidence of this woman's greed? She must have taken Geordie for all he had.

He took another sip of tea, more cautiously this time. The stuff tasted like dishwater. He set the mug aside.

"I understand you do no' believe me," he said with what he hoped was engaging earnestness. "And I am a rational, practical man, so I do assure you. But I have been a soldier a long while."

"A mercenary," she interposed, speaking the words with some distaste. What did she expect? He had left home at sixteen, forced to make his way, and met Geordie soon after. The two of them had earned their fortune in the world—survived. How dared she judge the means?

"A mercenary, aye, and a soldier. Geordie and I stood at Culloden."

"So Geordie did say. He used to get into fights over it, at the ale house. The first time, a crowd set on him, and he got the worst of it. My father made his acquaintance when he gave Geordie some rough assistance in the alley, after."

Finnan scowled. "Why should Geordie get into fights over it?"

She hesitated. "He refused to state on which side of the conflict he had fought."

Ah, and there lay the heart of the matter. And the accursed lowlanders had ridden Geordie hard for it, had they? Aye, Finnan should have been there, as ever, to stand at Geordie's side.

"I am sure," he said softly, "he owed your father a debt of gratitude." Finnan meant nothing of the kind. "And I know how grateful he was for your presence in his life."

"Then perhaps you will explain to me, Laird MacAllister, why you have turned on me? Why try to chase me from the glen?" She leaned forward on her bench, her gaze fixed on him. "Just what did Geordie's letters say? I think you must tell me."

"He spoke of your marriage. It was not all he had hoped."

Color flared in her cheeks. Hastily, she set her own mug aside and drew a breath. "What concern is that of yours, Laird MacAllister?"

"Everything to do with Geordie MacWherter concerned me, all danger or perceived danger."

"You consider me to have been a danger?" Again, her beautiful eyes widened. "Me? I would like to know how."

"There was that in Geordie's letters that led me to believe you had taken advantage of him."

"Was there?" She looked completely taken aback. Aye, a fine actress.

He held her gaze with his. "I stood to defend even Geordie's heart." Or avenge it.

41

The color in her cheeks flared still brighter. "You know nothing of the relationship that existed between me and my husband. It is not unusual that people should marry for convenience."

"Convenience?" It had been nothing of the kind. Geordie had adored her from the tips of her toes to that crown of golden hair. Finnan slid forward to the edge of his seat. "Did you not love him?"

The expression in her eyes changed, transformed from embarrassed affront to something far colder. She gripped the edge of her bench so tight her fingers turned white. "Laird MacAllister, you may indeed own this glen—every stick and stone, as you say—by whatever means you have stolen it. But you do not own me and have no right to the contents of my heart."

What heart? It was obviously as cold as her gaze had become. Aye, and he saw the truth now beneath the pretty picture she sought to present.

He said, hoping to catch her unawares, "Geordie wishes me to look after you. It is what he came to tell me last night. You see, he loves you still and wants for you to remain in the glen."

Chapter Seven

Jeannie looked up from the kale bed where she once more knelt, and sweated, beneath a clear, northern sky. Yesterday's torrential rain had flown as if it had never existed. The glen drowsed in a haze of peace so seemingly complete it felt obscene for so much disquiet to possess Jeannie's heart.

She decided she detested garden work just as much as did Aggie. The tiny black flies bit mercilessly and the stooping caused her back to ache. She marveled that her life could come to this: a scrap of garden and a small cottage spelled existence. Yet she'd become convinced that if the kale failed to flourish she and Aggie would never survive the winter.

With a sigh, she shifted along the row of struggling plants and thought about Dumfries. More precisely, she thought about Geordie, as she had ever since Laird MacAllister's visit yesterday afternoon.

What sort of letters could Geordie have written to his friend? What had they said of her? And what had she seen in Finnan MacAllister's eyes when he spoke of them?

The man was an enigma, a mystery, layers upon layers, each more bewildering than the last. He might smile at her, a seemingly winsome smile, even while that light which bespoke anger flared in his eyes. He professed to be a practical man, a soldier, even while he spoke of fairies, boogies, and ghosts. She considered herself a very fair judge of human nature, but she could not begin to guess what to make of the man.

Nor did she quite believe his claim that the spirit of her husband had persuaded him to call off his cruel campaign against her and allow her to remain here in peace. It made no sense.

Then again, the man was a highlander…

She sat back on her heels and brushed the hair from her forehead. She had met very few highlanders in her life. Geordie had been one, but Geordie now seemed as unlike his friend as day like night.

She remembered the first time she had seen Geordie MacWherter, big, burly, covered with cuts and bruises at the time. Appalled that her father should bring home a crony from the alehouse, she had tried to keep her distance.

But as he so often did, her father had called on her to provide hospitality, and she glimpsed something unexpected beneath Geordie's rough exterior—a gentleness, a longing, an almost childlike expectation. Yes, from the first, Geordie had disarmed her.

But she had never loved him.

Oh, she had cared, and she had felt for him, even pitied him. But pity did not win a woman's heart, at least not hers. It would be difficult, anyway, to love a man who spent most of his time drunk, who wept when in his cups and sometimes muttered about the past in a brogue too thick to let her understand.

Something rode Geordie MacWherter hard, a fool could see that. And as the tales went, troubled spirits were most likely to return to this world after their death. But the idea that Geordie had come now to speak to his friend—well, it seemed absurd.

She spoke aloud to the sunny day, there in her poor excuse for a garden. "If you are going to show yourself, Geordie MacWherter, do so now, here, when I need you."

Nothing. A breeze ruffled the stalks of kale, and a bird took wing at some distance and sang a sweet, heartbreaking song. No more.

She called a picture of Geordie up in her mind, as if that could summon his spirit. Well over six foot of strapping male he had been, a warrior out of training and beginning to go soft, the ale putting extra weight on his large frame.

His friend had not fallen out of training. It would be difficult to imagine a man in better form than Finnan MacAllister. And she had seen all of him.

But Geordie—Geordie had reminded her of a bear, big, slightly bewildered, and drowsy, but still very dangerous if roused. She had lost count of the brawls in which he had been involved during their acquaintance.

But certain things about him remained the warrior, no matter how intoxicated he became. He wore always a highland dirk in the cuff of his boot and could draw it before a man might blink. He wore his sandy hair long in the highland fashion and often half-braided like a man going into battle. And those sleepy hazel eyes could, in an instant, turn to granite.

He had never been anything but unfailingly gentle with Jeannie—sweetly earnest and mildly gallant. Her heart twisted just thinking on it. Had she loved him after all? Maybe, the way one loved a brother or a child.

No wonder Finnan MacAllister wanted to protect him. There had been that quality about Geordie, after all. But the very idea of him writing letters to the man… Geordie should have been far too inebriated to put pen to paper. Anyway, she did not believe Finnan MacAllister. She could not give credence to a word the man said, whether it concerned ghosts or otherwise. His lips might smile, but the look in his eyes suggested deceit.

She looked up again as Aggie hove into sight, a basket over her arm. Impatient, she demanded of her maid, "Where have you been? I wanted your help with the weeding."

Aggie made a face. Servants were not supposed to pick and choose their duties; Jeannie had let things get sorely out of hand.

"The ground is wet from yesterday's rain," Aggie pointed out. "You will be all mud."

"True, but the soil is soft, and the weeds pull out most easily."

"I have brought us eggs from Avrie House. We can have a good breakfast come morning."

Or a good supper tonight. Jeannie knew all too well not much else lay in the larder.

"And"—Aggie lowered her voice to a near whisper —"I have news."

"More gossip, you mean." Jeannie sighed. As well keep Aggie from gossiping as halt the rain in this place.

"No, legitimate news got from Dowager Avrie herself."

"You spoke with the Dowager Avrie?"

"No, but Dorcas and Marie got it straight from their mistress, as well as saw with their own eyes."

"What?" Despite her resolve, Jeannie's interest stirred.

"The Dowager's grandsons have come home, the sons of her dead son. And they have vowed to settle that Finnan MacAllister."

****

For a man who had achieved all his dreams, Finnan MacAllister did not feel as satisfied as he should. He sat brooding in the library at Dun Mhor, which had once been the favorite room of his father, Kieran MacAllister. Indeed, it was from this very room Avrie and his accursed men had dragged Kieran out to his doom.

All while Finnan lay upstairs in his bed unaware his father's life was ending, spattered in blood on the stones of the courtyard. Aye, and he had sworn vengeance on that blood, every drop of it. He had worked and saved and suffered, he had bought up debts on the sly until he owned Gregor Avrie, and then he had returned to demand payment.

Too late, it had been, to save his mother, who had died in exile, or his sister who had fallen into the hands of one of Avrie's demon sons. It had been eight years since he'd had word of Deirdre, ten since he had seen her. She had been only fifteen when the tragedy befell them. What sort of woman might she have become?

Agony stirred in his heart, which he had believed far too calloused to hurt so much. He had killed men, many men. He had lied, cheated, and traded his honor for money, all to get back to this place. And now that he sat here, he discovered it was not what he had anticipated.

Hollow. That described it. The house, with the Avrie clan chased from it back to the dowager's dwelling or out of the glen, proved just a house and far

47

too empty. The Avries had not suffered enough. He, Finnan, wanted more revenge.

But what? A vision of Jeannie MacWherter swam before his eyes. Aye, and he would have her sooner rather than later. That would be too easy, though avenging Geordie might soothe his pain.

Or would it? Avenging his father's death had not, despite all his longing.

The trout in the pool had bidden him choose peace.

The library door creaked open, and young Danny poked his head into the room. Finnan and Geordie had picked the lad up following the battle at Culloden—a mere boy, in truth—and Danny had served him willingly ever since, a passable valet and an even better groom, despite the loss of his right arm.

"The horses stand ready, Master, if you wish to ride out."

"I do." He could barely stand being cooped up with paperwork on this fine afternoon. Maybe viewing his lands would settle his mind.

Danny grinned. "Rohre is full of himself today."

Finnan grunted. He had bought the horse in Callander from a man he'd caught abusing the beast. The horse had a wild streak and a temper that proved he had not forgotten his past.

No more had Finnan.

Never mind, he had a taste for a wild ride. Perhaps that would chase Jeannie MacWherter from his head.

The great house of Dun Mhor lay at the northern end of the glen. An ancient place of stone built over the foundations of a roundhouse, it had housed members of Clan MacAllister since time immemorial—until the Avries took it into their minds to change that history.

The Avries were supposed to be sworn allies of Clan MacAllister, held under *geis*, and had lived under the protection of the greater clan before the MacAllisters' fortunes declined and the treacherous Gregor Avrie saw his chance. A deceitful plan, a dirk in the night, and Gregor supposed his future changed.

Finnan still remembered his mother rousing him from his bed, weeping. "You must go at once, Finn! Your father is dead, and you are his heir. They will kill you next. I could not bear it—anything but that. Take your sister and go."

But they had been unable to find his sister. And once he had crept to the courtyard, viewed his father's dead body and taken Kieran MacAllister's sword into his own hands, his mother, clearly terrified, had bundled him off through a hidden exit, giving him all the portable wealth on which she could lay her hands, including her own gold brooch and a pouch of small coins.

He thought on it now as he thundered up the glen, letting his eyes rest on every sweep of turf and high peak, how he had sworn vengeance and begged his mother to let him stay.

"Let me answer these vile wolves as they deserve!"

But his mother had wept harder. "They will murder you, Finn my love, and we will have nothing, nothing! At least I can live if I know you are somewhere in the world and can come back to reclaim your father's lands."

And so he had traveled everywhere in the world, but she had not lived. Word reached him but slowly through that family friend in Fort William. An illness, some said. Others whispered of murder, or suicide.

Where was Deirdre now, he wondered, as he fought Rohre for control of the reins. Reports there also varied. Some said dead. Some said mad. Upon his return, Finnan had served her husband's father—Gregor Avrie—as he deserved, but had caught not a glimpse of his sister.

Would he even know her now, after so long? Aye, but he would know her eyes, so like his mother's.

He tried to picture them and saw in his mind's eye, instead, Jeannie MacWherter's eyes, blue and innocent. Aye, she feigned innocence, but Finnan knew it very well for deception. And he vowed again, as Rohre pounded down the glen, Gregor Avrie would not be the only one he paid in kind.

Chapter Eight

Bright sunlight glittered off the waters of the burn as from shards of glass, blinding Finnan's eyes. When he and Rohre, with Danny's mount now trailing well behind, entered the copse of trees not far north of Rowan Cottage, the sudden gloom further dampened his sight. Indeed, not until Rohre's stride broke and the horse tossed his head did Finnan realize they were no longer alone.

A group of mounted men had ridden out of the trees onto the path, blocking Finnan's way.

His every instinct roused in response. Ten years away from home and he had been first and foremost a warrior. Before he could curse, he had his sword in his hand, the same razor-edged blade with which he had defended his life across Scotland. Blinking fiercely, he saw his attackers all came heavily armed.

But who were they? And from whence had they come? He controlled Rohre with iron knees, leaving his hands ready to fight, and the horse snorted.

Finnan spared a thought for Danny coming behind. If things got ugly, the lad would ride right into it. He eyed the mounted men, assessing his chances. Six of them, two planted abreast at the front, four behind. Finnan sneered; he'd faced steeper odds, though usually with Geordie at his side.

"Well," said one of the two men in front, "if it is

not the MacAllister cur who considers himself laird of this place."

Avrie. The name appeared whole in Finnan's mind, spurred by the hate he heard in the voice, and just like that he knew his opponents. How, though? The brothers Avrie—Stuart and Trent—had been conspicuously absent from the glen since Finnan returned and killed their traitorous father. But another thought possessed his mind. "Where is my sister?" he demanded.

The man on the left—was he Stuart?—tossed his head. "Lost to you, turncoat murderer. You will never see her again."

Rage rose to Finnan's head. "You think I will not make you pay for your crimes, even as did your accursed sire?" He tossed his head much as Rohre had. "Get you out of my way."

Stuart Avrie spoke again. "I think not. A coward such as you might find it easy to terrorize an old woman and a man on his own. But his sons are here now, and serving you notice we will answer you as you deserve."

Finnan's head jerked up further. "I am no coward."

"Nay? Is that why you stood against our Prince at Culloden and fought on the winning side?"

Finnan said nothing. He owed explanations to no one, especially these jackals.

"The Crown pays its turncoats well," said the second brother, who must be Trent. "And the dog came back to Glen Rowan a wealthy man. What does that tell you, Brother?"

"That he needs settling." Stuart gestured to the men at his back. "Take him." And the two of them rode away into the gloom beneath the trees.

Finnan understood the gesture: they would be elsewhere, with clean hands, when he was slain. But his lip curled in derision. And they called him a coward!

Still, his career and much of his future had been founded on just such strategy. Was it not why men of high renown paid mercenaries? And he liked these odds much better.

He eyed the wall of four men on horseback who faced him. Were they mercenaries as well, or just members of Avrie's household guard? Either way they were paid men, with little invested in the cause.

He knew how liberating it was to hold no stake in the outcome of a battle. It freed a man's emotions and let him concentrate on the matter at hand. Yet he could not, himself, be more invested.

As if to prove his point, he heard the approach of Danny from behind. He called out, "Go back, lad! Do not join me here."

"What? Why?"

Finnan did not need to turn his head to see Danny disobeyed his order.

He called again, "Stay at my back!" And he urged Rohre forward with his knees.

The men were not mercenaries, as he learned at the first pass. A mercenary would have employed far dirtier means to spear him than did his first opponent. Finnan, nothing loath to use every trick at his disposal, feinted and got inside the man's sword to slit his throat with the razor blade almost before the fellow could blink. He fell from his horse with a thud, and the animal blocked the others' way, further improving Finnan's odds.

The second man, a chancer, whirled his sword around his head and came in bellowing. Finnan ducked and barely saved himself from scalping.

He heard Danny holler from behind. While his opponent was overextended, Finnan launched himself from Rohre's back and took the man over backwards from his mount. They both landed hard on the track; the air left his opponent's lungs with a rush.

Rohre and the other animal danced, cutting off the two remaining riders. To Finnan's horror, he heard Danny come wading in.

The fool! The lad was no warrior, and he carried no sword, only the dirk in his boot. Filled with alarm on Danny's behalf, Finnan closed his hands around his opponent's throat and bashed his head against the ground until the man passed out.

He had dropped his sword in the fall but now recovered it before scrambling to his feet, his muscles working with well-trained efficiency.

The sight that met his eyes set his blood aflame. The last two guards had Danny trapped between them, the lad already disarmed. Even as Finnan watched, one man struck. His sword took Danny in the stump where his right arm should be.

Without conscious thought Finnan raised his sword and chirruped to Rohre. The horse, head high and nostrils flared, answered, and Finnan vaulted onto his back. They moved together into the fray.

He took the second man, who blocked his way, in the back between the shoulder blades, and cursed as the fellow fell. Rohre, now as enflamed as Finnan, shouldered the man's mount aside. Moving together, they were in time to see Danny's attacker stab the lad viciously.

"No!" Finnan bellowed the word, all his heart in it.

He watched Danny's eyes go wide, saw the lad slump over the neck of his mount as his attacker withdrew the blade.

"Face me!" he roared. "I am no unarmed lad. Face me like a man!"

The man jostled his horse and turned it in the limited space. His gaze flicked toward his fallen comrades and then locked on Finnan.

"I know what you are," he sneered. "Everyone knows. A traitor, a turncoat, a murderer."

Finnan's blood burned so hot he barely heard the words. All he saw was Danny doubled over in agony.

He urged Rohre forward, and the horse, picking up on his emotions, charged. Finnan's sword met his opponent's in the air with a wild clang. He felt his mind slip into fighting form—no distractions, few emotions, just total concentration.

For Danny, he thought when he marked the man's shoulder. *And for my Da*, when he slit the fellow's sword arm, causing him to drop the weapon. *For myself*, he thought when his blade kissed the side of the man's neck with swift competence.

He felt a flash of satisfaction then, for he remained untouched. Unlike Danny.

Swiftly, he dismounted. Rohre stood blowing air and trembling with reaction. Danny had tumbled from his mount during Finnan's last encounter and lay in a heap on the ground.

"Guard," Finnan told Rohre. He did not know if the two brothers Avrie lurked somewhere nearby, watching to see the outcome of their ambush.

He thrust the sword upright in the ground, ready to his hand, and knelt down beside Danny, laid hold of the lad, and turned him over.

Blood, a veritable river of it. The cloth Danny kept pinned over his stump had been shredded, but the wound in his chest caused Finnan's lips to tighten, for it was from there the bright blood spewed.

Yet the lad's eyes were wide open, stretched by shock.

"Master Finnan—"

"Hold on, lad. I will get you to safety."

Where, though? If he turned back for Dun Mhor there might well be another troop of men waiting for him. And he would have to pass by Avrie House.

But Rowan Cottage lay directly ahead. And the Widow MacWherter owed him, whether she knew it not.

Chapter Nine

Jeannie lifted her head as her ear caught the echo of a sound. She could not be sure just what she had heard—it seemed quite distant—but noises tended to funnel up the glen from afar.

Shouting? The clash of weapons? Absurd. Since Culloden, Highland men were not even legally allowed to own weapons.

She stood among the rows of plants and attempted to brush the mud from her knees before calling to Aggie. "Did you hear something?"

Aggie appeared from around back of the cottage where she had been spreading tea towels over the prickle bushes to dry. She shook her head.

Jeannie narrowed her eyes and peered down the glen. The sun, well on its way to set, showed her only a glare of brightness. After a moment, she bent her back and returned to work.

Not until many minutes later did Aggie return and cry, "Mistress, someone's coming!"

Jeannie abandoned her task and straightened again. Sure enough, two horses approached, led by a man on foot. The first horse, a big animal, had a coat that shone red-brown in the dying sun, as did the head of the man.

Jeannie swore softly, speaking a word no decent woman should employ, and started forward decisively. Oh, no—they were not having all that again.

57

She met Finnan MacAllister as he breached the rise that led to the cottage door. "You can just turn about and go, Laird MacAllister. I have no time this day for your tales and blandishments."

He kept coming. She saw his expression then, stark and grim, and the blood spattered on the hand that gripped the reins.

"Peace, woman. I am no' here for you." He gestured to the back of the horse he led where Jeannie saw what looked like a bundle. No, it was a man.

She gasped. "What has happened?" What had he brought to her door?

"I need a place to lay him down. I fear he is dying." Finnan stopped at Jeannie's side and turned to the bundle, which she now saw possessed a brown head and a young man's face. He already looked dead.

Instinct made her block the way. Trouble, that was what he brought, and Jeannie had already experienced enough of that in her life. Yet he slid the lad down from the back of the horse, which stood like a rock, and then lifted him in his arms like a child.

His tawny eyes, grave and intent, met Jeannie's. "I fear he is dying," he repeated. "I will never get him all the way back to Dun Mhor."

Jeannie made a swift decision. "Come." She turned and led the way into the cottage, catching a glimpse of Aggie's horrified face in passing. The cottage possessed but the two ground floor rooms, one of which was Jeannie's bedroom, and the loft. She knew MacAllister would never make it up the ladder with his burden, so she led him straight into her room and indicated the bed.

A small, bare place this was, with only the bed, a

single chest below the window, and the few meager possessions Jeannie had been able to bring from Dumfries.

Finnan eased the young man down on Jeannie's bed as tenderly as he might a child, and she got her first good look at the lad.

"Sweet heavens!"

Finnan MacAllister had not lied; the lad, sore hurt and awash with blood, looked past saving.

"What befell him?" A hunting accident? But these looked like no wounds taken in the hunt. The lad's clothing had been rent as with a sharp blade, and the blood came hot and fast.

Finnan shook his head. "An attack in the copse not far north of here. Danny is no warrior, and he was unarmed." Hard anger colored his voice, far too well disciplined at the moment to qualify as rage.

Jeannie turned to Aggie who, clearly aghast, hovered in the bedroom doorway. "Bring water and what bandaging you can find. Use a sheet if you have to." Jeannie possessed very few linens, but needs must.

She glanced at Finnan. "Who would do such a thing?"

"Avrie's men."

That made her stare at him harder. "Surely not. There is no one at Avrie House save the Dowager." Unless the rumors Aggie had brought home were true.

He flicked at her a glance sharp as a sword. "Her grandsons have returned."

Jeannie contemplated it even as she watched Finnan open the lad's rent tunic. His hands, already stained red, moved with the competence of one skilled in tending wounds.

"Have you been trained to treat injuries?"

"Nay, but a man who makes his way with the sword learns a few things about stanching wounds. That scar on Geordie's belly? 'Twas I sewed that up on a cold winter's day, with coarse twine."

Jeannie had never seen Geordie's belly, but it seemed no fit time to say so. The red cloth came away and the lad's chest into view. The stroke, high toward his left shoulder, had surely just missed his heart.

"Could be worse," Finnan grunted, clearly agreeing with Jeannie's assessment. "Where is your maid with those cloths?"

Jeannie, half dizzy from the metallic smell of blood, went to the door, where she was in time to take a basin from Aggie before its contents spilled. She bore it back to the bed and set it on the floor.

"Here, mistress." Aggie tiptoed in with cloths which Jeannie recognized as portions of her very best sheet. She sighed and folded a pad even as Aggie stood staring down at the lad—Danny, Finnan had called him—like a woman in a dream. "Is he dead?"

As if in response to her voice, the lad opened his eyes, wide and gray-blue, full of a sweetness that might belong to a child.

"What happened, Master Finnan?"

"You ha' been struck, lad." Finnan's tone, harsh and rough, belied the great tenderness with which he worked at the wound at Danny's shoulder. He bathed away the blood and revealed a ragged rent, the sight of which turned Jeannie's stomach queasy. Surely human flesh had never been meant to suffer such abuse.

The water in the basin immediately turned pink. Without looking at Jeannie, Finnan reached for another pad of cloth, which she folded as quickly as possible and handed to him.

"He has but one arm." Aggie whispered the words as if unaware she spoke.

"Hush," Jeannie told her even as Danny's gaze found Aggie's face. "Go and heat more water, quick as you can."

Aggie went, and Danny's eyes sank shut again. For a terrible moment Jeannie thought they had lost him, but his shallow pained breaths still came, far too fast.

She asked, "Did the stroke pass all the way through?"

"Nay, but 'tis a fearsome slash." Finnan's hands still moved in calm defiance of his anger. "Valiant men, to face a maimed boy."

Danny clearly possessed years enough to qualify as a young man, but Jeannie understood Finnan's sentiment and could feel the protectiveness streaming from him.

The blood had begun to well up from the folded pad of cloth. Finnan turned his head, and his eyes, tawny red-brown and with a flame of anger deep inside, met Jeannie's.

"I will need to stitch him up. Will you bring me needle and thread?"

"Yes." Jeannie stepped to the door beyond which Aggie danced, hands twisted in her apron, and requested the items. When Aggie brought the sewing kit, Jeannie picked out a needle and a length of thread with trembling hands and carried them back to the bed.

Another glance from Finnan. "Can you thread it?"

Jeannie sincerely doubted it; her hands shook like leaves in a cold wind. But she nodded and turned to the window, seeking both calm and light.

Behind her, she heard Finnan murmuring to Danny, soft words of comfort and reassurance. "'Twill be all right, lad. We have been in far worse places, surely you remember, and survived just as you will now. You hold strong, and I shall see you safe."

"Aye." The word was barely a breath from Danny's laboring lungs. Jeannie could hear the fear, though, as must Finnan, for he went on, "Trust me, lad. Have I ever let you down?"

He turned to Jeannie. "Where's that thread?"

She thrust the needle, now with a tail, into his reddened, slimy hand.

Tersely, he told her, "You will have to hold him. I need him still."

Without question, Jeannie moved to the other side of the bed. She placed one hand on the lad's chest, the other on his upper arm, and held tight.

She caught her breath, as did Danny, when the needle bit torn flesh.

Finnan began to speak, like a father soothing his son. "Do you remember that time the three of us—you, me, and Geordie—were caught in that high pass above Glen Lyon by that band of king's men? How many swords were against us then?"

"Ten."

"Ten, and no mistake, but we made short work of them. Would have taken our weapons from us, would they not? But we showed them right and proper. Easy odds."

Jeannie turned her head away, no longer able to watch the needle plunge through bloodied flesh.

"And," Finnan went on softly, "that time north of

Callander, in that ale house."

To Jeannie's surprise, Danny gave a laugh that shook his chest.

"Aye." Finnan supplied words for him. "They did not expect a one-armed lad to have a dirk nestled in his boot. You served them right well that day."

"Aye," Danny echoed softly.

"So what is a wee bit of a fight here in our own glen? We fight on our land, now. No success to them!"

No response. Jeannie stole a look to see the lad appeared to have fallen unconscious.

"At last," Finnan breathed. "Lass, hold him still."

She was certainly no lass, but as this scarcely seemed time to argue it, she obeyed and watched while he tied off the thread. The angry blood lessened to mere seepage amid the stitches.

"Will that hold?" she asked.

For answer, he held out his arms, the tattoos on which were liberally interspersed with white scars. "It always has. More water."

Jeannie released the patient even as Finnan turned to the wounded stump. Her stomach flipped over. "Aggie?"

"Here. Give me the basin." Steadier now, Aggie took the reddened bowl and languished a glance on Danny in the doing.

Jeannie experienced a flash of disquiet. She had supposed Aggie interested in the groom at Avrie House. This lad, with his redoubtable master, would not make a suitable substitute.

She turned her gaze back to Finnan. He appeared calmer now, but the anger still simmered in his eyes.

She blew out a breath. "Will he survive?"

"Oh, aye, no thanks to those who attacked us."

"Avrie's men." She had to ascertain it.

"Aye, so." He shot her a searching look. "You must ha' heard enough about the situation to know those of Avrie blood do not want me here. But this glen is mine. And, Mistress MacWherter, I always protect what belongs to me."

Chapter Ten

"I fear I will not be able to move him," Finnan told Jeannie MacWherter, nodding toward the lad who slept in her bed, "until I am certain that wound has closed. I am sorry," he added with what he hoped was well-feigned concern. "'Tis an inconvenience for you."

Jeannie stared at him with those wide, blue eyes. Bonny eyes they were, and no mistake. No wonder Geordie had found himself snared by them.

But Finnan was surprised by her mettle this day. She had barely protested his arrival with a wounded lad in his arms, and had assisted him with unshirking competence. Pity the woman was a deceitful lowlander, else she might be worth something.

"Come," she told him now, "and wash up at the hearth."

Ruefully, he looked down at himself, liberally splashed with blood on skin and clothing, most of it Danny's and some his opponents'. He nodded.

"I will sit and watch over him, mistress," the maid whispered.

Jeannie hesitated before nodding. What did she expect, that Danny would rise up and strangle the chit with his one hand?

"Call us, Aggie, if he stirs."

She led Finnan from the small bedroom to the other room, which served as both kitchen and sitting room, and indicated the pan of hot water Aggie had ready by the fire.

He went to the hearth and stripped down, removed his tunic and the shirt beneath, now ruined. He heard not a sound behind him, but Jeannie supplied a wedge of soap and a rough cloth for drying, laying both on the fender. The soap smelled like a summer's day, like lavender—like her. Ruefully, he acknowledged now he would carry her fragrance also, sure as if he had taken her in his arms and stolen her scent. To his surprise, the thought aroused him. He turned from the fire and caught her staring.

At him.

And what was that he saw in her beautiful eyes as they measured the width of his bare shoulders, his chest and arms, marking every tattoo? She had seen all that of him and more, yet she had not had her fill of looking.

He smiled to himself in satisfaction. It would be all too easy to use her desire against her, make her want him as Geordie had wanted her, and serve her in kind. For he recognized desire when he saw it, and after ten years at large in the world understood what women wanted. Aye, he knew how to bring a woman to the brink of abandon and satisfy her. He knew what made her scream and moan and come apart in his hands.

He needed to keep his eye on the goal here. The ambush and Danny's injury had distracted him, yet he played still another game.

Moving slowly in order to let her look her fill, he dropped his shirt beside the hearth. "Ruined," he said in lament. "I dare not put that back on."

He heard the catch in her breath when she said, "I have nothing to lend you, I am afraid."

"No matter." He gave her his best smile. "You have been naught but kindness itself. I would ask no more."

"May I offer you tea to settle your nerves? I confess, I could use some."

Finnan asked hopefully, "Have you nothing stronger?"

"Not in the house." She shook her head and moved past him to reach the hearth, so close her gown brushed his knees. He stood where he was, and when she straightened he had her virtually within his arms.

Her breath hitched again. He could feel the warmth of her combatting that of the fire at his back. He wondered what would happen if he kissed her, plunged his tongue into that pretty rosebud of a mouth. Would she protest? Or succumb to the want he saw brimming in her eyes?

Before he could decide, her gaze dropped; he felt her curiosity as she examined the tattoos that twined over his skin.

"Each of these has a story," he told her softly, and gestured to himself. As did each scar, truth be known. "This one here?" He touched the picture of a blade over his heart. "I got it after surviving my first battle. "This"—a swirling pattern on his upper arm—"after I saw the magic that lies in the other world. This"—he touched the twined hound high on his shoulder—"you will recognize, for Geordie and I had them together, and it signifies our oath of loyalty to one another."

She said nothing, and he gave her another smile, this one crooked. "But you saw all of me at the pool, did you not, mistress?"

Her eyes, blue as the sky on a day in May, came up

slowly to meet his. Would she step away? Move closer? Invite him in?

"There is much talk of you, Laird MacAllister. They call you a very wicked man."

"Who says this of me? My enemies? And would you take the word of the sort of men who could order the slaying of an unarmed lad?" He stepped still closer; now barely a breath separated them. "Or are you a woman to make up your own mind?"

Unexpectedly, wry light flashed in her eyes. "They say you have beguiled every woman in the glen. Given such powers of persuasion, I am not sure it is wise to trust my instincts."

"I can assure you quite honestly, I ha' not beguiled every woman in the glen." Not yet. "And what do your instincts tell you, Jeannie MacWherter?"

"That you are as dangerous as standing on a precipice over rushing waters." Yet she did not move away, and he saw the fabric of her bodice quicken with her heartbeat. Aye, there would be passion in her— searing hot—when he at last stripped her naked and took her, even as she desired.

He raised a hand slowly toward her hair. Gentleness, he knew, often accomplished what demand could not, especially when a woman had not yet made up her mind.

But he was not prepared for the sensation when his fingers met the softness of those yellow curls. This made the first time he had touched her, and the sweetness of it pierced him, speared through him with power that rocked him back on his heels.

It felt like sticking his hand in a fire and then wanting to keep it there.

And oh, but her hair, soft as thistledown, invited his fingers in deeper. He wanted to comb them through those yellow tresses, loosen the curls one by one to fall about her shoulders. He might, aye, be a wicked man, but Jeannie MacWherter posed a rampant danger to him.

Her hand came up and captured his, still in her hair. For an instant they stood so, fingers and gazes linked, while Finnan found himself suddenly fighting for breath. Then she drew his hand from her hair and stepped away.

He felt the loss of contact like a physical blow, like an icy blast at the coming of winter. It hit him so hard he could not speak.

And Jeannie? She stood for a moment with her back to him before she spoke in a strained voice. "How long will it be, Laird MacAllister, before you can move Danny?"

"Overnight, at least." He struggled to gather his thoughts, to keep his mind focused on his objective. "I apologize again, mistress, for the inconvenience to you."

She turned and faced him once more. "And how are Aggie and I to keep him safe from these enemies you insist abound here in the glen?"

"Well, mistress, I shall just have to stay here the night to guard him—and you."

****

Jeannie fought determinedly to calm her emotions and her mind. She considered herself first and foremost a practical woman. Even her marriage to Geordie MacWherter had been a purely practical matter. She usually did her best to keep her affairs and her life in order. But there was that about this man that knocked the very breath from her body and chased all power to reason from her head.

Maybe it was the way he looked at her with those intent, russet-colored eyes. That look said he knew things about her—it made her pulse speed up, caused her blood to race, made her suspect he knew even the thoughts in her mind.

By heaven, she hoped not, for they were scandalous, and they shocked her to her soul.

And when he had touched her hair, but the lightest brush of his fingers, she had felt it right through her like the blow from a weapon.

Oh, no, she could not deny Finnan MacAllister was a most dangerous and quite wicked man. And now he threatened—promised—to stay beneath her roof the night. By all that was holy, could she survive?

She had never been the sort of woman to succumb to a man's charms. In fact, she had always told herself a man's character mattered far more than his appearance. She'd kept her heart carefully unentangled till Geordie came along, and she had not fallen for him.

Now, terrifyingly, she could feel herself falling, precisely as if the ground beneath her feet had turned to water. What to do about it? She could not demand he leave, with his young groom hurt near to death.

That Finnan MacAllister cared about the lad she could not doubt. What a strength it must be to have such a man care to such an extent.

She took another deliberate step away from him, turned toward the cupboard, and pretended to search for the makings of a supper. It did not help; she could still feel him standing there beside the fire, gazing at her.

"You should be safe this night," he told her softly, the words bathed in that highland lilt that sounded so like a song. "The Avries will not bring violence to your door. You are on good terms with them, are you not?"

"Fair terms. I have met the Dowager Avrie, and Aggie is friendly with her servants." She resisted the desire to look at him again, just for the sheer pleasure of it. "We did hear a rumor her grandsons had returned. Also that you killed their father." She hoped she was not going to be caught amid some bloody, highland feud. "Was this attack today about revenge?"

He made a face and gestured with those beautiful hands. "Life is mostly about revenge, is it not, mistress?"

"Not in my experience." Wryly she added, "It is mostly about survival."

He moved at last to sit on the three-legged stool beside the hearth, affording Jeannie the enjoyment of watching his muscles flex again. "Revenge *is* survival."

"Perhaps, in your world." Jeannie reflected briefly on it. "I suppose if you murder a man's father you can then expect him to come looking for you."

"I thought the sons had taken flight like two carrion crows and were in hiding for fear of their own lives. I will be better prepared the next time I meet them."

She swung to face him and crossed her arms across her breasts. "And if you kill them also, Laird MacAllister? Will that not merely extend the violence on and on?"

"'Twill do more than that, Mistress MacWherter." He leaned toward her and his eyes glowed. "'Twill rid the world of a scourge of vermin. And, you ken, such vile pests must be eliminated wherever they are found."

Chapter Eleven

Jeannie stirred uneasily on the narrow straw pallet and reached for sleep that would not come. Aggie had insisted on giving Jeannie her bed in the loft and now slept in a nest of blankets on the floor alongside, but neither Jeannie's mind nor emotions would still.

Might as well try to sleep while a wolf prowled below; Finnan MacAllister remained at large in the cottage, watching over his servant and supposedly guarding the place.

She could hear every step he took, soft padding very much like the wolf she envisioned. He had added fuel to the fire and been in and out of her bedroom, tending Danny. Outside, the world lay still, the hush of the summer night seemingly complete. She counted Aggie's quiet breaths; she caught the murmur of Finnan's voice, if not his words, every time he spoke to the lad.

Was Danny awake, then? Better? Worse? How long could she lie here wondering? How long till dawn?

She knew she should stay where she was, difficult as that might be. She needed to keep well away from Finnan MacAllister and the danger he represented to her peace of mind. But lying there staring at the beams of the loft by the dim firelight that sifted up the ladder, she acknowledged keeping away served very little purpose. He already occupied a place in her head, and she could virtually see him moving about, those tattoos writhing above the muscles of his chest and arms, hair hanging down his back like the mane on a wild pony.

How might it feel to run her fingers through that hair, tangle them in the rough tresses? How might it feel to press herself against his hard body? To taste him?

Forbidden thoughts, wicked thoughts. It was as if she had caught them from him.

She groaned softly and rolled over, desperate to supplant him in her mind, but other thoughts, like sleep, would not come.

What sort of man was he? For weeks, Aggie had been bringing home whispers of him, gossip from the servants at Avrie House and others in the glen. Murderer, betrayer, mercenary. He had fought at Culloden—as had Geordie—and survived, but no one seemed sure on which side of that conflict he had raised his sword.

Her best source of information about Finnan MacAllister was now dead. Geordie had not liked to talk about his past. Even when in his cups he threw out only a few words before falling into brooding silence.

Indeed, Geordie MacWherter had spoken of his good friend, Finnan, seldom enough. He had mentioned him in passing, and also when telling Jeannie about the residence here in Glen Rowan his good friend had gifted him.

"Paradise on earth," he had claimed, his eyes hazy and distant with the drink. "A home at last, for I have never had one."

"Why do you not go there, then?" Jeannie had asked, nodding at the letter, covered with black script,

Geordie held in his hand.

Geordie had gazed at her with wistful eyes that retained that childlike innocence despite all he must have seen. "I would not go there alone, Jeannie Robertson. Will you marry me?"

She had refused him then, attributing the offer to the drink, of which he obviously had a skin full, and also later when he proposed a second time. She knew to her soul he deserved better, someone who could give him her whole heart.

But still later, after her father died and her situation worsened, Jeannie found herself in need of the protection the big, sandy-haired highlander offered. Marrying him had not been an honorable thing to do. Yet she'd been as honest with Geordie as she could. And he had taken her on her terms.

She had not made him happy. She'd known that on some level, even if she had not been aware he had written letters to his good friend, MacAllister. Complaining of her, apparently—for the proof of what Geordie must have told Finnan lay in Finnan's anger with her at their initial meeting.

But now—now he claimed Geordie's ghost had come to him and asked for his protection and forbearance on Jeannie's behalf. Finnan would have Jeannie believe his attitude toward her had changed. Did she believe it? Lying there with her eyes stretched wide in the darkness, she could not tell.

She heard Finnan murmur again, then followed his soft footsteps as they went to the fire, heard the splash as he poured water. With a sigh she sat up and slid from the cot.

She had gone to bed fully clothed, unwilling to

undress with that man in the house. She seized a shawl and wound it about her shoulders before going down the ladder.

No one in the main room. The fire burned steadily, and the kettle simmered, hot. She went to the door of her bedroom and peered in. One glance told her Danny had taken a turn for the worse. Finnan bent over the bed, on which the lad tossed and muttered words to which she heard Finnan reply.

"There, now, lad. Try to lie quietly. You'll tear open that wound."

"But they are coming for us! They will hang us for traitors. We must away!"

"Whisht now, Danny lad, you are safe. Did I no' promise to keep you safe?" The tenderness in Finnan MacAllister's voice, so much at odds with anything Jeannie had heard from him, went straight to her heart. Oh, but he had a beautiful voice when he did not threaten or beguile.

But Danny, if he heard, took no comfort. "They will put us all to death! Cut out my heart..."

"Easy, Danny. You know I will fight to the very death for you."

An avenging highland angel was he, standing between this lad and all harm with a drawn sword? Cursed if Jeannie was not convinced. She stirred in the doorway, and Finnan's senses, ever alert, detected the movement. He looked at her and straightened from the bed.

"Mistress, I hope we did not disturb your rest."

Jeannie answered with another question. "What is it, is he worse?"

"Fever has set in; he is out of his head." Slowly,

moving with that powerful grace, Finnan approached her. "It often happens with this kind of wound, but I confess I hoped for better."

"Of what does he speak? Whom does he fear?"

Finnan gave a wry smile. "Whom does a man not fear when caught in a fever? I have bathed his head and done my best to reassure him, but I do no' think he hears."

"Perhaps willow tea."

"Have you any?"

"I will brew some."

Jeannie turned away to the fire and expected Finnan to remain at Danny's side, but he followed her instead.

"I apologize again for this intrusion," he murmured. "I have turned your life on its head."

She glanced at him as she took the jar of willow bark from the shelf, trying to measure his mood. She began to suspect she could take at face value nothing this man presented.

"It cannot be helped," she returned. But yes, he had turned her world upside down, and yes, she found it difficult even to think clearly in his presence.

"I would like to say we will clear out of here come morning, but I cannot make that promise, with Danny this way."

"And, as you say, you always keep your promises?"

"Always." He spoke the word passionately, an absolute.

Jeannie nodded toward the lad in the other room. "Has Danny been with you a long while?"

"Ever since Culloden." Finnan fell silent for a

moment, and his expression turned bleak. "He never should ha' been there, a mere lad. I found him lying beneath a number of his fellows, all dead, bleeding from the wound where his arm had been. I only heard him because he sobbed for his ma."

Jeannie's throat tightened. So Finnan MacAllister truly did have a heart beneath all those tattoos.

"Given such a dire injury, however did you keep him alive?"

Finnan shook his head. "Last evening was not the first time I ha' stitched him up. Thought sure we'd lose him after Culloden. Geordie and I..." He stopped speaking abruptly.

Jeannie, curious, looked into his face. It had closed as if a shutter had come down.

Yes, and that matched the look she remembered seeing in Geordie's eyes whenever that battle came up: tight, arrested, fierce with pain.

Finnan sucked in a breath. "But, mistress, I will not sully your ears with such talk. 'Tis not something I would inflict on my worst enemy."

Secrets, Jeannie decided, lay behind those tawny brown eyes—some she did not want to know.

"Well, then," she said, "let us see if this tea can soothe young Danny's pain."

Chapter Twelve

Finnan followed Jeannie back to the bed, where Danny still tossed and turned, trying hard to rein in his emotions. What in hell was wrong with him? He had very nearly lost control of his tongue, and his feelings, a moment ago. Wooed, just like Geordie, by a pair of beautiful, wide blue eyes. He had to remember who, and what, she was.

Perhaps not his worst enemy, given the events of this day, but damn near. He cursed the Avries under his breath again. Let them attack him as they would, but falling on an unarmed lad, and one under his protection, just upped the score to be settled.

He would settle Jeannie MacWherter also, no question. But that would be easy and, aye, a mite enjoyable. He could not help but watch the sway of her hips as he trailed her back to Danny, and imagine what lay beneath that plain brown skirt she wore. Smooth and soft, no doubt, round white flesh he wanted bare beneath his hands.

That was not all he wanted. He needed to engage the wench's emotions and then break her heart, even as she had broken Geordie's. Turn about made fair play, to his mind. And engaging her emotions would not be difficult. A blind man could not miss the way she looked at him. Tempted already, she was. That blue gaze had been all over his body, had measured the muscles of his chest and arms and trailed the line of red-brown hair that led down into his rough kilt—and that more than once.

Oh, aye, he would have her on her back and screaming his name within the week.

But first he had to cope with these other complications. He'd not figured on Danny being so sore hurt and marooned here. The lad held Finnan's heart—what little of it remained whole.

"Lift him up," Jeannie bade him now, "and I will tip the cup to his lips."

Finnan did as bidden, and rested Danny's head against his bare shoulder. Ah, but the lad burned with fever. Jeannie leaned in, which brought her very close to Finnan indeed. He could catch the clean scent of her, and the golden shine of her hair.

Danny opened fever-fogged eyes and looked at her. "Ma?"

Jeannie shot Finnan a look of consternation but barely missed a beat. "Yes, son. Drink this for me; it will ease your pain. Then lie back and rest."

Danny, utterly trusting, drank the potion like a lamb. His gaze never left Jeannie's face as Finnan lowered him back onto her pillow.

"Ma, I hurt. No, do no' leave me!"

Jeannie froze in the act of stepping away. Danny's one good hand reached out, searching, and she clasped it.

"Stay with me, Ma. Where have you been? I searched and searched."

Finnan's throat tightened. He knew the story full well: not long before Culloden, Danny and his mother's nearby farm had come under attack by raiders. When the lad, off hunting hares, came home he found the cottage burned and his mother missing.

He had found her eventually, splayed on the hillside out back, violated and dead.

Jeannie MacWherter drew a breath, but she did not hesitate. "Of course I will stay with you, Danny. But you must lie quiet. I do not want your stitches to tear."

Without a word, Finnan fetched a stool from the other room and placed it beside the bed for her. She lowered herself onto it, looking every bit the compassionate angel. Finnan, watching as her fingers caressed those of the lad, had to remind himself again of her true nature.

He should not be surprised to find her a clever and deceptive creature. Geordie, despite his air of innocence, had been no fool. No man who had suffered the events and seen the sights they had together could be entirely gullible. And she had fooled Geordie completely.

No matter. He, Finnan, could be as deceptive as she.

Jeannie glanced at him precisely as if she could hear his thoughts, and he gave her his warmest smile.

"Only look how he settles for you," he crooned, for indeed Danny's eyes fluttered shut. He added truthfully, "He has wanted his ma for so long. But I doubt she was so lovely as you."

Some strong emotion touched her features before she schooled them. "She was beautiful, to him. I can tell by the way he looks at me. What happened to her, Laird MacAllister?"

"You do not want to know."

She gave a grim nod. "I am sometimes reminded

that this world in which we live is a terrible place."

Finnan could not but agree. "Terrible, dangerous, frightening…and beautiful. All the while I was away, the beauty I remembered here in this glen kept me whole and sane." Partly sane, by any road. It might be argued he had traded, to the demons that rode him, some of his sanity—or his soul.

She gave him another of those measuring glances. "Glen Rowan means a great deal to you. I wonder that you ever left."

Finnan hesitated. He had no intention of spilling his deepest feelings to her, and so murmured only, "Aye, well, needs must. But the place a man was born seems to always keep a hold on him."

She made a rueful face and said in a low voice, so as not to disturb Danny, "I was born in Dumfries, but I can admit to no longing to return there. Do you know what I remember about my home? Rain flavored by cinders, falling down into the wet streets. Drawn curtains and neighbors who never ceased their gossip. Oh, the Nith is beautiful with its stone bridges, but I confess I would not wish to go back again."

Yet that was just where Finnan meant to send her, with her tail between her legs.

He shrugged. "Dumfries—that is the lowlands."

She raised to him a blue gaze tinged with mirth. "Whereas, only the highlands are worthy of admiration."

"The highlands are the backbone of Scotland." That backbone might have been broken at Culloden—in fact Finnan knew it had. But, like Danny with his one arm, the sons of this land would fight on.

He propped himself against the wall at the head of

the bed. "Tell me of your life in Dumfries, Mistress MacWherter." He welcomed any details he might use against her. "Geordie said little enough of your situation there."

She appeared to think about it, and turned her gaze away from him. "It seems I have spent my whole life looking after other people."

Not what he expected her to say. His eyebrows jerked upward.

"My father was a curious man, a scholar and very well educated. He worked at the University of Glasgow for a time, but there were incidents, and they asked him to leave. He took his books and his opinions and his scandalous ideas and moved to Dumfries, where he accepted children of the wealthy class, to educate. There he met my mother. She was a chambermaid at his first residence. Very pretty."

She would have been, Finnan reflected.

"He ruined her," Jeannie said, speaking as distantly as if of someone else, "and then decided it would be good, equitable and just, to marry her and raise her to his level. My father was always an equitable man. He claimed to see no differences between the classes and, I think, more than half believed it."

"You were that child?"

She smiled bleakly, and her fingers, soft and gentle, caressed Danny's hand. "The only child they had. My father decided to educate me as I grew. My mother—" She paused abruptly.

Finnan asked, with unwilling sympathy, "Is she dead?"

"Probably, by now. I do not know." She shot him another look, this one defiant. "Why do we speak of this?"

"Because you said you have always looked after others." He nodded at the bed.

"I looked after my mother until she left. She went mad. Father claimed reason could cure her. It could not."

That sent a jolt of surprise through Finnan. "I see."

"No, Laird MacAllister, I doubt you do. My father drove her mad with his expectations."

"How is that, then?"

"She could not be what he wanted. You would have had to know him, if you were to understand. He could be very kind, very idealistic. He could also be so closed into the workings of his own mind he became unreasonable. Things to him were very simple and yet immensely complicated."

"You say your mother left him?"

"Left him, and me. I was ten at the time. I took over running the household, and took care of my father and every stray soul he brought home."

"There were many of those—stray souls?"

"More than you can imagine: thieves, prostitutes, swindlers, and some good people also, gone astray. He met them on the streets or in the ale houses. He began drinking after my mother left and never looked back."

And so was that all Geordie had been to her, another stray? Why marry him, then? Why bother to break his heart? Anger burned in Finnan anew, despite the way her words pulled at his sympathies. Yet she sat there stroking Danny's hand and said, "I understand how this lad feels, wanting his mother."

Aye, and no wonder she did not want to go back to Dumfries. And no wonder, with such an upbringing, she had grown into a deceptive and ruthless creature. Anything to survive.

Finnan understood that edict. But he would never harm those he loved.

"Is that how your father died?" he asked. "The drink?"

"My father," she said with an edge in her voice, "could drink vast amounts of whisky with very little apparent effect. He just became…more so. More intelligent, more dictatorial, more absolute. It was his arrogance that killed him. Oh, I am sure the drink contributed. His health and his body were both ruined well before the night he died."

"If you do no' wish to speak of it…"

"I do not. He was fall-down drunk that night, yes, and stuck his nose into business that did not concern him. An argument broke out." She lifted cool, blue eyes to Finnan's face. "I got all this from Geordie, you understand—I was not there. My father decided to tell someone how to treat his servant, got knocked down for his trouble, and hit his head."

Finnan contemplated it. Was that arrogance, or conscience? The man's daughter plainly thought the worst of the man.

"Geordie came and told me," she concluded. "I fell apart in his arms. We were already two months past due on the rent, had pawned most anything of worth. My father drank it all."

So she had decided to wrap Geordie around her finger, had she? Use his vulnerability against him?

Aye, well, any sympathy he might feel for her, reluctant or not, would not stand in the way of his intentions. But it might make him see her well-settled with a year's rent when he sent her back to Dumfries. If only for Geordie's sake.

Chapter Thirteen

"Are you sure you should move Danny so soon?" Jeannie asked as she stepped out into the morning sunlight. Golden radiance flowed over the mountains to the east and, as so often at this time of year, the air quickly warmed.

Just as well, she reflected, for Finnan MacAllister still went but half clad. The sunlight brushed his shoulders as he moved, and defined the muscles of his chest and arms.

Her fingers tingled, and she acknowledged how she wanted to touch him. What had come over her last night, speaking to him as she had in the depth of the darkness, telling him of her past? She so rarely confided in anyone. But something about the moment, or the man, had invited confidences.

She had to admit, Danny looked a bit better. The lad actually sat upright on the back of his horse, pale but able to speak.

As she watched, Finnan reached up and closed the lad's single hand more firmly about his reins.

"I have no wish to intrude upon you further, Mistress MacWherter," Finnan told her, and added softly, "You have been kindness itself."

Aggie slipped out the doorway behind Jeannie and went to Danny's horse, where she spoke to him.

Finnan stepped to Jeannie's side and gazed down at

her. "Geordie was right about you, it seems. He said you were an angel."

Among other things, apparently. Jeannie schooled herself to remember the anger Finnan had directed at her when first they met, and not fall victim to the seduction in those half-veiled eyes. *He's changed his mind about you,* her traitorous emotions whispered to her. *He's learned better.*

She said, "Are you certain you can get safely past Avrie House? Danny will not be able to stand another attack." She wanted to make it clear her concern was all for the lad and not for him.

"We will take a different route, up along the hillside. Trust that I know every path through this glen."

"Still, you might be better leaving him here and coming back for him with a guard." Jeannie looked again to where Aggie now leaned up to Danny's horse, her hand covering the lad's.

Finnan said ruefully, "I have no guards. Unlike the Avries, I ha' no force of hired men. And as I say, I would impose on you no longer."

Jeannie nodded, unwilling to admit she feared for him. Or how thoughts of him—of his safety, that was—would occupy her mind. She moved to step back, but before she could he reached out and caught her hands in his.

And just like last night beside the fire, when he had stroked his hand through her hair, the shock of it—the pure, searing pleasure—flared through her from where his warm, strong fingers clasped hers. Her gaze flew to his and held, caught like a hare by a hound.

What did she see in his eyes? It was difficult to

read his mood at any time, and now the light there held only mystery. Its gleam might be that of desire, or gratitude—or even malice.

Danger, her mind screamed at her a moment before he said, "Thank you, Jeannie MacWherter. You ha' been most kind."

He leaned toward her, and her pulse sped unpreventably. His lips found her cheek in a kiss that should have been chaste but instead burned like the touch of hot iron on her soft flesh. Ah, how she felt those lips! The warm, agile texture of them, sending ripples of awareness through her, seemingly carried by her accelerated heartbeat to that place where no man had ever touched her.

She ached to turn her head so her mouth met his, desired it with a deep and sudden hunger she'd never dreamed of feeling. Heart, mind, and body all reached for it, and only shock kept her still.

He straightened, withdrawing all the promised pleasure, and stood there looking at her. The newly risen sun made a halo of his hair, flamed red.

No halves for him, Jeannie warned herself. He is indeed a wicked man. But everything within her wished to experience, in full, his wickedness.

"You will have a care going home," she said in a voice that sounded nothing like her own. His fingers still held hers captive, and heat still thrummed through her in waves.

"Aye, you may rely upon it. And, Jeannie MacWherter, will I be welcome to call on you again?"

"Certainly, Laird MacAllister. Aggie and I will both be most anxious to learn how Danny gets on."

He bowed his head toward her again, and she

steeled herself for another brush with that impossible pleasure. But he only spoke in her ear. "I did no' mean that. I would like to call on you, Jeannie, the way a man calls on a woman."

Shock speared through her again with still more intensity, though she would not have believed she could perceive such shades of difference with all her senses scorched and burned.

Discerning her thoughts, no doubt from her expression, he asked, "Why look so surprised? You are a widow, after all. And I am alone in the world."

Alone in the world. Something in those words spoke to Jeannie, fell into the deep, empty place in her heart. *Not wise*, a tiny voice in her mind warned. *You know what he is—a wolf before the sheep. And anyone who can affect you so with one chaste touch could wound you very deeply indeed.*

Yet he stood there waiting, watching her with those mysterious eyes, irresistible as the summer's morning.

She attempted to draw her fingers away; his tightened, and a whole new wave of heat beat through her.

"I am sure that is not what Geordie—or the ghost of him—meant when he asked you to look after me."

"Perhaps not. But grieve for it as I might, Geordie has gone to his rest, while you and I remain."

Tell him no, advised the small voice again. *Send him from your door.*

But every other sense argued differently. She remembered him rising from the pool, every part of him naked to her gaze, the overwhelming, wild, and terrifying beauty of him. *Might I have that?* she asked herself, and the question shocked her still more deeply.

She was a widow, yes—one who had barely felt a man's touch. She and her husband had never lain together. He had kissed her on the lips—a sweet, whisky-flavored caress that had stirred her pity rather than her desire. Nothing, nothing like this. Was she to grow old alone, die without truly living, without tasting fire?

She lifted her chin and told him with what propriety she could muster, "Yes, Laird MacAllister, you may call on me."

Oh, and what was that she saw in his eyes? Satisfaction? Victory? Desire? For something flared there that made Jeannie's stomach flutter in response.

She drew her hand away again, and this time he let her. He made a slight bow that tumbled the wild hair over his shoulders. "Until then, Jeannie MacWherter. Be safe."

He turned from her, took the bridle of Danny's horse in his hand, and, leading the other animal behind, moved off. Aggie, a thoughtful look on her face, stepped away. Both women stood watching until the movements of the small party could no longer be seen down the glen.

****

Aye, and this would be easy, Finnan told himself as he moved off and away, his feet padding in whispers on the soft, green turf. Far easier than he had imagined at the outset. He had bedded many women in his time, and he knew full well when he had snagged one's desire.

Jeannie MacWherter wanted him, and he had not yet even kissed her on the lips. She wanted what she'd seen at the pool, and she wanted his mouth on her, everywhere.

He would be happy to comply—possibly the next time they met. He would, of course, have to get the little maid out of the way. Seduction never worked well with an audience. But he did not doubt he could have Jeannie in broad daylight, right in her cottage—Geordie's cottage that she had stolen—and in any position he chose.

The thought enflamed him. He pictured Jeannie on her knees before him, her golden tresses in a tangle and her lovely red lips parted in anticipation of what he would give her. He wondered again about the curves beneath that plain gown, how her breasts would look, how they would feel in his hands. But this was not about desire.

It was about revenge.

Of course he had the Avries to deal with first. He glanced over his shoulder at Danny. "All right, lad?"

"I will no' complain."

The words pricked Finnan. 'Twas something Geordie had always said, and usually with a touch of dark humor, when things were at their very worst. They might be hungry, wet, and cold, with battle wounds, and nowhere safe to lay their heads, but if he asked his friend how he fared, the response was always the same.

He gave a hard laugh now, grim in its acknowledgement of their situation. Surrounded by enemies once again, and him with paradise to hold and this lad to defend.

Yet the promise of Jeannie MacWherter lay before him.

Chapter Fourteen

Jeannie spread another cloth on the prickle bush and straightened her aching back. She and Aggie had been up doing laundry since before dawn, and it was now well after noon. Endless buckets of water had been hauled and heated over the fire, and countless garments and sheets wrung out. She tried to imagine doing this chore in winter, and failed.

Aggie looked as tired as Jeannie felt, her round cheeks red from exertion and her hair straggling down. She had stopped moaning some time ago, however, for which Jeannie was profoundly grateful.

The cottage lay peaceful and drowsy in the warm afternoon, bees humming among the heather farther up the hill, but Jeannie felt anything but peaceful inside. A day and a half it had been since Finnan MacAllister rode from her door, but she still had not been able to chase him from her mind.

She planted both hands in the small of her back and stretched, letting her eyes stray down the path he had taken away. Did she expect to see him returning? Her heart leaped at the very thought, and she forced herself to measure, instead, the deep hue of the sky and the white clouds sailing inland from the western sea.

Last night had been pure torture, a test of her endurance. How long had she tossed in her bed, trying to persuade herself to sleep? But every time she closed her eyes she saw him stripping the shirt from his body beside her hearth, laying those beautiful hands on Danny's head, leaning in to kiss her cheek.

What was it about the man? Aside from that faultless body, of course, and the wicked light in his eyes. Jeannie narrowed her gaze against the glare of the sun and forced herself into an honest acknowledgement of the truth: she had never seen a man as attractive as Finnan MacAllister.

And she had seen all of him.

The memory of it even now made her blush, yet she let herself relive it again: the wonder of seeing him arise from the pool dripping with water, the long, reddish-brown hair slapping his back, the tattoos that covered his body, and those well-defined muscles. Tattoos everywhere, even...

"Mistress, are you all right?"

"Eh?" Jeannie opened her eyes and looked into Aggie's concerned face. "Of course."

"Only, you looked like you were in pain," Aggie pointed out. "I will fetch us some water, shall I? You sit there a moment."

Jeannie complied and perched on the stone wall that hedged the yard, making sure she chose a place from which she could still see the track.

He had said he would come to call. He had, right before he seared her cheek with that burning caress.

What did it mean? His letters, still folded away in her chest and covered with his forceful, black writing, had expressed his hatred. But they were written before he met her. Dare she hope he had truly changed his mind? She did not know, but if she held to honesty she had to admit she hoped it was true.

Did highland men, moreover strapping warriors who walked about carrying the evidence of past battles on their bodies, truly believe in the existence of visiting spirits, or had he made it up? If so, why? She, herself, gave the tale no credence. She would rather think of Geordie at peace, the demons that had spurred him laid to rest.

As for Finnan MacAllister...

"I hope he is all right."

"Eh?" Jeannie started and nearly dropped the cup of cold water Aggie placed in her hand.

Aggie leaned against the wall, drank from her own cup, and said, "I have not been able to stop thinking of him."

Jeannie stared. Had Aggie, too, been taken by the auburn-maned half-god-half-man? And who could blame her if she had?

"Only imagine," Aggie fussed on, "losing an arm in battle, and him so young and handsome."

Jeannie breathed again. Aggie spoke of Danny. Hastily, Jeannie reordered her thoughts. "Yes," she murmured. She supposed Danny a winsome enough lad, with thick, brown hair and those wide, pain-filled gray-blue eyes. And she knew, better than anyone, how soft was Aggie's heart.

"What if they were attacked again on the way home, and him burning up with fever? I wish they had stayed longer."

So did Jeannie, if only so she might gaze on Finnan.

"And who could imagine the Dowager Avrie's sons doing such a thing?" Aggie went on. "Attacking in broad daylight."

"The two houses are at war," Jeannie said. "We are best out of it."

Aggie lowered her voice, even though no one but the bees could hear. "There is much hatred toward MacAllister among those at Avrie House. Dorcas says Laird MacAllister killed Master Avrie and so took the glen from him."

"It was MacAllister's first, to my understanding."

"Wicked highlanders," Aggie decided, "with their treachery and their back-stabbing."

Jeannie had to remember that Finnan MacAllister was indeed a very wicked man. Wicked enough to strip the clothes from her body? To plunder her with that bright, dangerous gaze? To touch her everywhere with those lips that trailed flame?

Suddenly she was on fire, far beyond the effects of the warm day.

"Yes," she murmured, "we are far better out of it."

Aggie shot her a look. "What will happen if the Avries take the glen back from MacAllister? Will we be asked to leave?"

"I hope not." But disquiet stirred in Jeannie's heart. How long had it been since she had felt secure? She could not even remember.

She pictured again the care with which Finnan MacAllister had tended Danny. What would it be like to have someone take care of her that way?

"I mean," Aggie rattled on, "I am not entirely happy here. It is dull, and I do miss Dumfries. But I am not sure I would like to go back now. And I know I would not want to leave without learning what has happened to that brave lad."

"I thought," Jeannie said absently, letting her eyes

wander to the trail again, "you were interested in the groom at Avrie House. What was his name?"

"Ronald. He is a fine-looking lad, as well, and with a bold pair of hands on him, but he is not a patch on young Danny." Aggie sighed. "Do you think if I walked to Avrie House I could get some news?"

"You may not have to." Jeannie's eyes, still narrowed, had detected movement on the trail. Her heart leaped painfully in her chest. Had he come? Did he keep his promise so soon?

There—she saw a glint of light on harness; a mounted man. No, two. Had he brought Danny back with him? But surely the lad should be home in his bed.

"Oh, look!" Aggie said unnecessarily, for Jeannie's attention was all on the approaching men. They slowed as they met the rise that fronted the cottage, and her heart plummeted. Strangers both, with fair hair that gleamed in the sun.

She unpropped herself from the wall even as they dismounted and approached the gate, which, as always, stood open. As alike as two hounds from the same litter they were, both tall and well built, with those shining caps of hair. They came armed, in leather, and in tartan that identified them.

The Dowager Avrie's grandsons, it seemed, had come to call.

"Mistress," said the taller of the two. "Good afternoon to you." His eyes swept Jeannie in a comprehensive glance. From the distance she could not tell their color, but something in the look filled her with caution, though his tone sounded courteous.

"Good afternoon."

"I am Stuart Avrie, and this is my brother, Trent.

And you, as our grandmother the Dowager Avrie has told us, are Mistress MacWherter." Stuart Avrie added deliberately, "MacAllister's tenant."

His voice changed at the speaking of the name MacAllister, from polite to dangerous, and hate twisted his handsome face. Beside him, his brother's hand flew, as if by instinct, to the hilt of his sword.

More wicked highlanders and—if Finnan MacAllister could be believed—those willing to order an ambush. And breaking the law by wearing those swords, no less. Ah, well, and the highlands proved, indeed, as lawless and wild as her father had always claimed.

Gathering all her composure, she stepped forward. "You are mistaken, gentlemen. I am tenant to no one. My late husband owned this cottage free and clear."

Stuart Avrie's face darkened. "And him friend to MacAllister, we are led to understand."

His brother gave Jeannie no chance to reply. Pushing forward, he asked, "Is he here?"

"I beg your pardon?"

"Is he here—MacAllister?" He eyed the door of the cottage, which also stood open. "Are you sheltering him?"

Jeannie exchanged incredulous looks with Aggie and drew a breath. "I assure you not. I assume he is at his dwelling—Dun Mhor."

"Nay," said Trent Avrie, with steel in his voice. "For we burned Dun Mhor to the ground last night."

Chapter Fifteen

Finnan MacAllister slipped out from the shelter of the trees and took a measuring look at the stars. Only a few hours until morning, and Danny slept peacefully behind him, under cover. They would make it safely through this night.

No moon sailed overhead, and that proved a benefit to a hunted man. Anger surged through him and soured his gut; it infuriated him that he should be chased like a hart on his own land. This place belonged to him both spiritually and by right, but he would stay hidden if he must.

The Avries would die. He savored that truth the way a man savors a draught of cold water after a long march. They would strangle on their own blood like their father before them, the treacherous bastards. But for the time being he had to play at ducking and waiting. He would strike when the moment arrived, not before.

He should have been more cautious withal—especially after that attack in broad daylight. He had let them harm Danny and attack his home. But he would have his own back; it was just a question of when.

And that meant his revenge upon Jeannie MacWherter would have to wait. Oh, aye, he would still extract what Geordie was due from her. Just not yet.

Upon the thought of her, he felt himself grow

aroused. He remembered how she had looked when last he saw her standing in the morning light at the door of Rowan Cottage. He relived the moment he had placed his lips against the soft warmth of her cheek and known the intensity of the heat that flared. She would be that soft—and hot—everywhere beneath those clothes. He promised himself he would one day measure the weight of her naked breasts in his hands.

Soon? Not soon enough.

He flicked his gaze northward in the direction of her cottage—Geordie's cottage, he corrected himself. Jeannie was but a parasite, like a flea, that currently infested the place. A stunningly attractive flea in which he ached to bury himself.

Could he destroy her by making her want him—more, by making her love him as Geordie had loved her? Cold-hearted wench. He wanted that heart in his hands, right along with those breasts.

But first he must settle Avrie's accursed spawn.

Hard to imagine now that for centuries past men by the name of Avrie had served his family loyally and well. MacAllister lairds had relied upon them in battle and friendship both, until one Avrie clansman got ideas too big for himself.

Finnan acknowledged he was presently at a disadvantage, his home heavily damaged, though certainly rebuildable—it had come under attack on numerous occasions over the past centuries and yet stood strong—the last of his family's retainers chased off for fear of their safety. He and Danny driven to the hills… He saw all that as temporary. He and Danny, with Geordie, had been in much more difficult places.

He let his eyes trace the outlines of Orion, who

hung above the glen. He remembered lying on a hillside far north of here, once. It had been after he and Geordie withdrew their swords from the service of a chief who refused to pay them. Before Culloden, that was. He had been sore hurting then, suffering one of the many injuries he had carried during his life. But Orion had seemed to point him homeward.

Now the warrior whispered that Finnan should turn his attention north, to Jeannie's door. Could he not hide there as well as elsewhere? Might he not kill two birds with the one stone?

There, in the darkness, he smiled.

****

Jeannie drew the shawl close about her shoulders and edged nearer the dying fire. August it was still, but who would know it, with the way the chill arrived with the setting sun here in these hills? Of course, the light did linger long in the sky, but now velvet dark hung outside the cottage, and the cold crept in.

She should be in her bed. Aggie slept soundly up in the loft, but Jeannie had arisen from her own cot, her thoughts far too full to afford any rest.

Those men today—Stuart and Trent Avrie—had they truly burned Finnan MacAllister's home? Did they hunt him like a fox on his own land? Did such things really occur here in the highlands?

What would they do if they caught him? Murder him in cold blood? A shiver traced its way up her spine, a shiver that had nothing to do with the chilly dark. She did believe they might, given the look in Stuart Avrie's cold eyes.

She remembered the man's parting words to her: "I urge you, Mistress MacWherter, to band together with us in our effort to capture this blackguard. No one is safe with him at large in the glen."

She should have asked. She should have demanded to know how they meant to resolve this situation, a circumstance that could never have evolved in Dumfries, where people tended to call the constables and only took matters into their own hands after too much whisky.

Need she remind herself she was no longer in Dumfries? This place, wild and lawless, seemed beyond the bounds of civilization.

She had been too stunned to ask the brothers Avrie anything. For an instant she had been sure they would push their way inside the cottage and search for MacAllister. But they had ridden away leaving her upset and, if she were honest, frightened.

She did not wish to be caught in the middle of some highland squabble. She would leave if she could; she had nowhere else to go.

The night seemed far too quiet, so much so she could catch the flutter of Aggie's breath from the loft, and even the crackle of the dying fire sounded loud. She contemplated throwing on more fuel, just for the comfort of it, but she did not know how they would ever garner enough fuel for...

What was that?

Her head came up as her ears caught a new sound outside the door. A brush of movement? Another chill chased her spine, this one pure, superstitious terror. Anything could be out there.

She did not believe in the existence of Geordie's ghost. She did not.

A soft knock sounded.

Jeannie, on her feet in an instant, froze where she stood, thinking of the wild stories Aggie had brought home from Avrie House of banshees, witches, boogies, all haunting the glen. Of course she did not believe in those things either, but she would be mad to open that door.

She eyed the bar that held it shut. Would that hold against a spirit? Against the ghost of Geordie MacWherter?

The knock sounded again, a bit louder this time.

"Who is there?"

If a deep, gravelly voice answered, she would shame herself on the spot. How might a ghost sound?

"It is I, Mistress MacWherter. 'Tis Finnan MacAllister."

Jeannie's heart leaped for a whole new reason. Relief and dismay combined to elevate her pulse.

She would still be mad to open the door.

Yet he had come back to her—no matter in the middle of the night. Her feet carried her to the door without her volition; her fingers lifted the bar and swung the panel open.

He stood there, hair mussed by the night wind, with Danny leaning against him. His eyes reached for her even before he spoke.

"I am that sorry to come so late, but I seek refuge—not for me, but for the lad. I ha' nowhere else to take him."

Jeannie stepped back, making of it an invitation. "Then, come in."

Chapter Sixteen

"You are a merciful angel," Finnan MacAllister said softly, his eyes on Danny but his voice a caress Jeannie could almost feel.

They had bedded the lad down in a corner near the hearth. He now slept, restless with fever.

That Danny remained very ill, Jeannie could not doubt. His skin burned to the touch and had a waxen quality. She could quite see why MacAllister did not want to keep him at large out on the hillside, but why did he have to come to her door?

Now she struggled to think clearly and found it far too difficult. Finnan MacAllister's presence affected her on levels she could barely understand.

Her awareness leaped every time he moved, flexed a muscle, every time he drew a breath. He had brought the fragrance of the night in with him, along with an underlying scent of pure male that roused all her senses.

She watched his hands as he pulled the blanket to Danny's chin and then touched the lad's forehead—graceful, strong, long-fingered hands covered with scars and those twisting tattoos. Strange how none of those scars diminished his male beauty.

"I hope you have hidden your horses well," she whispered.

"We did not come on horseback. We walked over the hills, and it took a toll on the lad. Still, we ha' come through worse."

She felt a sudden, consuming curiosity to know all he had been through, and what had befallen him. She might sit for days just listening to the music of his voice while he told her.

Beautiful hands, beautiful voice; but could she trust him?

Trust—such a fragile and tremulous thing. She had trusted her father, once. Trusted Geordie, as well. Geordie, at least, had not disappointed her; he had kept to his word. But this man beside her? Another matter completely.

He seated himself on the bench beside her, which put him less than an arm's length away. She might reach out and touch his hand if she chose. Move into his arms.

And what then? What if she followed a heretofore unprecedented impulse, leaned in and kissed him? Would madness ensue? Would she be lost?

She chose her words carefully and spoke, instead. "They were here this afternoon, the brothers Avrie, looking for you."

That made him stare, a sharp glance she felt like a touch. "Then I should not be here. I am sorry for drawing you into my quarrel."

"It seems far more than a quarrel. They say they have burnt your house to the ground."

He smiled, the last thing she expected. "Not quite. They stormed the place, aye, and gutted some of the rooms with fire, but Dun Mhor is built of cold stone and will stand long after I am dust."

"Yet they have chased you to the hills."

"I do not like the prospect of being caught like a rat

in a trap. Anyway, the hills are my true home. I ha' spent half my life in the wild."

Yes, and she sensed that about him, the stillness he sometimes achieved, and the canny, measuring glance as of some creature untamed.

"We will away now, if you wish," he added, very offhand. "The last thing I want, Jeannie, is to bring harm upon you."

He should not be so familiar as to call her by her given name, yet hearing it in that soft, musical voice rendered her incapable of minding.

"You can hardly move him now." She nodded at Danny. "And anyway, it is nearly dawn. Let him rest."

"The morning star was rising when I came to your door." He spoke the words like poetry.

She folded her fingers together in an attempt to discipline them. "How is it the Avries think they can hunt you like an animal? Are there no laws here?"

"There are, and far older than any known in Dumfries. The land makes our laws; the very hills do. The only right is survival. The land is mine, so do what they will the Avries cannot defeat me."

Madness, Jeannie thought. Did he really believe such wild assertions?

"If they catch you, what will they do?"

He gave a thin smile. "What I did to their father, and what he in his turn did to mine. But they will no' find it easy; I will not be caught unawares again. Now are you ready to reconsider and turn me from your door?"

Suddenly restless, Jeannie got to her feet. She took up the poker and stirred the fire, her face turned from him. "Murder does not justify murder," she said, "even in the highlands."

"I do not expect you to understand it," he told her. "But I will fight as I must. This place is my blood and my bones, and that of all those who came before me. All the while I roamed the world earning my way, I carried the love and duty of it, like a second heartbeat."

All those years he had been a mercenary. So perhaps killing meant little enough to him. It might be as easy as breathing.

He went on softly, "A man must make his way—a lad must, in my case, for I was scarcely more when I began. I left here with little but my father's bloodied torc, and his sword."

Jeannie turned her face and looked at him, searching. Could she even try to imagine the life he had led? Could he imagine hers, striving so desperately to hold together the pieces of a life already shattered?

Geordie had carried that same sense of fierce endurance beneath his pain and regret. She sensed no regret in this man, however.

"And how do you see all this ending?" she challenged. "They dispossessed you and your family, you murdered their father, so now they would kill you, as well. Will you live like a hare in the hills forever?"

"Better a hare free in these hills than a man anywhere else. But nay, 'twill not be forever. Only until they are driven back out of the glen."

"Or dead."

"Or dead."

A chill traced its way up Jeannie's back. Wicked to speak so casually of such an eventuality. The worst of it was she believed him.

"And what about Aggie and me," she asked,

"caught in the middle of it?" She could not hide in the hills, and she had nowhere else to go.

He, too, got to his feet and approached her. Before she could think to protest, he reached out and captured her hands.

And oh, the warmth of his touch went through her, chased like fever up her arms, heated the breath in her lungs, and rose straight to her head. It kept her motionless as he stepped closer and looked her in the eyes.

"I would remind you, Jeannie MacWherter, I am a man who keeps his promises."

And his threats. That she believed.

He stepped still nearer; now she could feel the heat of him all up and down her body. "And have I no' promised to keep you safe?"

"You promised that to the ghost of my dead husband." She said it wryly, combatting the feelings that assaulted her.

"A sacred vow, for Geordie and I are bonded even beyond the grave."

And so would he take what even Geordie never had? Jeannie had pitied Geordie MacWherter, relied on him, perhaps even felt for him sincere affection, but nothing that would persuade her to take the big, bluff highlander to her bed. Now, though, the impulse stormed her like a gale wind.

She had managed to live twenty-two years without experiencing this sharp and wild desire. Why now?

"And," she asked, her voice faltering as she gazed into his eyes, "how do you mean to protect me while fighting for your own life, and Danny's?"

"One thing I learned all those years roaming the

world was how to fight. Trust me, Jeannie. Once I take you under my protection you are safe, you are mine."

Did she move still closer then? Did she truly lay the palms of her hands against the warmth of his chest?

She could feel his heart beating, deep heavy thuds like the pulse of the world. She had a sudden, terrifying thought: this man could become her world, if she let him. Maybe even if she did not.

She told him honestly, "It is not easy for me to trust."

"Then," he whispered, "only let me show you my devotion."

His hands slid slowly up her arms in a tantalizing friction as he bent his head to hers. Still caught by what she saw in his eyes, Jeannie could not look away. His gaze held her fast as might a magical spell, even as his lips reached for hers.

He drew her up against him an instant before he claimed her mouth, so she felt all of him in a rush of pure, muscular heat. His lips seared hers, soft and persuasive yet hot as fire. Sensation speared through her from that point of contact and burned away any lingering hope of resistance.

Oh, and she had never imagined touching someone could feel like this. Darkness rushed at her on the wings of flame and pleasure as demoralizing as pain. She surrendered to it completely, as to sudden death.

His lips molded to hers, moved and wooed, coaxed her lips apart. He seemed to drink of her and then to pour himself into her like strong drink. His tongue slipped into her mouth, licked the insides of her lips, and stroked her tongue in an act of blatant intimacy that turned Jeannie's knees to water.

No one had ever touched her so. She knew she should haul on the strings of her sanity—her propriety—and push him away. But all she could imagine was his tongue touching her everywhere while she lay open and welcoming beneath it, naked and shameless.

Wicked.

He made a soft sound in his throat—satisfaction or demand—and it completed her undoing. She opened her mouth further beneath his, pressed herself to him, lifted her arms and wound them about his neck. Smooth, warm muscle met her fingers, and a tumble of hair like silk. His heart beat still more quickly against her breast, and hers sped to match it. She wanted to be inside him; she wanted him inside her.

Yes, and he came armed for it; she could now feel him pressed insistently against her and could not mistake that particular weapon. It should shock her further, make her pull away from him and flee. Instead she felt a rush of victorious joy that she had aroused him.

His tongue stroked hers and took up a deep, suggestive rhythm. Jeannie had never lain with any man, no, but she understood instinctively just what that dance meant. Had she any doubt, he pressed himself against her in silent demand, and she fought the desire to part her legs and welcome him in.

She nearly sobbed in protest when he broke the kiss and withdrew his tongue from her mouth. "Jeannie," he said raggedly. "Jeannie, Jeannie—"

She gasped and threaded her fingers through his hair. Determinedly, she reached for his mouth again—wet and hot, *hers*. This time she slid her tongue between his lips, coaxed his tongue to her bidding, and when he thrust it upon her, a mad idea burst to life in her mind: she could slide down his body, take him into her mouth just as she had that tongue.

Doubly wicked! But he made her feel wanton and abandoned, and all those things she had never expected to be.

His hands, that held her so fast against him, slid softly downward, caressing her body as they went. Pleasure, still more intense, pierced her to the marrow. Surely she would die if she did not have this man.

Again he broke the kiss, but it was only to slide that irresistible mouth of his across her cheek and shiver little kisses to the corner of her mouth.

She tried to recapture his lips with hers, needing it badly, and he gave a soft, low laugh that vibrated through her. By heaven, but she longed to hear that in her ear, in the dark.

"So beautiful," he murmured. "Do you ken how beautiful you are?"

She little cared if that were true, so long as he believed it, so long as it made him want her. So this was how good women went astray…

"Please," she begged, and captured his mouth again. He tasted like nothing she had ever known: honey, and the best whisky, and danger.

His hand moved once more, caressing its way up her body, and found her breast. Jeannie stopped breathing and the world stood still.

Surely she had been made to fill this man's hands? To lie beneath him? To give and give, and give.

****

This will be entirely too easy, Finnan MacAllister

thought in satisfaction. Already Jeannie MacWherter melted in his hands like frost in the sun.

The lying hoyden—how was he supposed to believe a woman who burned with such passion would have kept Geordie or any other man from her bed? Yet he had Geordie's own word on that, his letters written out of an aching and sorrowful heart.

She will not love me, Finn, not in the way a woman loves a man or even as a wife accepts her husband. 'Tis proof, had I needed it, I am but a blight on this world.

Finnan had heeded the sadness those words expressed, but taken up completely with his struggle here in the glen had he neglected the deeper darkness in Geordie's soul? Geordie had often expressed an almost childlike idealism, all too easily disappointed. He possessed little of the hard cynicism Finnan had learned to wear like armor, and that protected him yet.

It did protect him, he assured himself, even as he kissed Jeannie MacWherter again, his tongue mimicking the action his loins ached to complete. She proved a far too potent temptation.

And he could have her here and now on her own hearthstones, with Danny but an arm's reach away, if he wished. The risk and danger of the prospect further enflamed him, the chance of the lad waking to see them moving together, him spearing the woman as she deserved.

And she did deserve it.

He shifted his hand on her breast—soft, delectable warmth—and sought her nipple with his thumb. He now had his tongue so far down her throat it was an act of copulation of itself, and he clearly felt her stiffen as pleasure shot through her. Deliberately, he slid his fingers down the neck of her gown. Ah, but for a creature of hell she was heaven to touch.

Yet Finnan did not believe in heaven—only hard-won retribution.

Jeannie arched her back and pressed herself into his palm, a willing offering. He knew then without question that he had won.

Was it too soon to push her to complete the act? He had her well on the hook now and did not want to frighten her off. Yet he ached so to plunge into her, he did not know that he could endure.

Fiercely, he reined in his impulses. He must make her want him beyond all reason, needed to play the role of protector to the hilt. He needed her to love him, not just give in.

But it would be hard to draw away now when the spell he wove held them both fast.

He stopped kissing her but left his hand inside her bodice in a blatant act of claiming. The contrast between her soft, mounded flesh and taut nipple goaded his desire. He felt wild to open the garment and replace his fingers with his mouth.

He pictured all the ways he might have her: on her knees; or on her back, spread for him like a holy offering.

He managed to say, "I am that sorry, Jeannie. I ha' overstepped myself." And he tried to withdraw his hand.

Her fingers flew to cover his and pressed them to her breast. She licked her lips, and a wild woman looked at him from her eyes.

"Please, Finnan."

The first time she had spoken his given name, and

said it with that sweetness she wore like a cloak—almost believable. *Almost.*

Chapter Seventeen

Outside the cottage a cock crowed, heralding morning. Jeannie heard it like a woman emerging from a dream, or more correctly one freeing herself from enchantment. For Finnan MacAllister had surely woven a potent spell.

She contemplated it, not sure she believed in dark magic. As a girl, she had attended the kirk, expecting it to afford her some comfort and peace. It never had, because the minister spoke only of ruination, sin, and sacrifice.

Ruination and sacrifice she had found in her own home. Sin, it seemed, found her only now.

Would it be such a sin to haul Finnan MacAllister away into her bedroom? To peel the clothing from that beautiful body of his, divest him of the rough, woolen kilt, and have him all for her own?

Unquestionably.

And she cared for her immortal soul, did she not? Of course she did. Well, perhaps.

He still held her pinioned against him, one arm hard across her back. His other hand remained thrust inside her bodice. Sweet heaven, how could she have let that happen? She looked down at her own body and saw his long fingers cupping her breast. A new, potent wave of desire assailed her.

But she was a sane, rational woman, and the

cockerel had called her to herself. She released Finnan's wrist and fought her way free.

Her dress, disconcertingly, gaped open. When had he untied the front of it? The shawl she had been wearing lay in a heap on the floor. The sheer impropriety of it brought heat over her in a rush.

Looking up, she encountered his gaze: bright with danger, hot as fire, and yet guarded. What did she see there besides admiration? Ah, but he liked what he had seen of her, and what he had felt. Triumph flared through her again.

She took another decisive step backward, out of his reach this time. "Laird MacAllister, I do not know what came over me," she began.

"Or me." He bent and caught up her shawl from the floor, offered it to her. When she took it, her fingers brushed his, and she recoiled as if burned, and clutched the woolen fabric to her bosom.

Earnestly, he asked, "Can you forgive me? I have no excuse save for your beauty, and the fact that I have been alone—far too alone—a long while."

Jeannie, her thoughts scattered, did not know how to reply. The cottage seemed suddenly too small to contain both of them. She wanted to run out the door into the dawn.

Yet the remnants of his magical spell held her, and she knew, disconcertingly, if he snapped his fingers she would be in his arms again. She turned and fled to the only place she could, her bedroom. No door but only a curtain separated it from the other room. It seemed a woefully inadequate barrier now.

Outside the single window, gray light gathered, the half radiance that filled the glen at dawn. Her cockerel crowed again, and she blessed him. What would have happened but for his cry? Might she and Finnan MacAllister both be in this room by now?

She eyed the bed and wrapped her arms tight about herself. She had heard about the act from women she knew, not the least Aggie, led astray in Dumfries by a young doorman at a neighboring house, who had soon abandoned her. It could be awkward, uncomfortable, even painful.

With Finnan MacAllister, Jeannie believed, it would be none of those things.

She had to regather her sanity, needed to go back out there and act the mistress of this place. He was just a man. One with a magical touch, a hard, beautiful body, and delicious lips. Mating with him would be like mating with liquid fire. Taking him into her mouth...

She stopped herself there and tried to think of something—anything—that would dampen her imagination. Surprisingly, an image of Geordie MacWherter flickered to life in her mind—Geordie, with his wide, sorrowful gaze and the well of deep sadness he seemed to carry around with him.

Ironic, that the memory of her husband should now deliver her from temptation. Hastily, she straightened her clothing and bundled her hair into a respectable knot. Before she finished, she heard voices from beyond the curtain—that of Finnan MacAllister, which now seemed to have become rooted in her soul, or perhaps a bit lower down, and Aggie's lighter tones. She pushed her way back through the curtain. Aggie bent over Danny's makeshift bed, her hand on his forehead, and exclaimed in concern.

Finnan MacAllister—but no, she would not look at

him.

"He is burning up," Aggie said, "and will not wake."

Jeannie swept forward to examine the lad. Two flags of bright color flew in his cheeks, and he tossed, restless.

"Go and dress yourself," she told Aggie more brusquely than she intended. "It is not proper for you to appear in your nightclothes."

Did she hear a faint snort from Finnan MacAllister's direction? Still, she would not look his way.

"I did not know they were here," Aggie began, in defense of herself.

"Just go."

Foolish, for it left Jeannie alone with Finnan again, the last thing she wanted.

"Danny seems very ill indeed," she said. "Have you dressed the wound?"

"I was just about to, when your maid appeared." Finnan approached, and Jeannie's entire body went on alert. She had never suspected she could quiver with awareness. Hastily, she stepped away.

"Jeannie," he said, and the sound shivered through her. "Jeannie, will you not look at me?"

She would have fled once more, but his fingers snared her wrist. She shied from the immediate rush of pleasure.

"I am that sorry," he told her in a low voice. "I have made things uncomfortable between us."

It had not been all his doing, the kisses, the touching—she knew that very well. Yet she said, "You have made things impossible between us. You will have to leave." Because now she could not trust herself near him.

"Aye," he agreed. "Just as soon as I can move the lad."

And when might that be? Danny had arrived on his feet last night but did not look capable of standing on them now.

Aggie came clattering back down from the loft and tied her apron around her waist.

"Please heat some water so Laird MacAllister can tend Danny's wound, and then make some porridge," Jeannie bade her.

Aggie nodded and leaned in close to Jeannie. "Have you told him those men were here yesterday afternoon?"

"I have. He will be leaving as soon as possible."

Aggie did not look happy, but she went about her duties without further comment. Finnan MacAllister stepped away as she gathered a basin and bandages—further inroads on Jeannie's best sheet. She wondered what thoughts occupied his mind and then cursed herself for caring. Last night had been a rush of madness, now over and done.

Yet when he began peeling the bandages from Danny's wound, she followed the gentle movements of his fingers, all too aware of the way the thick auburn hair spilled down the back of his neck. She had touched that hair, tangled her fingers in it. She had been cupped by that hand, had pressed herself against that lithe body.

By heaven, was this a disease that afflicted her?

Danny stirred when the bandage came away, tossed his head restlessly, and moaned.

Jeannie bit her lip; the wound looked angry, the

flesh red and puffy around the stitches.

"Inflamed," she whispered.

"Aye, it looks bad," MacAllister agreed. "But he has been through far worse."

"What if the Dowager Avrie's grandsons come back?" asked Aggie, from the hearth. Aggie had never been the sort of servant to speak only when spoken to.

"Surely they will not," MacAllister replied, "if they ha' already been here looking. They have no reason to believe you in league with me, have they?"

"None besides the fact that you once owned this property," Jeannie said.

He looked at her, and his gaze skittered over her body, from her lips downward. "Still, that does not lead them to think you would protect me." He corrected softly, "Or, us." He turned his attention back to Danny. "By any road, we will be gone before you know it. Have you any herbs in the house? Yarrow or comfrey? This wound needs to be packed."

Jeannie shook her head. "I have never needed to grow my own cures; there were plenty apothecaries in Dumfries."

"This glen is my apothecary. I need to go out and search."

Into that gray dawn? Jeannie glanced toward the door even as all her instincts rose in protest. "But…"

"Just for a wee while; I promise I will come back for him."

"Is it safe?" she asked, without intention. Finnan MacAllister was not hers over whom to worry. And he could quite plainly look after himself.

"They may be watching the cottage," Aggie added, proving she, too, felt protective.

"Just try and keep him quiet until I return." Finnan moved to the door in that soundless way he had.

Let him go, Jeannie's common sense told her, and pray he does not return. Better if he walked straight out of her life.

But he gave her a smile before he slipped out the door, and she felt its effect all through her body, down to her toes.

By heaven, what had come over her? She raised both hands to cheeks as flushed as Danny's.

"Mistress, are you ill?" Aggie inquired.

"Yes. No. We find ourselves in a perilous situation, Aggie."

"Yes, mistress. But we cannot turn our backs on them, can we? Not with this poor lad so sore hurt."

Jeannie very much feared she would not be able to turn her back on Finnan MacAllister, not for any reason.

Chapter Eighteen

Finnan whispered a prayer as he cut the stalks of yarrow with his dirk—no prayer ever heard in any kirk, this, but one far older, that flowed from his heart. Long ago he had learned not to take anything without permission.

That was why Jeannie MacWherter would be begging for him before he took her.

And the ancient laws decreed he give thanks for all that came to him.

Oh, aye, he would thank her most generously after, just before he broke her heart.

By God, why could he not manage to chase the woman from his mind? Was she not just a woman like every other he had rowed in his arms, with two legs, two breasts, a mouth, and a well of heat into which he might pour himself? Only, she was not like every other woman—those lips of hers tasted wild and sweet, and his fingers craved the feel of her soft flesh.

He straightened from his place on the hillside and let his gaze find the new dawn. He had to go carefully, here. He would have her, just as she deserved. Yet he needed to remember this was not about pleasure, but retribution.

He might take his pleasure, as well.

That thought curled seductively through his mind. Aye, he might—over and over again, before she learned not to trifle with a highlander's heart. The treacherous wench. The beautiful, irresistible she-demon.

Nay, but that was an exaggeration. Jeannie MacWherter might be a scheming little baggage, but she was a flesh-and-blood woman, no demon. He would leave her with a lesson before he chased her away out of his glen.

The morning light blurred before his eyes as he contemplated how he would have her. There, in her own bed? Out here on the hillside, a willing sacrifice made to this place and Geordie's memory? Aye, that would be sweet.

He was already up and hard beneath his kilt just thinking about it, so beguiled he almost missed the movement along the floor of the glen below.

Instinct honed over many seasons in the field corrected his error. He blinked, and his surroundings came back into focus.

A party of men on horseback, a patrol. Searching for him. Aye, and the hounds were abroad early this day, hoping to catch him unawares, no doubt.

He stuffed the cut yarrow into his pouch, turned, and, very like a deer, loped up the hillside. The search party headed toward Jeannie's cottage, but even as he gained greater height and crouched down to watch they veered westward and away. He breathed a bit more easily. Four riders; he knew he could take them with his sword, but he would prefer to avoid such an encounter if he could.

He stood still as a rock and watched them wind away and disappear into the mist. Then he murmured another prayer beneath his breath, for protection this time, and started down.

He had almost reached the cottage when a bird fluttered near his shoulder and away again. He paused, looked for and found it perched on a prickle bush. A highland grouse—Geordie's bird. Geordie had always favored it for its courage and ability to conceal itself, and had one tattooed on his cheek.

"Hello, old friend," Finnan said softly. "Have you come to visit with me?"

No exaggeration to think the spirits of those on the other side came in the guise of birds. Had Finnan not seen crows take the souls of many after a battle? The crane was said to bear the task of carrying souls to the next world, but Finnan knew different. For fighting men it was the crow.

The grouse fixed him with a beady eye that held all Geordie's sadness and vulnerability.

"Do not worry; I will settle her," Finnan promised.

The bird ruffled its wings in distress.

"You always did have a soft heart," Finnan told it. "No one knows that better than I. And no doubt where you are now some of the pain she caused you has faded away. But I ha' taken a vow of vengeance on your behalf, and you know I never leave go of my vows."

The bird opened its beak; Finnan almost expected Geordie's voice, low and deep, to issue forth.

"There is but one thing," Finnan confided. "I shall need to plunder her in order to see her set right. I hope you will not mind that, where you are."

The bird gave a wild cry and flew away. Finnan took it for permission.

****

"They turned away to the west," Finnan said softly to Jeannie even as he packed the yarrow into Danny's

123

wound. He did not want the maid, who seemed an excitable creature, to overhear. He did not need her fretting and greeting.

Give Jeannie MacWherter her due; she did not seem the sort to greet. He sensed strength beneath all her beautiful softness.

She turned those clear, blue eyes on him but said nothing. Her head, bent over the basin she held, nearly touched his.

He went on, "I do not doubt they made to cross the burn at the rock ford not far from here, to search the other side of the glen. That should remove the threat a wee while."

She nodded. "And as you said, why should they come here, when they have just been?"

"Aye, and they have no cause to believe you would succor me. It might be safest if you put about the tale, through your maid, perhaps, that you fear and despise me."

Her steady gaze did not waver from his. "What makes you think that would be a tale?"

"Ah." He allowed one corner of his mouth to twitch upward. "So you are still holding those letters against me."

"They were hard and vicious."

I am hard, whenever I am near you, Finnan thought ruefully.

"And frightening to a woman with nowhere else to go."

"I regret that." He let his eyes caress her face, allowed his admiration to show. "I had not met you then. I had only what Geordie wrote to me by which to judge."

"He never said he wrote you letters."

Finnan would wager not.

"I wish you would tell me what did he write, that gave you so harsh an opinion of me."

Anger licked at Finnan's soul. "That you did not love him." Would not, no matter how Geordie tried.

"Well, that is true. He knew it at the outset. He said he did not mind."

A man might say many things, as she would learn to her sorrow.

"No matter now," he told her, and smoothed Danny's bandaging in place. "The yarrow should dim the pain from that wound. But I hate to move him again."

"Stay then," she urged, her gaze fleeing his at last.

He felt it then, how close he stood to having his way with her. He said, "I dare not."

"Why?"

"A thousand reasons, not the least of which is what passed between us last night."

She bit at her luscious lower lip. He ached to do the same. "We might try to overlook that," she said, "since we were both at fault."

"That is generous of you. I know I overstepped myself, and quite honestly I do not know that I would not do the same again."

"Oh!"

"I will take to the hills. But I would ask of you one last boon: might I leave the lad here one more night? If you agree, I thought we could conceal him in your loft."

"Well—" He saw the thoughts move behind her eyes. Leaving Danny here made a reason for Finnan to return. "All right, just for the one night, mind."

"Aye, sure."

"But I do not see how you are to get him up to the loft."

"Leave that to me."

He stepped away from the sleeping lad, brushed past Jeannie, and felt the contact all down his body.

"Aggie," she bade the maid, "come sit beside the patient. Wring the cloth in cool water, and lay it on his brow."

"Gladly, mistress."

Finnan experienced a flash of misgiving. He did not need the maid succumbing to any inconvenient attraction. When he and Danny left here for good, they would break all ties, clean.

He watched as Aggie settled herself cozily beside Danny's makeshift cot. When he turned back, Jeannie MacWherter once more watched him. She could not keep her eyes away, it seemed.

"I will be off out of here before dark," he told her.

She hesitated before she said, "Must you? I was just out at the well, and the weather is on the change. Rain coming, so I do believe. Surely no one will be hunting you in the wet."

She did not want him to go. A good sign.

But he shook his head. "I've no wish to endanger you." And if he stayed, could he have her in her bed this night, the two of them entwined and making their own heat while the rain fell outside? Aye, that image would haunt him while he slept in the wet.

"At least take a good meal before you go."

"I will, that."

She turned to the fire, but not before he saw the gladness fill her eyes.

****

Before dark came down, he carried Danny up to the loft like a sack over his shoulder. The maid had jumped to offer her own bed and now fussed around it, adjusting the pillow and blankets.

"I will just make sure he is comfortable, shall I?" she asked as Finnan and Jeannie went back downstairs.

"You will no' let her sleep up there with him?" Finnan asked, only half concerned. In some matters, Danny must look after himself.

"Certainly not. There will be no impropriety here."

Was she sure?

"Aggie will bed down in my room."

He took up his plaid, against the rain that now crashed down, along with his sword and leather pouch.

Jeannie reached out and touched his arm, her fingers immediately skittering away again. "Are you sure you should not stay?"

"Never say you are worried for me?" He raised his hand and touched her cheek very gently. "No need, Jeannie. I am a survivor, me."

She shivered beneath his touch. "I do not doubt that. Yet the night is filthy wet."

"I will stop by some time tomorrow when I think it safe, to see how Danny fares. I hope I will be able to move him then."

Her eyes searched his. "And should he take a turn for the worse, instead?"

"Then signal me. Wave a white cloth in the air from your back garden. I will keep an eye on the place and come should you need me."

She nodded but did not look happy about it. Finnan smiled to himself. Aye, he had already half won, but best not to press her too soon. Make her want it; make her beg.

"Until tomorrow, then," she said.

"Aye, and thank you. How could I ha' been so mistaken in the woman Geordie wed? Clearly, you are an angel."

He bent his head then to kiss her cheek, an intended mark of gratitude. His lips skittered along the warm velvet of her skin as she turned to catch his mouth with hers. For an instant, Finnan went still, both breath and heartbeat arrested, as her sweetness flooded upon him.

Hot, blinding, lips parted slightly beneath his, her mouth lured him in. He dove into her without further invitation, his tongue a sword meant to wound her mortally.

But swords, as he should know full well, were two-sided, and he felt the backlash of the passion that pierced her.

Danger, his mind screamed at him. *Do not lose yourself in punishing this minx.*

Failing to heed his own advice, he captured her face between his hands so he might kiss her still more deeply. Her fingers came up and curled around his wrists, but not in an effort to prevent the embrace. Instead, it felt as if she grounded him, clung the way her legs might around his waist in a still more intimate situation.

He broke the kiss only because he needed to breathe. His heart pounded up in his ears, and every impulse demanded he take her to her bed.

She withdrew from him, but not far; her lips whispered against his when she said, "Be safe."

"I will."

"Come back soon."

Haste ye back. The old highland words of parting. But this was no highland woman—he had to remember who, and what, she was.

He straightened. "Aye."

She released his wrists and he felt the loss, deep. With a supreme act of will he left her and stepped out into the rain.

Chapter Nineteen

"I think he is some better—Danny, I mean. He is asking for his breakfast." Aggie's face shone as she delivered the words. Her worry seemed to have cleared like last night's rain.

Jeannie knew very well Aggie had crept up the ladder to the loft not once but three times during the night. On the last occasion, near dawn, she had stayed and only came down now with the glad tidings.

Jeannie had heard Aggie's every movement because she had been unable to sleep, her mind too full of images and emotions. How many times had she relived the kiss she and Finnan MacAllister exchanged at parting?

What was a woman to do with such feelings?

"A good sign," she said now. "Why do you not start the porridge? I will go up and check on him."

"His fever must have broken, for his forehead is cool."

Jeannie raised her eyebrows at her maid. How often had Aggie put her hands upon the lad? And could she truly censure Aggie, when she ached to touch Finnan?

"It was a quiet night but for the rain," Aggie went on.

"Yes." The storm had moved eastward over the hills before dawn. Beneath its dying rumbles, Jeannie had been sure any number of times she heard Finnan returning, looking for shelter...for warmth.

She went to the door now and drew it open to peer out. The fresh, matchless highland air poured in upon her, so unlike the coal fugue of Dumfries. Rays of sunlight angled over the eastern hills, and mist rose slowly from the burn. It looked like a world newly made, out of which a god might come striding.

One of the old gods, that was—the sort her father used to study in his books—with a rack of antlers on his head, perhaps, or a mane of auburn hair and a body to bring a woman to her knees.

When would he return? And when he did, would he kiss her again?

She had to stop thinking about it. She felt like she had caught Danny's fever.

Determinedly, she shut the door and turned to find Aggie's gaze upon her. "Are those men out there?" Aggie asked uneasily.

"I see no one."

Aggie shivered. "I thought about it all night, them storming the cottage and hauling him away." She lowered her voice. "He is so brave! Imagine losing an arm and yet going on with such courage."

"Yes," Jeannie could only agree.

Aggie stepped closer. "Faith, mistress, I do not know who or what to believe any more. That man, Laird MacAllister, is denounced as wicked, and a traitor, as well." She widened her eyes. "They say he turned coat at Culloden and helped the British against his own kind. But he does not seem like that when he is with Danny, does he?"

He did not.

"Yon lad adores him." Aggie jerked her head toward the loft. "Would follow him through fire, I think."

"We do not know the whole tale." But Jeannie would like to. "And it is a fatal mistake to judge before knowing all." That much her father, with his scholar's mind, had taught her. "Never mind that now," she went on briskly. "Get Danny fed and go about your day as usual, just in case anyone is watching."

****

The day proved a long one. Jeannie, following her own edict, worked all afternoon in the yard, weeding and pampering her plants, hands calm but emotions in turmoil. She lost count of how many times she raised her eyes to the path. She dared not look to the hills where Finnan might be concealed, for fear of giving him away. But her tension built as the hours crawled by.

He will come at dusk, when it is safer, she promised herself. Even she could not declare Danny unready to leave. The last time she checked on him, he and Aggie had been chatting away to each other double time, the girl seated by the side of the lad's cot with idle hands.

Jeannie should have chastised her but had not the heart. Let the lass have her few moments of pleasure, so fleeting. Danny would soon be gone from their lives.

Both he and MacAllister would.

At nightfall, Jeannie went inside to find Aggie preparing supper. Aggie's cheeks were flushed pink, but that might have been due to the heat of the fire on a warm day.

Or a few kisses might have been stolen in the loft.

Who was Jeannie to censure?

Shocked at herself, she told Aggie, "It has been a quiet day. No sign of anyone searching."

Aggie gave her a bright-eyed look. "And so, mistress, were you on guard as much as at work in that garden?"

Perhaps so, but Jeannie refused to acknowledge it. "We will need those crops if we are to survive this coming winter." Yet she could not even imagine winter now, or much beyond the moment she next saw Finnan.

Aggie only nodded. "I have supper nearly ready. If Danny's master does not come for him, shall we keep him here a second night?"

"He will come."

"Because Danny seems so much improved, yet his fever may yet return. You know how it is with fevers—they do rise at night."

"I cannot imagine the laird failing to collect the lad."

Yet supper time came and went, and Finnan MacAllister did not appear. To be safe, Aggie carried Danny's meal up to him, and she remained there well after. Jeannie could hear the two of them conversing in low voices, the soft music of Danny's words followed by Aggie's familiar tones.

Jeannie, with no appetite of her own, went to the door and threw it open. It must be later than she thought, for soft dark filled the glen, gathered like a living presence.

She stepped outside and quickly shut the door. A faint breeze greeted her, coming from the west, and in the east the stars emerged one by one through the last of the gloaming.

But for the whisper of the wind, her ears caught no sound. She stepped out down the path, enjoying the cooler air against her skin after the close warmth inside.

The glen had swallowed Finnan MacAllister as if he had never existed. What if he were no real man at all, but only a spirit? Immediately, she chided herself for the fancy. That had been a flesh-and-blood man she held in her arms.

She stepped through the gate in the wall and into deeper darkness. The path wound away northward, but he would not come by the path.

She raised her eyes to the hills that lay like the shoulders of great, slumbering beasts. A stream ran through a copse of rowan trees behind the cottage, and it was there she directed her steps. Beneath the branches she stood and breathed in the night.

"Jeannie."

He materialized beside her, very like the spirit she had just imagined him to be. His warm fingers caught her hands, and all her senses leaped, instantly aware. Suddenly he filled her—the height of him, the nearness, his scent as he stepped closer, coming at her out of the night. She caught a gleam of light from eyes that might belong to a feral beast, and a glimpse of a tattoo as he raised an arm to draw her in.

"What are you doing out here?" he whispered. "It is not safe."

And what did she care for safety, when he occupied her world? Gone, it seemed, was the practical woman who had striven so hard to keep an ordered household and an ordered life in Dumfries, denying to the world any suggestion her father might be less than he seemed, less than respectable. She had hung on so long. Surely she deserved to let go now, here in the dark.

She raised her face toward him and said, "Fortunate you found me, then."

He drew a hard breath an instant before he bent his head and captured her lips. It was, Jeannie thought wildly, as inevitable as the tide, as the setting of the sun and the rising of those stars. Inevitable as eating when hungry, or drinking when dry.

Drinking deep.

So did he drink from her, claiming her mouth and making it his to plunder. He kissed her slowly, thoroughly, and with perfect dominance, and before it ended Jeannie clung to him, heart pounding.

"Well, now," he murmured, his voice a soft caress in her ear. "Never tell me you came out here looking for that?"

Wicked. But she had, she had.

For answer, she kissed him again, reached for him blindly. This time she slid her tongue into his mouth, marveling at the heat of it. She explored the inside of those supple, honeyed lips and stroked his tongue softly. She felt the pleasure of it spear through him, and wondered again what would happen if she applied her tongue elsewhere on his body.

But he broke the kiss once more, and his hands caught hold of her, steadying. "Jeannie, Jeannie, what are you trying to do to me?"

She guessed she had done it already; she could feel him hard beneath his kilt at the place where their bodies met. A rush of victorious gladness possessed her: he wanted her. That he could not deny.

She had no words to ask for what she desired. She

had never yet requested it from any man, had been unable to imagine doing so before she met him. Now, though, she suspected she would bargain whatever she must to the devil for but one more kiss.

Yet she had no notion of how a woman seduced a man, only the insistence of her pounding blood.

"Finnan," she said softly, deliberately. She wished to claim the man to whom she would give herself.

She stepped away, and he let her. Soft starlight, mingled with the last of the gloaming, filtered through the tree overhead, affording just enough illumination as she reached up with unsteady fingers and began to unlace her bodice.

Finnan caught his breath. For an instant he did not move but merely stood there, a perfect silhouette in black and silver.

I must be mad, she thought quite clearly, yet her fingers continued to move without her conscious permission, opening the front of her gown and sliding the fabric back from her shoulders.

She wore nothing beneath, and felt his gaze touch her, tactile as his fingers might be. The soft night air poured over her skin, and her arousal intensified unbearably. Why did he not reach for her? Must she beg?

As if he heard her thoughts, he moved suddenly, jerked to life, and caught her with both hands. His palms slid against her skin, gentle as the air, until they cupped her breasts.

Pleasure kicked through Jeannie, so intense her knees nearly failed her.

But she could not fall; he held her now—his strength and grace suddenly possessed her, and he spoke her name once again, bent his head, and laid his mouth to her breast.

Chapter Twenty

Steady on, Finnan MacAllister told himself even as he tasted the sweetness of Jeannie MacWherter's flesh. *You do not want to abandon the target here, nor lose your head.*

But he knew he had quite possibly already lost his head, at the precise moment she loosened the fabric of her bodice. Beautiful she was, and he could not ever remember being so hard.

Still, this was a boon to his plans. No question he had her on a string; this proved it. He had not expected her to offer herself so soon.

And now the night sang its song all around him, the rowans—enchanted trees—lent their blessing overhead. He had Jeannie MacWherter in his arms, and a right fine armful she made, too.

He parted his lips to take more of her into his mouth, let his tongue swirl around her nipple—the hardened pebble of it made a delectable friction—and suckled deeply. He felt her tremble and then, distinctly, take flame.

As easily as that, she was his. The wanton baggage—she had no doubt given herself to countless men in the past.

Then why not Geordie? The question appeared unbidden in his mind. Was it because Geordie was a highlander, and foreign to her? But so was he, Finnan, yet she clung to him as if she might never let go.

She moaned in wordless protest when he released her breast, and he let her hang there wanting it while his eyes feasted on her, even as his mouth had. His desire raised another notch.

By all the spirits of the fire and air, she was lovely to look upon, and even better to taste. Her breasts, full, round, and high, made a potent temptation. The skin of her throat shone in smooth perfection, and her eyes...

They reached for and beseeched him with a look such as he had never seen.

Slowly and deliberately, he reached up and put his fingers through the soft, silken mass of her hair, found the pins, and let the locks fall one by one. They whispered against her bare shoulders, and he leaned forward to taste the place where curls met flesh.

Aye, and he could lose himself in this woman, right enough. He closed his eyes, savoring the flavor of her skin, but those tight nipples below made far too tempting a lure. He slid his tongue down and latched on again.

"Finnan," she breathed, and her hands came up to cradle his head, to urge him closer. She tangled her fingers in his hair, her touch like fire.

Aye, and he wanted to feel her beneath him, willing, hot, and pleading. He sank to his knees, taking her with him, and laid her down in the soft grass.

The rest would be easy as cutting butter with a hot knife, he told himself. But he wanted to relish this. And he wanted her thinking of Geordie when he entered her.

Without taking his mouth from her breast, he reached down and slid his hand beneath her skirt, traced a path up along her leg. Her heat increased as he moved upward—the gods bless her, she wore only a thin pair of bloomers, no real barrier to his invasion. He let his fingers brush her curls and felt her reaction all through her body.

He released her nipple, kissed a trail to her lips and said, "You have only to tell me 'no,' Jeannie. I will take nothing you are not willing to give."

She whimpered like a distressed child. The little trollop, did she even have the ability to say no? And if she did, could he stop now?

But she failed to utter the word, and he let his fingers brush her intense warmth more closely. Wet for him she was, and ready.

He had the sudden, overwhelming desire to plunder her first with his tongue, but that would come later, when she was utterly and completely his.

"Ask me, Jeannie," he bade her. "You must ask."

Instead, she reached for his mouth, captured it, and wooed his tongue until it entered her mouth again. At the same moment, she parted her legs just enough to let him inside.

Ah, so that was the way of it. Nothing loathe, he thrust a finger into her slick heat, testing the waters. A helpless sound came up from her throat and into him.

Aye, he had her where he wanted her now. He had only to make her remember Geordie, and complete the deed.

But he could barely think straight with her so hot and soft beneath him, and with the ache of his own need.

Her back against the grass, and her mouth still clinging to his, she helped him as best she might while he removed her bloomers. Her skirt was now bunched up around her waist, and he hastily thrust his kilt to one side. He could feel her heart beating an accelerated pace all through her body and into his.

He released her lips and reared above her to admire the picture she made spread there on the ground, hair and skirts all about her, to imprint it on his mind so he would never forget. He palmed one of her breasts and said, "Are you certain you want this, Jeannie? Do you want me to stop? I would do nought to violate Geordie's memory."

Her expression went blank. Aye, Finnan thought bitterly, and she barely remembered her husband. His anger flared, but it did not make him want her any less.

"Ask me, Jeannie," he insisted in a whisper. "You must ask for it."

On fire as she was, he expected her to implore. Instead she lifted her chin and said in a voice that quivered, "You are a wicked man, Finnan MacAllister—a wicked highlander."

Aye, he was, and unrepentant.

"But I want you." She added deliberately, "I want this."

A wave of savage satisfaction tore through him, so tangled with need he could barely distinguish it. She had used Geordie and, aye, he would use her as she deserved.

He positioned his weight between her thighs, and she arched into him. She twined her arms about his neck even as he came down on her, her entire body a ready welcome. He slid into her as perfectly as if she had been made for him, and the shocking pleasure of it possessed him so completely he almost missed what else he felt—the slight resistance of a woman being plucked.

For the first time.

Astonishment gripped him, nearly as complete as his pleasure. But he could not gainsay it: Jeannie MacWherter had been a virgin when he entered her.

But how could that be? Aye, well, he knew Geordie had not had her, but such a scheming, calculating wanton must have made her way through a score of men.

Still he caught himself, held the impulse that bade him pound into her, and moved softly instead, giving her time to accept the length and heft of him. When she sighed and relaxed in his arms, when her legs reached up and clung to him, only then did he flex and begin to move inside her in a gentle rhythm that required all his will.

His mind still reeled from the surprise of it, but need rode him far too hard now to allow contemplation. Everything about her drew him to her like iron to a lodestone. He felt her wild response when the friction their bodies made reignited her, and her heat roared at him out of the darkness.

Consumed him.

Nay, not quite. He retained enough sanity to let him withdraw at the last instant and spill his seed on the ground. He wanted revenge, not a permanent tie to her.

That for you, Geordie. But he lied: what he had just done, he had done for himself. How deny it when he still held her, more than half naked, in his arms? And aye, she quivered against him, clearly flicked by the last echoes of those flames as by a whip.

And what to say to her now? That he had just used her, that she—and the act—meant nothing more to him than relieving himself? He wanted her to feel Geordie's pain.

But nay, that meant taking her body was not enough. He must break her heart.

Chapter Twenty-One

Oh, what had she done? Jeannie asked herself the question, as might someone emerging from a mad dream. She had never considered herself a foolish or precipitous woman. Yet she had just welcomed Finnan MacAllister between her legs—a place where she had allowed no man.

And now her sanity returned slowly, in pieces. The sounds of the night came to her even as the pounding in her ears—her heartbeat—calmed. She heard the rustle of the branches overhead, the buzz of insects.

She would have bites in the most shocking places.

She could feel Finnan's breath coming softly between those irresistible lips of his. What made them so irresistible? Was it their strength? Their warmth? Their wild flavor? He still lay on top of her, the graceful length of him a balm. One of his hands rested, in a gesture that hinted of possession, on her bare breast.

Did she want for him to own her?

Yes, oh, yes. But he did not, even though she had just given him the greatest prize a woman could purportedly bestow on a man. She still owned her own soul.

Or did she?

She could not deny the magic inherent in the night surrounding them, and in the act they had just committed. If magic could steal a woman's soul, hers might now be at least partially in the hands of this particular man.

She should be shocked that she could consider such a thing, that she could be lying here, out of doors, completely open to him and with no wish to cover herself.

Instead, she wished it were daylight so she could see that body of his, trace the tattoos with her fingers, especially that one on his... Desire convulsed her again when she thought of that part of him.

He stirred against her. The intimacy of it lent another stab of desire.

"Jeannie," he said.

Oh, the musical lilt of his voice! She wanted nothing more than to hear it sing through her, unending.

"I had no idea you were—untried."

Ah, that. She lay staring at the outline of the rowan tree overhead and acknowledged the need to explain.

"Geordie," he said.

"I never lay with him." She said it plainly, honestly. Could she prevaricate with this man who had touched all of her?

"Why not, if he was your husband?" Had a note in Finnan's voice changed, become hard and sharp?

"Ours was not that kind of marriage."

"How is that? I know he loved you."

And how to explain the way things had been in Dumfries? Finnan had not seen his friend in some time. Would he even believe the man Geordie had become?

"He fancied he loved me, perhaps."

"If he said he did, he did. I knew him, knew the strength of his heart."

"I do not doubt he had changed since you journeyed together."

Finnan stiffened in her arms. "Impossible. Geordie was the truest man I ever knew."

Yet Finnan had not witnessed his disintegration as Jeannie had. Finnan had not watched as Geordie lost himself by bits to the drink and whatever private demons rode him. Jeannie, who had, could not even say what they were.

She said none of that now, for Finnan MacAllister had never come to Dumfries. He had been busy with whatever devilry had taken place here in the glen—the same that now left him running like a hart over these hills. He had known a different Geordie MacWherter than she.

"Geordie and I had an understanding."

"Did you, so?" He hauled himself up above her, and his hand withdrew from her breast. "So he understood why you did not welcome him to your bed? 'Tis plain enough you do not mind a man between your legs."

Jeannie's every instinct went on alert. She studied the shadow he made above her against the lighter darkness. She could not see his eyes, but she felt his emotions strike at her like blows.

Why was he so angered? And where was the man who had just held her so tenderly, moved inside her gently for all his strength and passion? Flown…

Before she could speak, he demanded, "Are you sure Geordie comprehended how you used him?"

She gasped. This was the man she had first met by the pool, he who had flared to rage when he tumbled to her identity. Had he never put those feelings aside after all? Then what had this night been about?

Very carefully, she said, "Geordie understood I was prepared to give myself to no man." *Until now, until you.*

He got to his feet and turned away from her. The starlight slid over his shoulders and flowed like water over the sculpted muscles of his back. Jeannie's heart twisted in her chest with dismay and helpless attraction.

"What is it?" she asked softly, but he did not reply. She scrambled to her feet also, unsteady and all too aware of stings in unfamiliar places, and tried to smooth her skirt down over her knees. Her world tilted, and she almost fell down again, realizing that everything— everything had changed.

She wanted to turn and run, haul her bodice back up over her breasts and scamper off through the darkness, bar her door against whatever this was that flared between them, never let him in again. She had made a great and terrible mistake, the worst any careful woman could make. And yet he stood there tearing at her with his fathomless anger, a god in black and silver.

"Finnan," she breathed, and her voice did not sound like her own. Instead it seemed to come from the night, on a breath of hopeless enchantment.

Yes, she should move away, flee and hide herself. Instead she took one long quivering breath, stepped forward, and placed her hand on his shoulder.

He stiffened like a man being touched by a hot brand, every muscle rigid. "Why are you angry with me?"

For an instant she thought he would not respond. It felt as if he had closed a door against her, even though the mane of his hair spilled over her fingers where she touched him, and his scent filled her, lifted her.

"Finnan," she said again, as if that could claim him. She felt his muscles quiver against her fingers as if he fought some great battle, and he sucked in a deep breath before he turned.

And that helped her little in the end, for she could not see his face clearly in the flickering light. His voice came at her out of the darkness. "Angry? How could I be angry with you, Jeannie, when you have just given me so great a gift?"

"You are angry," she insisted. "I am no fool."

He gave his head a sharp shake, and the hair rippled over his shoulders. "I am but thinking I should not have taken what my friend enjoyed not."

Was that it? He felt some kind of misplaced guilt? But surely he saw it was up to her, Jeannie, where she bestowed herself?

And what to say to him? That she had never wanted to throw herself, wanton, at Geordie? That she had never considered, with Geordie, the thoughts that now pounded through her mind: that she might run her tongue all over his hard body; that she might kneel before him and perform an act she had, before this night, barely let herself imagine.

She said none of that. Instead she stepped forward, pressed herself into his arms and felt her still-bare nipples peak against his flesh.

"Jeannie." The word came from him in a growl. Suddenly fierce, he caught her between his hands, a grip that stopped just short of punishing. "Go home. Shut your door. Save yourself."

Had he read her mind? Did he have that power? She struggled to see the expression in his eyes and failed. He was but a mysterious presence in the dark.

"Why?" she asked even though she already knew the answer.

"Because I will break your heart."

****

And why had he said that? Finnan demanded of himself even as he caressed Jeannie MacWherter's soft flesh between his hands. Why warn the wanton vixen? Was it because desire still pounded at him? But nay; he could control mere physical reactions. Could he not? Yet Jeannie wielded a powerful magic. And she must be an actress beyond compare, for she projected a vulnerability that spoke to every protective instinct he had ever possessed.

Aye, warn her, the devil in him applauded, *make the game a challenging one. That will render it all the sweeter when you break her.*

Sure, he had to keep in mind this was all about revenge.

Yet his hands slid without his permission down her bare arms to her hands. He wanted another sip from that sweet mouth of hers, longed for it the way a man half sotted longed for more whisky.

She did not speak, and he could barely see the expression in those wide eyes, but her whole body cried agonized hesitance. Aye, a fine actress was Jeannie MacWherter. She thought to play upon his sympathies even as she had upon Geordie's.

Yet she had remained virgin. That fit with none of the opinions he had formed about her.

She spoke at last in a breathless voice. "I do not doubt you are right."

But she remained where she was, pressed against

him and looking like a wanton angel with her dress down around her waist. Because he could not help himself, he slid his hands from hers and across that silken skin until he cupped her breasts. A gasp issued from between her lips.

The soft mounds of her flesh filled his palms and spilled over. Perfection. He was already up and hard against her again; she must feel the evidence of his arousal.

Would she accept him a second time? The mad question tore through his mind even as he watched her lean into his touch.

He knew it then—he had her, quite utterly, in his hands.

Make her want for it, the devil said now, changing his tune. *Make her beg. You want her on her knees.* He did, in more ways than one.

"Go home," he told her instead, even though his body screamed in protest.

"I will." But she did not move, and his thumbs moved of their own accord to find the tips of her breasts and tease them into tight peaks. Her hot mouth called to him—but if he gave in and kissed her, he would never have the strength of will to leave her wanting.

Instead he released her from his hands and used them to tug the fabric of her bodice up over her shoulders, covering her bosom.

She helped him and retied the bodice with her own hands. To his surprise a wry smile curved her lips. "I cannot imagine what you think of me."

"That you are gey beautiful," he said with absolute veracity. "And that I have taken what I should not."

He lost sight of her face in shadows as she bent and

shook her skirt down over those slender legs. Next she bundled her hair into a rough knot that would not stay where it belonged. He had lost all the pins.

"There. Do I look a respectable woman?"

She did not; she looked like one he needed to plunder all the night long.

"I must go back and face Aggie."

"And I must collect Danny, and be away."

She nodded, hesitated, and raised a hand toward him. Half breathless still, she asked, "When will I see you again?"

And there it was, he thought, the question that proved he had her securely gaffed. A second question lay within the first: *When will I lie with you again?*

In his many years away from home he had loved any number of women, if only in the physical sense. Almost without exception they had asked him that, be it in demand or longing. But Finnan MacAllister had rarely stayed anywhere long enough to spend more than one night with any of them.

Now he said, at the devil's bidding, "It might be best if you do not."

She went still, and he felt her denial come at him out of the dark. Before she could ask why, he spoke again. "'Tis safer for you, Jeannie, if I keep away. 'Twas kindness itself for you to house Danny for me, but I would never forgive myself if I led the hounds that chase me to your door."

"That makes some sense." Her hands rose, and she tried again, unsuccessfully, to bundle her hair. It took her a score of heartbeats to say, "But I could meet you away from the cottage. Here, perhaps."

He smiled to himself under cover of the shadows.

"And should the Avries' hunting party come upon us when we are together? You would be ruined in more ways than one."

"True."

"Come." He reached for her hand. The way back to the cottage was short, and the light increased slightly when they emerged from the rowan copse. He stole another look at her, just because he could not seem to help himself: that disobedient, golden hair tumbled about her shoulders, and those lips that had clung to his so wildly were swollen. He ached anew to have her again.

But, by all the gods, he must have some self-discipline.

At her door he paused and reached out to smooth her hair. The warm curls clung to his fingers; he had best not touch her at all, if he wanted any hope of controlling himself.

"I must look…" she began, before words failed her.

She looked like a woman who had just been well-tumbled and needed it over again. But he did not say so.

"Go inside and pretend naught has passed between us," he bade.

She gave him an incredulous look and went.

Chapter Twenty-Two

Steady rain dripped off the branches of the trees, struck the plaid Finnan wore over his head, and seeped through the wool to trickle down his neck. He sat huddled in a stand of pine, safe from the hounds, or so he hoped. Danny, exhausted and once more pricked by fever, slept behind him, under cover. Even the wet would not rouse the lad now.

The moments spent at Jeannie MacWherter's cottage had been the last rest either of them had known. All day yesterday the Avries' men had chased them about the glen, keeping them always on the move. Two groups of hunters combed the hillsides, one led by Stuart and one by Trent Avrie. Trent's group had almost had them this afternoon, half way up the slope above Dun Mhor. Danny had stumbled and gone down; Finnan had climbed the rest of the hillside with the lad slung over his shoulder.

And got away. But for how long? He could move like a deer, but it could not be denied Danny hampered him. And with the return of the lad's fever, Finnan could only ask so much. Danny needed rest and had been on fire when Finnan tucked him away among the trees.

Surely they were safe for a time. On a night so filthy wet, even his pursuers must be loath to venture out. Danny would catch his breath and be stronger in the morning.

But Finnan did not like keeping still; he never had, and now, surrounded by danger, he felt as if he had a prod at his back. Inactivity gave him too much time to think, and while he could unquestionably use an opportunity to figure how he would get out of this tangle, he could concentrate on only one thing.

Jeannie MacWherter.

She had haunted him ever since he walked away from her door. The feel of her flesh seemed to linger in the tips of his fingers, and his cock had been up more than down. Even now, beset by damp and exhaustion, the very idea of her had him stirring.

If ever a woman had been made for plundering, it was she. He relived again the moment he had plunged into her: her heat and tightness, that telling moment of resistance. And then the way she had clung to him with arms, lips, and those inner muscles. She fitted him the way a finely made sheath fit a sword.

By all that was holy, he had to stop thinking about it or he would embarrass himself here in the darkness, and he had not done that since he was a green lad. He had to stop thinking of her. Or if he did he must focus on his revenge, because this was all about Geordie. Jeannie had denied Geordie everything Finnan had enjoyed yestere'en. *Remember that, my lad*, he told his cock.

It refused to listen and bade him instead remember the scent of her, filling his senses when she became aroused. Her desire had beat at him like a wall of fire.

Perhaps, his maddened brain whispered at him, taking up the demand started lower down, he should punish her again soon. *Now*. He might walk to her door and—

Nay, but Jeannie MacWherter's cottage lay down a rocky slope at the other end of the glen. He and Danny should remain safe here.

Curse it.

For she would be so warm on a wet night. He imagined how she might strip the dripping plaid from him, and then all the clothing beneath. He thought on how her narrow white hands might move over his body, collecting moisture, followed by her lips and then her tongue.

What was it about the woman? She exerted a powerful attraction. He pictured the men of Dumfries lining up behind her like dogs behind a bitch in heat.

But that line of men included Geordie.

In truth, she had been fortunate it was Geordie she had wed, else she never would have remained unplucked. Any other husband would have pressed his suit, claimed his rights, and had her. Geordie, beneath all his muscle and brawn, had been a gentle soul and almost ridiculously courteous to women.

As two young, wandering mercenaries, they had both received more than their share of female attention wherever they went. He could remember many a time a woman had been drawn to the big, sandy-haired highlander, like a bee to honey.

Why not this time?

Jeannie hinted that Geordie had changed since Finnan last saw him. But Finnan knew that for a lie. He had the letters, after all.

Upon the thought, he reached into his leather pouch, wherein he kept his treasures, and extracted a folded piece of paper. Only three letters remained, and he kept them with him at all times. The others Geordie had sent were all destroyed, some to wet and one to fire. He should not expose one to the rain now. But he needed to remind himself just what Jeannie MacWherter truly was.

He smoothed the oft-folded paper open on his knee. Barely enough light remained for him to catch the words scrawled there. In truth, he had no need to. Everything Geordie had written was more or less inscribed on his memory.

Unlike him, Geordie had not received a decent education while young. When they met, Geordie had barely been able to write his name. Finnan had taught him that and enough to let him get by, in their quiet moments and over the long winters when time weighed heavily upon them. As a consequence, he knew Geordie's hand as well as his own.

Which of the three missives had he drawn from the pouch? Was it the one that began, "Finn, I have met an angel," in which Geordie poured out all the tender emotion in his heart? Was it that written after his marriage, that expressed his disappointment? Or the final outpouring of grief that held all Geordie's pain and inability to comprehend why the woman he adored did not love him?

He could see enough words on the page to tell it for the last. Quickly, he folded the paper and tucked it away again.

The words filled his mind:

Why will she not love me? I would give anything— all the days I have left of my life—for her to take me even once to her bed. But she does not look at me the way I wish. She does not see me the way I wish.

It is some terrible punishment, Finn. Fate is repaying me for all the evil I have done: the men slain for silver, the homes burned at the direction of some vile chief. And Culloden. She sees all that when she looks at me. What we did at Culloden. That is why she breaks my heart.

Finnan closed his eyes and stopped trying to remember. *Culloden.* Aye, it always came back to that. No man who had been there could have come through that battle unchanged.

A thought stole into Finnan's mind: maybe Jeannie was right in that Geordie had altered a bit in Dumfries. But the truth of him, the loyalty that made up Geordie's heart, could not alter.

It was a sin to throw the love of such a man, unstinting and genuine, back in his face. But that Jeannie had done, hard-hearted woman that she was.

Did that make Finnan want her any less? Damned if it did.

****

Jeannie looked up from the doorstep where she sat spinning wool, and the spindle went still beneath her hands. After two days' rain, this morning had dawned awash with heavenly blue, smeared like watery paint across the sky. She had taken her work outdoors, and Aggie had walked to Avrie House to see what she might learn.

As an agent, Aggie left much to be desired. Impulsive and voluble, she had little talent for deception. But she was Jeannie's only choice, and Jeannie knew she would go mad without news.

She fumbled with the wool in her lap and tried to concentrate on the task at hand. In no fit state of mind

157

for spinning, her usually competent fingers had gone all clumsy, and the yarn broke time after time. Yet winter would soon be at their door with cold and snow. They would need warm clothing.

Frustration caused her to mutter a word oft-spoken in the taverns from which she had coaxed or dragged her father. She wanted to lay the spindle aside, wanted to walk down the path and meet Aggie.

Or anyone else who might be on his way.

Why did he not come? He had said he would. Two nights since they had lain together, and both endless.

Her cheeks grew warm just thinking of what had passed between them there in the dark, all she had done and permitted him to do. It almost seemed like some wild dream, but the next morning at first light she had walked back to the rowan copse and found her drawers lying there abandoned, like cobwebs on the grass. He had taken them off her, slid them down her legs with those strong, clever fingers, and she had offered herself to him as a willing sacrifice.

How could she have done such a thing?

How could she live if she did not have him again?

Other evidence had marked her body that next morning, as well, signs she could not deny. Tenderness in places never before touched by any man. None of that kept her from wanting him.

The thread broke again as her fingers jerked, and she swore still more woefully. She laid the spindle aside as a bad bet, got up, and walked down the path.

Warm air poured over her skin like water. The glen was beautiful in this weather, but she could not imagine surviving here in winter. Lest it be in Finnan MacAllister's arms.

What was the matter with her? Why could she think of nothing but him? But she remembered his hand sliding slowly up her leg, and her knees trembled beneath her.

Aggie had been gone most the afternoon. Surely she must come soon. They had agreed she should go for a gossip with her friends in the kitchen at Avrie House; Aggie seemed almost as hungry as Jeannie for news.

Upon that thought she caught movement along the path, and her heart leaped sickeningly, but it was only Aggie after all. She came with a hurried step, and when she drew near enough Jeannie saw the tension in her face.

"I wondered when you might come," Jeannie greeted her.

Out of breath, Aggie said, "I hurried back. Dorcas and Marie kept me long and had much to say. This chase is all they want to talk about."

"Come, sit and tell me over a cup of tea."

It did not seem strange for Jeannie to swing the kettle over the fire and serve her maid, even less so when Aggie drew a handkerchief from her pocket and unfolded it.

"They plied me with cakes in plenty, mistress. I saved you some."

The frosted dainties thus revealed looked a treat, but Jeannie set them aside, too hungry for news. "What did you learn?"

Aggie drew a deep breath and blew it out again. "Well, the Avries have not yet taken their quarry, but not for lack of trying. Dorcas says her masters have had men up and down the glen day and night—even in that filthy rain we had—but they have failed to catch him."

159

Jeannie shivered. What if a troop of Avrie household guard had come upon her and MacAllister in the rowan copse? The pure humiliation of it heated her cheeks again.

"Where could the laird and Danny be?" she asked. "They have not returned here."

Aggie widened her eyes. "That is the question on everyone's lips. They do not call Master MacAllister 'laird,' of course. They refuse to acknowledge him as that. They have many other names for him, some I dare not repeat."

Jeannie said nothing, watching the emotions flicker across Aggie's face.

"And the things they say of him!" Aggie made a quick gesture, the sign against evil.

"Like what?"

"That he is not only a man and murderer of men but possessed of magic, as well. They say he uses the dark arts to conceal himself about the glen and performs pagan rites—even sacrifices—to protect himself."

Jeannie remembered Finnan MacAllister leaning over the injured Danny and whispering a prayer—or had it been an invocation? She said, "Who knows what goes on in this uncivilized place? Yet how long can he and the lad hide themselves? They will have to go to ground eventually."

"Not at Dun Mhor. The Avries have men keeping watch over the ruins. If the laird and Danny set one foot there, they are snared."

Despair flooded Jeannie's heart. "But how can such a thing end?"

"In death, I fear," Aggie pronounced, her usually

benign expression hard and tight. "You mark my words, mistress, for they mean to slay the laird if they find him—and no hero's death, but by blood and by flame."

Chapter Twenty-Three

As soon as he heard approaching horses, Finnan MacAllister swung down from the tree in which he perched and alighted on the path. The long twilight had just descended, that time when shadows competed with the half-light of gloaming and men's nerves stretched tight. A perfect time for a surprise attack.

He recited a silent charm for protection as he leaped, and felt the familiar confidence return. His dirk, clenched between his teeth, tasted of metal, and even before his feet hit the ground his sword came to his hand.

He had been in one-sided fights before. And he had faced four-to-one already in his own glen; these odds did not really seem so bad.

The first man went down without even knowing whom he faced; Finnan's sword took him in a fell swoop, and he tumbled from his horse into the path. The other three men—none Trent or Stuart Avrie—quickly tried to maneuver their mounts in the narrow space. Finnan had chosen his place of ambush well, trees on one side and hard granite on the other.

"'Tis he!" Finnan heard one of them yell. "The demon!"

Demon, was it? Finnan grimaced even as he leaped for his second man. It would be easy to disable the fellow's mount, but Finnan did not like harming horses;

he had served in far too many campaigns when they were hired, same as he. And he could think of no better way to bring himself ill fortune than to bleed one.

The gods knew he had ill fortune enough.

That thought became his last before he switched off his mind and took on the warrior's mien. Years spent serving as a mercenary had taught him the necessity of it: complete and intense concentration kept a man alive, and no room for pity.

Save for the horses.

Two more men went down in quick succession, one to his sword and one to his dirk—dead or severely wounded; he did not have time to tell. The fourth man decided quite wisely to make a break for it, but Finnan hauled him from his mount and threw him to the ground, with the point of the dirk at his throat.

"Now, then," he said as he crouched above the fellow and tried to catch his breath. "You will give me some information before you die."

In the gloom beneath the trees, he could barely see the fellow's expression. Wide eyes caught what light there was and reflected it in a slick shine.

Finnan let the dirk bite a bit deeper. "You will be a hired sword." Not so different from him, then. "And with no real investment in this fight. Is it worth the dying?"

The man made a spasmodic movement but did not speak.

"How many hired men do the Avries have on hand?" Finnan demanded. It seemed like a small army. Finnan did not understand how they could afford it.

"A score," the man croaked out.

Finnan's brows jerked up. "Fewer now," he

returned seriously. "This will not end well for any of you. If I let you go, will you tell the others to clear off?" He bared his teeth. "This glen belongs to me. It will always be mine. Trent and Stuart Avrie—"

A flicker in the man's eyes, or perhaps pure instinct, warned him just in time. He bounded to his feet and whirled even as the sword of his first opponent, not dead after all, swooped past his head. Finnan swore to himself and rued the fact that he had not made sure and slit the man's throat. Now he would have to face both of them.

But nay, for he heard the man behind him get up onto his horse and away—going for help, most like. Avrie House lay not far off. Reinforcements would come soon, which meant Finnan needed to end this fight swiftly.

His opponent streamed blood from the wound at the side of his neck that Finnan had already inflicted, but he had a firm grip on his sword and a terrible grimace on his face. Finnan, with his sword in one hand and the dirk in the other, whirled like a dancer and attacked the man from behind, making the most of the limited space.

A deadly and desperate fight ensued over the bodies of the two fallen men, while the dark increased by the moment. Like fighting a shadow, Finnan told himself, one with a deadly blade. He could hear his opponent grunting and gasping with every blow rather than see him, and the breath began to heave in his own lungs.

End it, he told himself, but at that moment his opponent leaped.

Finnan felt the man's blade make contact with his

left arm. The dirk fell from his hand.

Anger ignited inside him then: it had always been so, on the field. Had not Geordie said Finnan fought like a boar, and like a maddened boar once blooded?

He swung his sword in a blur that caught the last of the light and, speaking another charm, completed a wide sweep that parted his opponent's head and body.

The corpse fell with two separate thuds that he heard rather than saw. He stood with his heart pounding, alone.

But not for long.

He had to get away from this place, as the fox leaves the hunt. He needed to find Danny, get the lad up and moving. Not easy with the fever that beset the boy every time night came.

Swiftly he took stock of himself and swore bitterly. Another scar to add to the number; for his left arm had been laid open in a long cut. He could not go dripping blood in a trail.

He fumbled on the ground, recovered his dirk by feel, and then wrapped his arm with his plaid.

A score of men, so his opponent had said. Only seventeen now. But this time he had not come out of it unscathed.

****

Danny tossed in a restless sleep as Finnan reached him, burning with fever and difficult to rouse. Their hidey hole lay high above the glen. From here, by day, Finnan could look out and assess Avrie's movements, but now he saw only darkness and little pricks of light—torches, perhaps—heading out from Avrie House to the place he had just fought his battle.

He unwound his plaid from his arm and rewrapped

the wound in a shirt that would never again see service, and once more assessed himself. Only minor cuts, besides this one. He had to get moving, and Danny with him.

But the lad made a nearly dead weight and mumbled fretfully when Finnan got him up.

"Come, lad," he said grimly. "We must find a better hiding place until morning."

He had in mind a stony copse at the south end of the glen, where they had concealed themselves before. Half way there he knew Danny would never make it so far—nor, to be honest, would he. He paused to gulp a great lungful of air and saw that Jeannie's cottage lay almost directly below.

Refuge. But why should he think of her that way? She had no real reason to help him, and her cottage, this night, could prove more trap than haven.

Yet if he might leave Danny there once more he could move far more swiftly, lead the hunters on a true fox's chase.

Danny made the decision for him—he went down and would not rise again. Finnan carried him the rest of the way and bore him, like an oversized child, to Jeannie's door.

The maid Aggie, and not Jeannie, answered his knock, and the blood drained from her face in horror.

"Oh, mistress!"

And then Jeannie stood there, her gaze reaching for Finnan like welcome. "Come in."

"They are after us, or soon will be." It seemed only fair to warn her.

Her only answer, a gesture, swept them in. Aggie shut the door behind them and barred it carefully.

"Lay him down beside the fire," Jeannie instructed. "Aggie, run and fetch the blankets we used before."

Tenderly, Finnan placed the lad where indicated and then stood back, watching Aggie fuss. He realized belatedly that both women stood in their nightclothes; he must have flushed them from their beds. To be sure, the night was now well advanced.

"His fever has returned," he told them unnecessarily. A hectic flush mottled Danny's cheeks, and Aggie had already placed a soft hand on his head. "If I might just leave him here a wee while, I would be most grateful. I ken fine 'tis not your fight, this. And I will no' stay to endanger you."

Jeannie turned her head to look at him. Her hair, loose down her back, tumbled like a river of golden silk; she looked impossibly beautiful. Did she know that when she stood so, before the fire, her gown became damned near transparent? He glimpsed everything he had already touched, and his throat went dry with longing.

This was no' the time for such thoughts.

Her face paled. "You are bleeding. Your arm—"

He looked down at himself in rueful acknowledgement. Not only did the wound on his arm bleed, it now dripped through the wrappings and onto her clean floor.

"I am that sorry." He tried unsuccessfully to stanch the wound. "There was a fight back down the glen."

She spoke a word no respectable woman should know. "Sit down. You can go nowhere like that."

"But—"

She fixed him with a fierce, blue gaze. "Sit." She planted a hand in the center of his chest and pushed him down onto a stool. To his surprise, his legs collapsed and he sat. "Someone must see to that wound. Aggie?"

But the little maid, completely occupied with Danny, did not so much as turn her head.

"And it seems," said Jeannie MacWherter through stiff lips, "it must be me."

Chapter Twenty-Four

So God did answer prayers, Jeannie thought, but not always in the way one wished. She had asked most ardently to see Finnan MacAllister again. Just now, lying in her bed, she had longed for it in a decidedly impious fashion. And so he came, but so sorely hurt her hands shook and her heart quailed as she surveyed the wound.

His left arm had been laid open from the shoulder nearly all the way to the wrist. She could not see how deep the wound went for the welling blood. How had he ever managed to carry Danny, so? And how did he remain upright on the stool now?

She looked into his face and was caught by the light that simmered in his eyes—bright, wicked light. She knew in that moment what filled his mind, and it was not his wounded arm.

Heat raced up her body and engulfed her face. She turned from that look and asked Aggie sharply, "Is that water hot yet?"

"Almost, mistress."

"Bring me bandages—tear up the last of that sheet. And fetch a cloth to hang over that window." She wanted no one peering in from the dark upon this well lit tableau.

Finnan spoke as Aggie hurried to obey. "I do not wish to endanger you."

169

"You are here now," she answered shortly. "Do you think you have been dripping blood on the ground all the way here?"

"I hope not. They will track me like hounds. 'Tis why I must leave. Be a merciful angel and wrap that, but then I will away."

"This needs more than wrapping. Do you want to end up like him?" She gestured at Danny. "How easy would you make it for them?"

"'Tis not your battle," he said again.

Jeannie did not argue it further. She accepted the cloths Aggie fetched and did her best to stanch the wound. But just touching Finnan, even in so rudimentary a manner, started up a steady hum of desire. She bit her lip and did her best to avoid his gaze.

What was she to do with these feelings, with the impulse even now to lean down and cover his mouth with hers?

Aggie brought the basin of hot water, and Jeannie set about cleaning the wound while Finnan sat quietly beneath her touch, as if he felt no pain. The man might be made of granite for all the reaction he showed.

"How did you get this?" she asked when the worst of it lay exposed.

"Sword," he told her shortly, and his breath hissed between his teeth—perhaps not so unmoved by pain after all.

"It will not stop bleeding and needs to be stitched," she told him firmly.

"Will you do it?"

She did look up and meet his gaze then. It looked feral and dangerous, and she faltered. "Me?" Before he could answer, she told Aggie, "Run get the needle and thread…again."

"We had best not make a habit of this," Finnan said with a touch of humor, when Aggie went into the other room.

Jeannie wanted to make a habit of him. Should she mind in what condition he came to her door, so long as he came?

She thought of all her fancies these past nights, of the two of them lying together performing shocking and exquisite acts upon one another. Her cheeks heated further.

"Have you a flask?" she asked him.

He shook his head. "Nay, why?"

"My father, who was widely read, used to say whisky—any liquor, really—could be used to purify a wound. This looks ragged and very dirty."

"Blood will wash it out."

"As it did for Danny?" She looked up once more and caught him peering down the front of her night rail. Ah well, nothing she could do about that now, and he saw nothing he had not already held in his hands.

But he said, "You are very beautiful, Jeannie MacWherter. I suppose a thousand men have told you so."

Only one, and Finnan did not want to hear about him.

"You are a wicked man," she told him. "Cannot even a mortal wound dissuade you?"

"This is no' mortal—just an inconvenience." He dropped his voice for her ears alone. "You are all I have been able to think about. The taste of you, how warm you were when I—"

"Here, mistress."

Aggie stood by with the needle already threaded. Suddenly, though, Jeannie felt unequal to the task.

Finnan assessed her with a measuring look and took the needle from Aggie's fingers. "You steady my arm," he told Jeannie, "and keep the blood sponged away. I will do the stitching."

She knelt on the floor beside him and gripped his arm in both hands. Their heads bent so close they touched as, with another sharply drawn breath, he began the work.

Before he finished they were both sweating, and Jeannie's hands trembled badly. Thirty painful stitches he had made, for she counted them.

What kind of strength—mental and physical—kept a man upright in his seat through such an ordeal? Finnan had turned pale as milk, but his hand remained steady and firm. A woman could only admire such a man.

In truth, she felt much more than admiration. At that moment, kneeling beside him, she experienced what she never yet had toward any man: a stir of the heart.

Nonsense, she told herself sternly. She could not possibly be falling in love with Finnan MacAllister, not when she had kept her heart whole so long. He was completely and utterly unsuitable—the last man in the world she needed: wild, dangerous, *beautiful.*

He looked up and caught her gaze with his, which was full of ironic light. "Well, now, that was no' so bad. I thank you for your assistance."

Jeannie, still shaking, got to her feet. "We are not done. You stay there while I wrap the bandages. Aggie?"

Aggie, who had stood and watched the procedure despite herself, stepped up with the remains of Jeannie's best sheet cut into strips.

"Aye," Finnan said, "and then I will away."

Jeannie glanced at him. "You are going nowhere. Aggie, make the laird some tea and then take an extra blanket up to the loft."

"He's sleeping there?" Aggie squeaked.

"No, I am. The laird will take my bed."

Finnan parted his lips to protest, but Jeannie's gaze met his like a crossed sword.

"'Tis no' safe for me to stay here," he told her. "I refuse to bring trouble to your door."

And she replied, "I do not wish to hear your protests. We will worry about the consequences come morning."

****

Jeannie MacWherter's bed, soft and comfortable, should have drawn Finnan into exhausted sleep. He had been living rough for days, laying his head on boulders and bracken, and his weary body craved this haven.

But his mind stayed vigilant even once his body relaxed and the cottage became quiet. He listened for every sound inside and out—heard the women murmuring to one another in the loft before they slept, heard Danny stir restlessly. He listened to the wind rise outside and fooled himself there were footsteps.

His arm throbbed with a steady ache in time with his heartbeat. He throbbed elsewhere also and ached for release. Jeannie's bed smelled of her, a delicate and beguiling scent, and prompted a host of memories. Her golden head had lain on this pillow—he recalled burying his face in her hair when they lay in the rowan copse. He thought on the perfect globes of her breasts, glimpsed down the front of her night dress, almost enough to distract him from his stitchery.

By all the gods of this place, how was he to sleep, with her under the same roof?

Upon that thought, his ear caught a sound, and then a succession of them, inside the cottage rather than without. A shadow stirred in the doorway of the room, and then a miracle came to him on soft, bare feet.

She wore only the night rail and floated like a spirit, being nearly soundless. In the dim light—for she had hung a cloth over the window—he could barely see her, just the blur of her pale clothing as she moved.

But he did not doubt her identity, and the breath caught in his throat. "Jeannie?"

"Hush, we do not wish to wake the others. I came to see how you fare."

Liar. 'Twas not why she came. Finnan's every instinct told him she answered the same desire that rode him here in the dark, and his heart leaped with hope.

She paused beside the narrow bed and regarded him. He wanted so to reach for her, but in this game he played she must reach for him.

She whispered, "I hoped you slept."

Liar, again. Whatever she desired, she did not want him insensate.

"I cannot sleep," he told her. "My mind is too full." As well as another aching part of him. But this was no rowan copse out on the hillside. Would she truly give herself to him here under her own roof, with the others within hearing distance?

While still he wondered, she reached out and her cool fingers found his forehead. "No fever yet."

He asked, his voice a taunt, "Never tell me you were lying up in that loft thinking about me?"

"Yes." The word whispered between her lips. "I feared you might be unconscious, delirious, or cold."

"So have you come to keep me warm?"

In answer, she slipped into the bed.

Chapter Twenty-Five

Jeannie had never before had a man in her bed, had never wanted one. No sane woman should, she told herself fiercely even as she eased her body between the blankets and against Finnan MacAllister's. Oh, she might have imagined it back in Dumfries, tried to conceive what it would be like. Nothing she had ever imagined compared with this.

And she would defy any woman to keep away. Had she not tried to argue herself out of this while lying in Aggie's cot up in the loft? As well try to keep wasps from a honey jar.

This particular bed was too small for the both of them. And Finnan MacAllister was not in any way a small man. She found herself lying half on top of him, and the sensation was...

Stunningly wonderful.

Full contact she had from her breasts on down, and she could feel all of him, hard muscle and more.

"I would not hurt your arm—"

"Jeannie," he breathed and swallowed the rest of her words as his mouth captured hers in a wild demand.

And oh, she had craved this, the heat and sweetness of it, the claiming. His lips molded to hers, and his tongue invaded her, making his desire more than plain. She melted like tallow when the candle is put to flame.

Take me, she begged him in her mind even as his

tongue caressed hers intimately and his hands, already moving, spread their heat through her night dress. He should not be using that arm, she thought quite clearly, an instant before all rational thought flew away.

His hand slid from her shoulder downward and, as if in answer to prayer, paused to cup her breast. Fire raced through her from his fingers, a potent conflagration.

He broke the kiss, and his breath whispered over her lips as he spoke her name again. "Jeannie."

She moaned and gave him little kisses, rained them upon him. She caught his lip between hers and sucked it in. She wanted him inside her so much she could barely breathe.

No one had ever told her a woman could ache for the taste of a man, or for the feel of him hard between her legs. But every part of her cried out for him now.

Following her desire, she let her hands move also, stroked the muscles of his chest, fingers trembling with delight. Daring in her need, she continued to trail her touch downward. He lay more than half undressed, chest bare, stomach bare except for an interesting and tantalizing pattern of hair. Her fingers encountered no barrier until they met with his trews. She explored the laces, her fingers intelligent in the dark, and untied them with an agility she might never have imagined.

He moaned then. Even as she slid her hands around him in a deliberate caress, he made a sound deep in his throat and kissed her once again.

And oh, he felt hot, so hot, the burning brand of desire. Like a woman drunk with delight she slid fingers that seemed suddenly too small for the task up and down the length of him. His whole body jerked in response.

Now she broke the kiss and began to withdraw from him. "I am sorry. Should I not—?"

"Do you not dare stop." The growl of the words made her shiver. She caressed him still more deliberately, sliding her palm up and down the great, hot length of him.

"What do you want, Jeannie MacWherter?"

Must he ask? It had to be more than plain. A woman did not present herself at a man's bedside, did not caress him, unless she ached for the act. But for some reason he wished her to say the words.

She would beg, if she must.

"You. I want you."

"What do you want of me?"

Oh, and he was wicked—*wicked*—making her admit it. But a sob came from her throat as she caressed him faster. "This."

"And how do you want it?" His must be the voice of the devil coming out of the darkness.

"Any way you will give yourself to me."

He moved then, sliding himself beneath her so she fully straddled his hard body. His hands drew the night rail up past her legs, her buttocks, her shoulders. When he pulled it off over her head, her hair tumbled about the both of them.

So now very little lay between them. His trews gaped open, and she could feel him prodding between her thighs. Her bare stomach rested on his, her breasts abraded by the hair on his chest.

Would he enter her now and end this exquisite ache?

But no, for he slid down in the bed, his hands at her

waist, and his mouth latched onto her breast.

So intense was the pleasure, Jeannie nearly cried out. Only the knowledge that Aggie would hear her and come running prevented it. What if Aggie brought a light and saw the two of them this way, devoid of covers and shame? Somehow the fear of discovery only heightened her pleasure.

She cradled his head—hair like silk—as his hungry mouth plundered her, and pressed herself closer. The ache between her thighs intensified, and tingling spread throughout her body, like that before a thunderstorm.

"Give yourself to me, Jeannie." His breath whispered across the damp skin of her breast. "All of you."

"Take what you will." Jeannie had never imagined offering all of herself to any man, but he was not just any man. He was a god, hard and vital in the dark.

Slowly, deliberately, he lavished the attentions of his hot mouth on her other breast, until her body thrummed unbearably and she begged, "Please."

"What more do you want?"

"You!"

"Then taste me."

Did she dare? Given, the idea had been in her mind almost from the first moment she saw him arise from the pool, every part of him dripping wet. But this act, surely, was more wicked then all the rest.

Still, she parted her lips and let her tongue taste his lips, slide downward from there and taste his chin, and the skin of his throat and then his chest, picturing the tattoos there as she did. He tasted salty and wonderful and so utterly male it nearly cost the last of her senses. She released the idea of right and wrong from her mind and continued to work her way down.

The muscles of his taut stomach trembled beneath her mouth. When she slid still lower and once more curled her fingers around him, he moaned like a man in agony.

Now it was he who said the word, "Please."

He slid into the hot cavern of her mouth like iron covered with warm satin. She closed her eyes, reveling in the pleasure and power of it as he arched off the bed.

Hers, hers, hers.

Yes, and this act might well be a wicked one. Delightfully so.

He began to move beneath her in a seductive rhythm. The tension in her body built, and her world narrowed to nothing but this man, this joining. When he drew her mouth from him at last and hauled her up, she nearly cried out again. In one swift movement he flipped her beneath him on the bed and entered her in a burst of pleasure that caused the light to explode behind her eyes.

And then they both lay breathing raggedly, his body draped atop hers while the waves of pleasure receded. Not far. She sensed he had only to move in order to send her soaring all over again.

Her mind, reawakening, tried to comprehend what had just happened. Here, in her own bed.

How would she ever be able to sleep here without him?

****

By all the gods of the earth, sea, and sky, what a woman! The thought dominated Finnan's mind even as the last sparks flew from his inner vision and the soft darkness came down.

Fool, fool, fool.

What voice was that, making itself known now that he could hear it? Moments ago he had not been able to listen. There had been only the pleasure and the desire.

She would have done anything for him. He knew, without question, he had held Jeannie MacWherter in the palm of his hand, right where he wanted her.

Trouble was, she had held him, as well.

And he had made a fatal mistake, spilled his seed inside her where he did not want to leave it.

Och, but the heat and tightness of her after she had her mouth on him proved irresistible. He defied any man to do better.

At the thought of any other man claiming Jeannie, fierce desperation swamped him. Nay, nay, and nay.

His arms tightened around her instinctively, and he kissed the skin of her shoulder where his mouth had come to rest. By all that was holy, he already wanted her again.

She stirred against him and whispered, "Your arm—"

Aye, his arm. He had probably torn all the stitches, and cursed if he cared, though now as the urgency fled it hurt like a bastard.

"I am well enough," he told her, a mere breath in the darkness. Did she know that he remained still inside her? The very thought had him hard again.

She threaded her fingers through his hair, and he shivered in response. He had not meant it to be this way. He wanted her in thrall to him, not the other way round.

He wanted to break her heart.

He reminded himself of that even as she brushed

her lips across his brow in a gesture of such tenderness it made him catch his breath.

"I had best return to the loft." Yet she lay where she was, and him still inside her.

He fought a brief inner battle and said, "No, stay where you are."

"But Aggie—"

"I can hear her snoring. She will not wake before morn. And surely"—he lifted his head and traced her lips with his tongue—"I can keep you awake until then."

"You should rest."

"Do you suppose that likely if you go from this bed?"

"No."

"Then stay with me and afford me what relief you can."

In answer she captured his hand and carried it to her breast. He teased the nipple into a tight bud, which made him lengthen and harden further inside her.

"Jeannie," he said hoarsely, "will you accept me again?"

She stretched and arched beneath him. "Only try and leave me, my Laird Finnan."

Chapter Twenty-Six

Jeannie stood with the pale light of morning flooding in through the open door of the cottage and felt her heart break.

Finnan MacAllister had risen from her bed at the first hint of dawn while still Aggie slept, and donned his clothing with his back turned. Unable to guess the thoughts in his mind, Jeannie had scrambled up also, snagged her night rail from the floor where it lay in a heap, and crawled into it, her heart thumping all the while.

How could she persuade him to stay? She must persuade him.

But nothing she had said then or since turned his mind. She believed she spoke reason all the while she changed the bandages on his arm, when he bent over Danny who still slept fitfully, even when Aggie clattered down from the loft and gave her a shawl—and a shocked look—to cover her near nakedness.

It did not matter how she appeared; Finnan MacAllister would not stay.

"I'll not endanger you," he said decisively, even as he slung his bloodstained plaid over his shoulder and hefted his leather bag. "The Avries are bound to come looking. I will appreciate it if you keep Danny one more day."

"And you will return to see him?" Jeannie leaned

toward him as she asked, her whole body aching for his touch. Was this how men felt in the thrall of whisky, as if they might die without just a bit more? She experienced a flash of sympathy for her father, and Geordie.

She would not ask Finnan to return to her, no. But to Danny? Surely.

"I will try to collect him when 'tis dark. I hope he will be able to travel by then." He adjusted the leather bag and winced when he moved his left arm. It must be painful, but she would never have guessed that, last night.

The memory of his touch still whispered over her skin as he stepped out the door with her following.

Morning mist clothed the glen and rose sluggishly, lit by the new sun. A fortuitous time for him to be away, but she wanted to bury both fists in his plaid and hold him.

"I will worry for you," she said helplessly. *Long for you*. But she did not add that. Could he not see it in her eyes as he turned and looked at her?

Oh, and he appeared like a young god with the hazy light dancing around him, hair warmed to red, and that dangerous, seductive brightness in his eyes.

"And I for you," he returned. "Danny makes a dangerous presence in your home. Should they come to your door, do not let them in for any reason."

"How am I to keep them out?"

"Tell them your maid is ill, raving. Say it is some vile contagion." He smiled ruefully. "I do not doubt Aggie can play the part. Meanwhile I will do my best to keep the hounds away from here."

"How?"

"I will allow them a glimpse or two of me and then lead them a hare's chase down the other end of the glen."

Jeannie's eyes widened in horror. "But you are not fit, hampered by that arm."

"Fit enough for the task." Just as in her bed. "And I can move much more quickly without Danny."

Jeannie, not happy with the plan, did not know how to dissuade him, and fell silent in dismay.

His gaze caught hers. "Thank you, Jeannie."

"For keeping Danny? I do not mind."

"Nay." He leaned forward, and she felt his lips, a source of warmth in the cool morning air, touch her cheek. In a whisper meant for her ears alone, he said, "For last night."

Jeannie's heart broke into still more jagged pieces, and she spoke the words she had vowed she would not. "You will return?"

"Aye, tonight. Keep him quiet till then." And just like that he stepped away and disappeared into the mist as if he had never existed.

Jeannie stood on her doorstep a moment longer, arms wrapped about herself, eyes searching for a hint of him and but one thought in her mind: When he returned tonight, would she have him in her bed again?

She reentered the cottage, only to be met by Aggie's accusing stare. The maid bent over the hearth, stirring a pot of oatmeal, but all her attention focused on her mistress.

"I am that shocked, mistress, truly I am."

"Eh?" Had Aggie observed Finnan's parting kiss?

Aggie waved a hand. "For you to appear so, barely clad, in front of a man. You do know, mistress, in

185

strong light he could see right through that night dress?"

Jeannie drew breath to speak, but Aggie did not give her the chance. "And," she added with heat, not like the servant she purported to be but the friend she truly was, "you were with him last night."

How did Aggie know that?

She need not ask; all fired up, Aggie rushed on. "I woke in the night, and you were gone from the cot in the loft. I grew worried that the lad, here, had taken a turn for the worse and you had risen to help tend him. But when I peeked down the ladder, Danny still slept, and no one else was in this room."

"Oh."

"Oh," Aggie emphasized, her cheeks turning pink. "There was but one other place you could be. And I heard whispers—"

Had she, by God? And what had Aggie overheard Jeannie say? She had done her best to keep quiet even in the throes of intense pleasure, but the small cottage afforded little privacy.

Her face, too, flamed with heat. She crossed her arms over breasts still tender from the ministrations of Finnan MacAllister's mouth.

"I went back to my bed," Aggie said self-righteously, "not knowing what to think. I never heard you come out of your room till dawn."

"But Finnan heard you snoring." Finnan, holding her against his muscular body, all of him hard.

"That," Aggie said with dignity, "was Danny."

"Ah." It seemed passion had fogged both their minds.

"Mistress, what were you thinking? I know you are

a widow and have had a man before"—Aggie lowered her voice—"although you and Master Geordie never did share a room."

"It is certainly none of your business, Aggie," Jeannie said gently. But it was—the two of them had thrown their lot in together here, and she represented Aggie's only security.

Aggie drew herself up. "Maybe not. But I worry for you, mistress. A man like that! All the other women he has had—it is wicked."

"And..." Jeannie held Aggie's gaze. "Can you blame me? Have you looked at him? I cannot help myself, Aggie. In truth, I cannot."

For once in her life Aggie seemed at a loss for words. She turned back to the pot of porridge and stirred fiercely.

"It may well end in tears," Jeannie admitted, "but until then..."

Until then she would be left wanting Finnan MacAllister.

****

Danny's fever broke late in the afternoon, and he awoke clear-eyed and full of questions.

"Where is Laird Finnan?" he asked even as Aggie fussed over him, adjusting his blanket and sponging his brow. "There was a terrible fight—"

"There was," Jeannie told him, and took the seat beside his cot. "He brought you here, and I patched him up before he left again."

Aggie shot her a scandalized look but said nothing.

"He means to come and call for you tonight," Jeannie went on.

"Unless the Avries catch him," Danny moaned. "I

should be wi' him, standing at his back."

It occurred to Jeannie that Danny, now clear-headed, might make a wonderful source of information about the man who wholly occupied her mind—and Finnan MacAllister did so occupy it.

"Bring a cup of that broth," she bade Aggie, "and see can we get it inside our patient."

Aggie bustled and obeyed; she still refused to meet Jeannie's eyes.

"Tell me," Jeannie urged when Danny had taken his first sip of broth, "of this quarrel between the Avries and Laird MacAllister."

Danny considered her with an intelligent gaze. "Surely you know? The story is all over the glen."

"We have had only bits and pieces of it. I would know the truth."

"Aye, mistress, but you may not like the truth."

"Try me."

Again the lad measured her with his eyes before he spoke. "This glen has been MacAllister land since time out of mind. Laird MacAllister's father's father's father reigned here, and Finnan is the last in a very long line. When I met him—" Abruptly, Danny's gaze clouded. "When I met him he had been dispossessed, his father foully murdered by those who should have been loyal to him, and his sister either stolen away or murdered also."

"Sister?" Jeannie could not help but exclaim.

"She disappeared the same night his father was murdered. He never did discover whence. Try as he might, he has not been able to glean word of her, and he fears her dead."

"The Avries," Aggie breathed, caught by the tale

despite herself.

Danny's expression softened as his eyes found her face. "No doubt."

"But why?" Jeannie wondered.

"Why did the Avries commit such foul deeds against their sworn lairds?" Danny shrugged. "For years they were ghillies to the MacAllisters, both favored and protected by the chief's house. But a strain of madness, so I think, entered the mind of Gregor Avrie, he who was father to yon Stuart and Trent, and turned his heart and mind. He decided he had some claim to the position of laird. And he took control, murdered my laird's father, and drove Master Finnan from the glen."

"Someone must know what's happened to the sister," Aggie insisted.

"And," Jeannie objected, "wouldn't the former laird's men stand with him?" She had heard tales of how these highland clans were ready always for a fight or vengeance.

"Aye, and so they did. My master says this glen was a far different place then, full of clansfolk both MacAllister and Avrie, many joined by ties of blood. Most are gone now, chased away or dead, for Gregor Avrie brought in a hired army, and after the old laird's death blood flowed right well."

Aggie voiced the question Jeannie longed to ask. "But Laird Finnan came back and murdered Gregor Avrie?"

"Aye—after ten years away serving as a mercenary, and after Culloden broke the backs of the clans."

"Those at Avrie House," Jeannie said softly, "claim Finnan MacAllister fought on the wrong side at

Culloden—stood against the clans."

Danny's face closed abruptly. "Anyone who can say that does not know him. His heart is all for loyalty—though not necessarily to any prince."

And that did not make an answer, Jeannie thought ruefully, even as Danny buried his face in his cup and went suddenly silent.

It seemed she would have to get the rest of the story from the man himself—if she ever saw him again.

Chapter Twenty-Seven

Breath came hot and painful in Finnan MacAllister's lungs, and he wondered with pitiless honesty how much farther he could run. He had been over the glen like a hart since leaving Jeannie MacWherter's door—a hart well-hunted. Now night gathered over the mountains to the east, and he could not imagine where he would find the strength to go on. Hunted on his own lands, but not defeated—not just yet.

His left arm hurt like fire and would be damn near useless in another fight. His sword—already well-wetted with blood in not one but two encounters—had barely been out of his right hand. He ached for food and rest.

He ached for Jeannie MacWherter.

A wonder he could spare a thought for the woman, in his present straits, yet his mind returned to her again and again. He remembered the feel of her silken tongue gliding over his skin and the heat of it when she accepted him. She was like a fever in his blood.

But he did not see how he would get back to her cottage this night. Certainly he could not lead the hounds that pursued him there, if only for Danny's sake.

For Jeannie's sake.

He watched a line of torches, held by men on

horseback, go by below him, and his tension eased a bit. He bent to a rivulet, a mere trickle of sound in the descending dark, and drank his fill. That answered one need. He eased down beneath a tree and, for the first time in hours, laid his sword aside.

Free, for the moment. Free to think on Jeannie.

What was it about the woman? Aye, well, he knew fine what it was—not only beautiful, with that air of impossible innocence, but she tasted like heaven on his tongue. No wonder Geordie had tortured himself over her.

Nay, but he had to keep his eye on the truth: 'twas she who had tortured Geordie.

He remembered again the way she had felt when he slid into her for the first time, searing with heat and so tight. And the way she had moved beneath him last night, in breathless invitation.

He shifted where he crouched, in an effort to ease the sudden tightness in his groin. Oh, aye, he wanted her again, would have her again. But probably not tonight.

And when he had her, he promised himself—when next he splayed her hot and quivering beneath him— would he break her heart then? Would he have his pleasure and then his revenge?

"All for you, Geordie," he whispered into the darkness, and knew he lied.

****

Finnan MacAllister failed to come and collect his man when the dark descended like a deep blue curtain over the glen, even though Jeannie, Danny, and Aggie sat up talking long into the night. At last Danny fell into a fitful doze, and Aggie retired to the loft, but Jeannie dared not take to her bed.

She knew the scent of Finnan MacAllister remained there, along with his essence. She supposed she might strip herself naked, crawl among those blankets, and revel in memories. But she felt far too restless.

When the cottage lay quiet, she stepped outside and into the beautiful night. Stars spread overhead like bright clusters of jewels, or the eyes of pagan gods. A clear night, and not the best to be abroad and hunted. She stood silent, with her breath held, but heard nothing. No shadow stirred, approached, or transformed itself into Finnan MacAllister, and she trailed back inside, disconsolate.

By dawn, her desire had reached fever pitch, but he did not come then either. Danny was up by first light, moving under his own power and seeming as restless as Jeannie. She watched Aggie fuss over him, watched them converse together with their heads close.

She dissuaded the lad when he said he wished to leave.

"Laird MacAllister promised he would come and collect you. He will do so when he thinks it safe."

Twice before noon they heard and glimpsed mounted parties that rode by and splashed through the ford that lay not far off, and Danny hid in the loft. But the horsemen did not stop at the cottage, and at last, in mid afternoon, Danny fell into a doze, with Aggie nodding beside him.

Jeannie, unable to quell her uneasiness, went out into her garden. Here the warm sun found her, and she told herself digging in the dirt would bring a measure of calm. But the surrounding quiet called on the sleep she had missed the past two nights, and she was more than half asleep when the first pebble landed beside her.

And from whence had that come? She raised her eyes to search for a source, and a second pebble joined the first, just beside her knee.

The third gave her a direction—a lone pine just up the slope from her garden wall. And did her eyes catch a hint of movement there?

Abandoning her hand trowel, she got to her feet. Her heart began to pound double time. She narrowed her eyes against the glare of sunlight and saw—

A flicker of well-known plaid: MacAllister tartan.

She allowed her gaze to sweep the immediate vicinity, searching out danger. Then she gathered her skirts, climbed the wall, and went up the slope, keeping her eyes down as if searching for herbs. Through the coarse grass she swept, and the bracken, and beneath the branches of the pine.

And there he stood, whole and breathing—the answer to all her prayers.

Oh, and he might as well be the spirit of the place, his hair the color of the tree bark behind him, his eyes full of reflected sunlight, far more handsome even than she had remembered.

And she had remembered him generously.

"Whisht," he said at once. "Speak softly; sound carries far too well."

She nodded, her throat tight with desire.

He reached out and drew her closer beneath the branches of the tree, his hand warm on her bare arm. His gaze moved all over her, like fingers in the dark.

"How fares Danny? I did not dare come last night and risk leading the hounds to you."

"He is much better." Somehow Jeannie drew her gaze from his lips. "Sleeping now, but he was up earlier and clear in his mind." She barely breathed the words.

"Good. Keep him for me until nightfall, if you will. We will away then."

"And, between now and nightfall?" Jeannie stepped still nearer to him, close enough that she could catch the wild, dusky smell of sunshine and pure male. His hand still grasped her arm, and her breath came more quickly.

"You must go back down and pretend I am not here."

"No."

"No?" He quirked an eyebrow and parted his lips, no doubt to protest. Jeannie did not give him the chance. She rose on tiptoe and covered his open mouth with hers.

Ah, bliss! The taste of him flooded upon her and promptly seduced all her senses. She had been craving just this, with every heartbeat.

This, and far more.

She raised her hands and pressed them against his chest even as she consumed him with her mouth. She wanted to draw his soul from him, possess it, own it— own him. Could such a man, so wild and wicked, be owned?

After a stunned moment, he began to participate in the kiss with enthusiasm. His tongue swept Jeannie's mouth, trailing heat, in blatant domination. Jeannie's knees promptly wobbled, and she tumbled forward against him.

The kiss ended on a ragged gasp, and she gazed up into his eyes. What did she see there? Desire, yes—raw hunger that matched hers. And something more, far harder to identify.

It occurred to her, the thought bright and terrifying: if she did not turn around now and go back down the hill it might be she who lost her soul.

God help her, she did not care.

"Let me stay," she whispered, begged.

The dark, unnamed emotion in his eyes flared. Just so must the devil look, she thought, when he drove a bargain. But Finnan said only, "Nay, Jeannie, 'tis not safe. Should we be caught up here—"

Without so much as a glance behind her, she told him, "You can see for miles."

His hands steadied her, restrained her. "And do you suppose I could spare an instant to keep watch, if I had you naked in my arms?"

For answer she took a step away from him, but only so she might raise her hands to her bodice. She saw a great breath expand his chest when she began to unlace the fabric there, but he did not move or reach for her.

She kicked off her shoes next and then took the pins from her hair one by one even as he had that other night, and scattered them on the ground.

If this keeps up I will not have a pin to my name, she thought. *Please God it keeps up.*

"Jeannie," he said when she unfastened the ties on her skirt and let it fall about her ankles—only that. The warm summer air found her flesh even as she revealed it to him a bit at a time—feet, legs, and, as the loosened blouse came off, breasts.

And then she stood shameless before him— trembling with eagerness, wanton. Free.

"Now you," she whispered. "I want to see all of you."

The only part of him that had responded so far stood beneath his kilt—that, along with his ragged breathing, he could not hide. He remained unmoving as a stone when she unlaced his sark and pushed her hands inside to meet warm, supple skin. She dragged her palms ever downward until they encountered him through the rough wool.

He jerked to life then, seized her with hands less than gentle. "You are a witch, Jeannie MacWherter."

She wished she were. She would weave a spell over him, make him remain always with her to do her bidding.

Perhaps she still could.

With a small smile, her eyes never leaving his, she fell to her knees.

****

Finnan struggled from the great depths of passion and tried without success to reach for his sanity. Overhead, through the branches of the pine beneath which they lay, sunlight glinted and dazzled his eyes. A thought teased at him as from a great distance—there existed some danger, and he should keep watch.

But Jeannie MacWherter, warm and completely naked, lay in his arms, and he could spare little attention for aught else. His entire body still quivered from the sensation of her mouth on him, hot and eager, so eager. He wanted it again, wanted her again, wanted nothing else.

She stirred against him, and he responded like a man in the throes of torture to a hint of pain. So aware was he of everything about her now, even her breathing felt erotic.

She laughed softly, and he nearly convulsed.

"What?" He tangled his fingers in her glorious hair and drew her head back so he could gaze into her eyes. They smiled at him. By all the holy gods, a man could lose himself in those eyes.

The corners of her luscious mouth quirked. Och, that mouth!

"It is a dragon," she pronounced.

"What is?"

Bold and shameless, she held his gaze. "The tattoo that decorates your manhood. I confess, from first I saw you, I wondered."

"Ah, that."

"Did it not hurt?" She planted a small kiss at the corner of his mouth as if to assuage any lingering pain.

"I do no' recall. I was drunk at the time." He reflected with what remnants of his mind she had left him, "It did smart a bit the next day."

"Poor dragon." She ran her hands down his body and captured him. He came up between her fingers again like a raised sword.

"I told you I wished to see you," she whispered while her hands did magical things. "All of you."

"Ah." The capacity for thought fled him. There existed only the softness of her breasts, the heat of her hands, and the blue of her eyes. He must keep sight of his goal here, though—remember that he meant to trifle with her heart.

"Why a dragon?" she persisted. "And did you need to be upstanding while it was put on?"

Perhaps. The tattoo artist, down near Falkirk, had been a lass, and not ill-favored. "A dragon is powerful magic," he told her.

"As are you."

He kissed her deeply, and she continued to massage him all the while. She broke the kiss and slid over his body to straddle him.

"Tell me about this one." She touched his shoulder. "And this, and this." *Touch, touch*, like sparks of fire.

"Why?"

"Because they are beautiful, and I want to taste them all."

He growled, seized her hips, and positioned her where he wanted her. "Later."

"Now."

A battle of wills, was it? He smiled to himself. He had begun to learn of this woman; she would not be able to hold out long against him.

She bent forward and ran her tongue across his taut stomach. "Tell me of this one."

"Victory tattoo got after a battle."

"And this?" She moved to his right bicep, her hair trailing across his skin.

"Got that after I saved the life of a chief. I was in his hire—" He caught his breath. She had moved lower, far lower. He tangled his hands in her hair. "Ah—"

"And this?" The top of his left thigh, very nearly where he wanted her. He struggled to recall the marking there, and failed.

"And this?" Not waiting for an answer, she skittered her lips and tongue upward until they reached the skin above his heart.

He froze. "I told you of that one." Geordie—the intertwined hounds they both shared, the brand of their sworn loyalty.

How could he have forgotten?

Her blue eyes swam back into his range of vision. Aye, beautiful she was—the witch.

"What is it?" she asked in a whisper. "What troubles you?"

"You must return below. Gather your clothing and go."

"But we are not finished."

"We are."

"Most assuredly, my laird, we are not."

Anger raced through him, combining with the passion he could not deny. He had a cruel and sharp tongue when in a temper, but he held it now. He would not spoil all the work—glorious work!—he had done.

How far could he push her? How much could he make her want him before he broke her in his hands?

He allowed himself another, small smile. By faith, he was indeed a wicked man.

"And," she wondered, "what does that expression mean? An instant ago you looked ready to throttle me."

Could she read him so well? "I think only of your safety, Jeannie, and that you should not linger here and so risk yourself."

"At this moment," she confessed, "I care little for risk." She leaned up and whispered against his lips, "I want to stay."

"Then best to ask me prettily," he bade her.

And she did.

Chapter Twenty-Eight

"My son is dead." The Dowager Avrie spoke the words in a stark, level voice that nevertheless betrayed her pain. "Have you any idea how that feels? As a woman—a widow who has lost her husband—you should."

Jeannie carefully set down her tea cup and looked at her hostess uncertainly. The old woman must have been beautiful once. Her white hair, piled atop her head, still showed a few threads of red, and her blue eyes remained bright. But her skin had become pale and translucent as old paper, and the severity of her expression chased from her any real attractiveness. Upright as an iron rod in her chair, she betrayed no hint of actual compassion toward her guest.

Jeannie struggled to decide how to respond. A messenger had brought the invitation—or should it more rightfully be called a summons?—this morning, that the Dowager Avrie wished to entertain Jeannie MacWherter for tea. Not wanting to arouse suspicion, Jeannie had come.

Now she strove to compose herself and said, "I am so sorry for your bereavement, Lady Avrie."

"My son Gregor was a good man, an extraordinary man, one in a thousand. He did not deserve to be foully murdered."

And what of Finnan MacAllister's father? Jeannie

wondered as she strove to keep her own face expressionless. Had he deserved to be cut down, his family shattered and his son driven out, all to satisfy another man's greed? Revenge, as she knew, was an old game in the highlands—tit for tat, cow for cow, head for head, even woman for woman. But the situation in the glen now went far past tit for tat.

"Fortunately," the Dowager continued with a touch of savage pride, "my grandsons have returned to set things right."

And what of this woman's daughter-in-law, Jeannie wondered, the mother of those sons? A woman did not achieve the title of Dowager Lady unless there existed a Lady Avrie. But Jeannie saw no evidence of her here or anywhere.

"Forgive me," she said, investing her voice with a full measure of curiosity. "What has this to do with me?"

The Dowager Avrie swept her with a cold stare. "This monster my grandsons hunt was friend to your late husband, was he not? A close friend. 'Tis why you are in possession of Rowan Cottage."

"Well, yes."

The Dowager's chin lifted a notch. "I brought you here to request your cooperation—woman to woman— and your assurance that you will do nothing to aid this vile murderer, despite that relationship."

Alarm raced through Jeannie like liquid fire. How was she to convince this old woman with the sharp eyes of a blatant lie? For she knew to her soul she would do anything to protect Finnan—throw herself to a pack of wolves, if necessary.

Back in Dumfries, she had learned to lie. Once an

honest, truthful girl, she had been forced to grow into a duplicitous woman who assured her father his acquaintances from the tavern had not called for him and, indeed, that establishment was closed today. Surely she could deceive one old woman?

"I do assure you, Lady Avrie, though my husband was associated with Finnan MacAllister years ago, that was long before my husband and I met. I have absolutely no acquaintance with the man." *His tongue, sliding over her flesh, his fingers invading her, his body claiming hers in an act of flagrant completeness...* "Your grandsons have already impressed upon me how dangerous he is. I want only to keep out of what sounds a dangerous situation."

"It is most important you offer him no succor, give him no aid of any kind. My grandsons have him well trapped and are watching his every move, tightening their net around him."

Jeannie's heart began to struggle in her breast. Was it so? Did they, then, know that she and Finnan had been together? Did this old woman play at a game of her own? Jeannie would not put it past her.

Danny had left her cottage early this morning, slipped out into the mist to join his master, and much recovered. Had his departure been observed?

"And," she asked, knowing she should not, "what will your sons do with this villain once they catch him?" It should be of no concern to her; she would do much better demonstrating indifference. But to save her life she could not manage that.

The Dowager Avrie's eyes gleamed. "He shall be treated as he deserves."

Jeannie trembled and strove mightily to conceal it.

"You will call the magistrates? Cause him to stand trial?"

The Dowager gave a thin smile. "That is not the way things are done here in the highlands. We make our own justice."

"So you mean to kill him." Jeannie had no idea now what showed in her face. With panic beating at her, she scarcely cared.

"How, Mistress MacWherter, would you deal with a savage dog? Would you have it stand trial, or would you make sure it will never harm anyone else?"

"Even a dog deserves its life. And we speak not of a dog but a man."

"That is where you are mistaken. Finnan MacAllister is nothing more than a mercenary, a turncoat. Does he deserve to breathe the air of this blessed glen?"

And, Jeannie thought indignantly, who had driven Finnan MacAllister to the life of a mercenary? Who had forced him from his ancestral lands?

"A man," she said carefully, "will do as he must to survive."

The Dowager gave her a long look. "You have a woman's heart, soft and sympathetic," she observed then with no hint of kindness, "and so easily deceived. Do not be mistaken in the nature of this particular man, Mistress MacWherter. We speak of a dangerous felon who needs to be put down as swiftly as possible. Indeed, I thought to bring you here today and offer you our protection."

"Protection?" Jeannie faltered.

"Aye, so. He is capable of occupying your house if he goes to ground, of murdering you and your lass, or worse." The old woman's eyes gleamed precisely as if she could see Finnan's handprints all over Jeannie's skin. Heat flooded her. Did the Dowager know the truth?

"May I suggest," the Dowager went on, "you allow my sons to station a number of their men on your property? That way, if MacAllister does attempt to use you, they may intercept him before any harm is done."

"That will not happen," Jeannie said. "He will not approach me. As you say, he knew my husband, not me."

"He will still consider that property his, no matter he deeded it to your husband under law. What is law to such a man?" The Dowager Avrie leaned forward in her chair and fixed Jeannie with a still more demanding stare. "I urge you, place yourself under our protection."

A reasonable enough offer, Jeannie thought, given the situation here in the glen. And what excuse might she give for failing to accept it?

She twisted her fingers tightly in her lap. "I do appreciate your concern, Lady Avrie. But I am an independent woman and have been for some time, comfortable looking after myself."

The Dowager Avrie did not so much as blink. "I am afraid I shall have to insist. I will send two of my grandsons' men to accompany you home. They will remain and stand guard on the road to your cottage, and watch the ford, as well."

Jeannie's heart faltered in her breast even as she fought to keep from revealing the extent of her dismay. No, and no. How could Finnan return to her then?

How could she go on living if he did not?

Surely the Avries had seen something that made

them suspect her.

A tight smile curled one corner of the Dowager's mouth. "I assure you, my dear, it will only be until the blackguard is caught and dealt with."

"I see."

"And then life here in the glen will return to normal. We will rebuild Dun Mhor and take up a peaceful existence there. You will be most welcome to stay in the glen. Though the rest of that traitor's lands will be forfeit, we will gladly leave Rowan Cottage in your possession."

Jeannie fought an inner battle to hold back the words she wished to say, and failed. "How can that be? You do not hold ownership of Dun Mhor."

"I do not, no. But with MacAllister dead, it will pass to my grandson, Stuart."

"How is that, if you do not mind me asking?"

"I do not." A small flash of satisfaction ignited in the Dowager's eyes. "It comes to him by right of marriage. You see, he is married to Finnan MacAllister's sister—the last surviving member of her family, as she will then be."

"Oh!" Jeannie gasped.

"Indeed." The Dowager folded her hands. "My grandson struggles on her behalf. Once that renegade is dead, she too can take her rightful place."

"But MacAllister is her brother."

"And she will do what is right. My grandson has taught her well about obedience."

Jeannie's heart sank. Did Finnan know his sister was here in his enemies' power?

The Dowager tipped her head as if reading Jeannie's expression. "Perhaps you would like to meet her before you go."

Jeannie's gaze stole to the door. "Is that possible?"

"It is." The Dowager rang the bell at her side. When the servant whom Jeannie recognized as Marie came, she bade the woman, "Please ask Mistress Deirdre to step in."

Jeannie got to her feet when, a few short moments later, a woman entered. It had crossed her mind while waiting that the Dowager Avrie—obviously a cagey old vixen—might have fed her a tale. But she could not mistake the woman she now beheld for other than Finnan's sister.

Tall she was, slender, with a head full of auburn hair worn simply in a braid down her back. Her face— beautiful, severe, and undeniably feminine—yet carried the set of Finnan's features in the cheekbones, nose, and eyebrows. Had Jeannie needed further confirmation, her gaze met Jeannie's in a fierce stare; the tawny eyes might have been Finnan's own.

"Deirdre, my dear," the Dowager said brightly, "I wanted you to meet our neighbor, the Widow MacWherter. She is going to help us bring your brother to justice."

Chapter Twenty-Nine

Finnan MacAllister edged out from under cover of the sentinel pine on the slope above Rowan Cottage and narrowed his eyes to peer through the gloaming. A perfect day it had been in Glen Rowan, warm and with fair winds chasing white clouds like sheep across a field of blue. Now the light lingered late in the west like a benediction, but he knew all too well it held no blessing for him.

Two men in Avrie colors stood guard on the trail at the rise that led to Jeannie's gate. He cursed softly as he watched them settle in for the night and felt Danny move up to his side.

"What is it, Master Finnan?"

Finnan did not answer at once. Anger, dismay, and, were he honest, alarm pounded up through him. Why would the Avries feel it necessary to post watchers there? Had he been seen going or coming? Had he placed Jeannie in danger?

And how was he to reach her now? He choked back his desperation and, without looking at Danny, said, "Trouble for those two lasses below, if not us. Careful," he warned as Danny took an incautious step forward. "Do not let yourself be seen."

Now it was Danny's turn to whisper a curse. "I never should have gone there, sick with fever or not. Now Aggie is in danger."

Finnan slanted a cool look at his companion. "Aggie, is it?"

Danny's expression turned grim. "She is a sweet lass with a kind heart. I would not like aught to happen to her, especially because of me."

"The two of you grew friendly, did you, whilst you lay ill?"

"More than that. She is the sort of woman a man could get used to staying with for good."

"Oh, aye?" Surprise made Finnan withdraw all his attention from the scene below and bestow it on Danny instead.

"Does not seem to mind the places I ha' been or the things I have done—nor the loss of the arm. Never thought I would find anyone like that." Danny sucked in a breath. "But I am in no position to do aught about it, am I?"

"And that is my fault, lad. I have brought you to all this." *And her.* Only look at the danger in which he had placed Jeannie. Finnan caught himself up harshly. What matter—he wanted only to destroy her, did he not?

Nay, that was not all he wanted. He ached to taste her lips again, plunge himself into her heat, or even just gaze into her eyes.

"I do not mean that, Master Finnan," Danny avowed. "You know all my loyalty is yours, no question."

"I do know that, lad, and I am grateful."

"Only, what are we to do? Chased we have been over the rocks of this glen for days, and with your arm refusing to heal... Your gey big house stands guarded, and the cottage below. How are we to defeat them all?"

Finnan MacAllister gritted his teeth. "'Tis time we

fought back, Danny my lad."

"But how?"

"By turning into shadows—spirits, if we must. By enlisting the help of the glen itself."

Danny shivered. "You ken fine I do no' like it when you begin talking of magic."

"'Tis the only thing that will save us now." Finnan gazed seriously into his friend's eyes. "You do not have to stay, you ken. No dent in your loyalty if you go. 'Tis my fight, this."

"And since when has one of us had a fight without the others?" For a moment, Danny's open face clouded. "I am that convinced we—the three of us—should never have parted ways in the first place, nor let Master Geordie go off by himself."

Finnan shrugged uncomfortably. "He'd had his fill of killing, could stomach no more. Should I have dragged him into this slaughter?"

"I do no' ken. But I am sure had we stayed together he would still be alive now. You always looked after us, Master Finnan, always."

Finnan heard Jeannie say again, "Where were you when Geordie needed you in Dumfries?" He had been turning himself into a hare here. One more thing for which he could feel guilt.

He became distracted from his thoughts when the cottage door opened and Jeannie emerged, barely visible in the dim light. She carried a white cloth in her hands and did not so much as glance at the guards along the way before she walked round the side of the cottage. There she paused and flapped the cloth the way a woman might shake away crumbs from a table covering after a meal.

Finnan's eyes narrowed. A signal? He watched as she marched deliberately to the rear of the tiny building and spread the cloth over the prickle bushes. Then she went inside and shut the door firmly.

The dark was now almost complete. Even in the west the light sank into a mere haze that reflected off the burn. Had he not seen them, he would not know the guards were there on the rise.

Nor would they be able to see him very easily.

"Jeannie needs to speak with me," he told Danny softly. And he to her.

"But 'tis too dangerous, surely."

Finnan drew himself up. "The Avries have overstepped themselves this time. Let them deal with the spirit of vengeance."

****

Finnan held himself still as the trees beneath which he had paused, the dirk clutched between his teeth. He thought about the night, listened for the way the breeze bent the gorse and rough grass. He imagined himself invisible, even his breath suspended.

He heard the two guards speaking to one another in low voices, never suspecting they were overheard.

"Damned fine-looking woman," one of them murmured with a lecherous undertone. "And we are not getting paid enough to stand out here all night when there are warm women inside."

His only reply came as a grunt from the second man.

"'Tis my opinion this fellow they are chasing will never be caught, by any road. He is a phantom. How long have we been after him now?"

Finnan bared his teeth around the blade in a grim

smile.

"No phantom, he," the second man said, "but a turncoat. Took pay to kill his own kind at Culloden."

The first man ignored that opinion. "You keep watch here; I am going to see if I can get inside yon cottage."

"To what purpose? Those are respectable women."

"And maybe lonely. I have a flask here. Do you really want to spend all the night out on this trail?"

The second man never answered. Finnan had moved, silent as the shadow he imagined, and muffled the fellow from behind with an arm about his throat. The dirk swung up in a short vicious movement, and Finnan lowered his victim softly to the ground.

One taken care of, but he had to silence the second man also. He saw the fellow swing round with the gleam of wide eyes alerted by instinct.

"Donald?"

Finnan leaped for him out of the deeper darkness and bore him over backward before he could draw his sword. The dirk, already well-wetted, did its work again, and Finnan breathed a fierce prayer of gratitude before dragging both men off the trail into the gorse.

His arm, stiff and enflamed, screamed at him as he wiped his dirk on the grass and returned it to his boot.

The cottage door opened and light spilled out. He saw Jeannie's golden head, and his heart leaped disconcertingly. By all that was holy, he had missed her. And not just her kisses.

Still silent, he started up the trail to her gate. He felt it the instant she caught sight of and recognized him. She hurtled through her doorway, leaving the brightness behind.

They met at the gate, and she threw herself into his arms. Her hands caught at him and his, equally eager, caressed her hips even as he drew her nearer.

She did not speak, not in words. Instead she reached for him with her lips, bestowed small, desperate kisses on his mouth, his cheek, his chin. He felt her tremble.

"There now, lass," he murmured, trying to tell himself he remained unaffected by the greeting even as his heart pounded and he went lightheaded.

"I was so afraid for you," she told him between the kisses. "Are you all right? Are you whole?"

Finnan's heart thudded perilously. This, he reminded himself, was the woman he lived to punish. He could not let himself care for her; he would not.

"You signaled me?" he asked.

"Come inside out of the light." In defiance of her own words, she held him there and kissed him, keeping him in the radiance that spilled from the cottage. Her mouth, hot and hungry, pulled at him, very nearly irresistible.

If he died now, he thought as his tongue swept the inside of her mouth, if a troop of the Avries' men should come up behind and strike him dead, it might very well be worth it.

She broke the kiss and tugged at his hand. "Come."

As soon as she had him inside, she shut the door and turned to her maid, who stared. "Cover the windows, Aggie—quick."

Aggie did not move. "What has become of those men out there?" Her gaze dropped to Finnan's hands. "That is blood!"

"They ha' been removed," Finnan said baldly, and

the lass's eyes widened with alarm.

"Where is Danny? Is he all right?"

"Up on the hillside."

Jeannie had hurried to cover the windows when Aggie did not comply. She turned back, and Finnan felt her gaze all over him, full of distress.

"Your arm—"

"Sore, that is all. I am fine." Better now—well enough, certainly, to ravish her on the spot, if only her maid were out of the way.

"Did you signal for me?" he asked again.

She nodded, a grave expression filling her eyes. "I needed to tell you: your sister is here in the glen—at Avrie House."

Chapter Thirty

"Deirdre? Here?" Finnan spoke the words and swayed where he stood. Jeannie wanted to reach for him again, for she saw the color drain from his face. She nodded and wondered why he took the news so hard.

"How do you know?"

"I saw her today at Avrie House. Here, come and sit down."

She drew him in beside the hearth even as Aggie seized a shawl and pushed past them out the door. In truth, Jeannie barely saw her maid go, focused as she was on the great well of pain that had opened in Finnan's eyes.

She shoved him down onto the bench. He leaned forward and forced his hands through his hair, looking like a man who had received a blow.

"I believed her dead. Truly, I did not know, but I told myself she must be. Perhaps I even prayed so." He looked up, and his gaze scoured Jeannie's. "Are you certain? How did you know 'twas she?"

Jeannie crouched beside him and laid her hand on his knee. "She has the look of you. And the Dowager Avrie referred to her as her grandson's wife."

Finnan shuddered. "Did she say which of those vile blackguards wed her?"

"She is wife to Stuart, so the Dowager said."

"I will kill him. So I swear upon all that is sacred to me."

Dismay flooded over Jeannie. "Finnan, I did not tell you this to intensify your hatred or so you would spill more blood. I thought it would do you good to learn what happened to her. All these years of wondering…"

He gave her a wild stare.

Jeannie went on, desperate to soothe him. "She did not look unwell or particularly ill-used." Grave and unhappy, perhaps, but strong for all that.

Bitterly, Finnan said, "They took her against her will, and Gregor Avrie wed her to his son in order to legitimize any claim they might have here. Once I am dead—"

He stopped speaking abruptly. Alarm flared in Jeannie's heart. It made a valid reason, beyond highland spite, for the Avries to see him slaughtered.

"I must get word to her that I stand ready to help her," he said. "Let her know rescue is at hand."

"But, Finnan, how are you to rescue her, and you hunted like a hart these many days?" Jeannie knew this man by now, understood the depth of loyalty that possessed his heart—for this place, for Danny, for Geordie. How could she expect him to withhold it from his sister? Yet the prospect of him endangering himself terrified her.

She knew then that among all the things she had given Finnan MacAllister—her virtue, her concern, her peace of mind—foremost she had given him her heart. She loved this man desperately and completely, and the truth of that frightened her more than anything, for she had no evidence that he would ever love her in return.

"I ha' just killed two men," he told her harshly, "and I can slay as many more as need be. I will take them one by one in the dark, if I have to, and so free her."

"A valiant enough plan," Jeannie said ruefully, "but impractical, I fear. You are exhausted and badly injured."

"And armed with my anger. I need only deal with them one at a time."

"Well, it will not be tonight. Give it some time and catch your breath. Stay here the rest of the night."

His gaze seared her face before he looked to the door. "Danny—"

"I suspect Aggie has gone to him. Do you truly wish to interrupt them? Let them have their time, Finnan, for it is precious for them as well as us."

He continued to gaze at her as if trying to see inside her, and Jeannie hid nothing from him. If they were to have only this moment—only this night—she would give him all she had, including her honesty.

After a moment a new emotion flared in his eyes. What was it? Gladness? Relief? Passion? The corner of his mouth lifted in a half smile, and he raised a hand to cup her cheek.

"Jeannie," he said—only that, but coupled with the brush of his fingers it set her heart into a new rhythm, double time.

"Finnan." She turned her face into his touch and kissed his palm, still splashed with blood.

He sucked in a great breath. "'Tis madness for me to stay here tonight."

"Surely not. The Avries have posted their guards. They will suspect nothing."

"And should they come searching and discover the fate of those guards? Or if new men come to relieve them?"

Jeannie got to her feet. "Then I had best get that arm of yours tended quickly and see you rest as best you may." Before he went from her again, as he must. Jeannie's heart twisted in her breast. He might be the wrong man for her to love, yet she was his this night and for all time.

****

"Tell me of your sister," Jeannie urged as she soothed Finnan's arm with cloths soaked in witch hazel. "Tell me what happened that night you left the glen."

Finnan sipped the willow tea she had brewed for him and looked again at the door. He did not want to speak of that; he barely wished to remember that night. Yet Deirdre was here in the glen. Duty beyond even what he owed Geordie called to him.

Best to finish with Jeannie MacWherter here tonight, and be done. He had seen what lay in her eyes, knew he held her in thrall. As with a defeated opponent in battle, he had only to lay the final stroke.

Yet he felt less than sure he wanted to do that, when it came to it. He no longer knew how he felt about this woman—warm, vital, and so bonny it hurt him to look at her. She possessed grit and courage as well as beauty. But he had made a vow, and the man he was would not let him shrink from it.

Anyway, he thought now, even had she been the bonny angel she appeared, there was no future in it. Aye, best to break it with her now, before she saw him lying in his own blood beneath an Avrie sword.

For he could not be certain he would survive this

battle.

He said nothing at all, and she smoothed the ends of his bandage with those careful fingers and rose from the floor where she knelt.

"Come," she urged. "Rest until Aggie returns."

"I cannot rest. I must remain vigilant."

She tugged at his hand and drew him into the bedroom where they had been before. Immediately a score of memories flooded his mind—the heat of her welcome, the scent of her, and the taste on his tongue. And aye, if he were to break her heart this night, should he not take her body first?

He stood unmoving, his heart at war while she began to remove his clothing and then her own. The only light came from the other room, yet he could see her—oh, aye—when she unfastened her bodice and shed her skirt. Naked, she stepped into his arms and pressed herself, trembling, against him.

"Please," she beseeched. "I must have you this night."

Somehow, by a miracle of will, he held himself back. "I thought you wished to hear a dire tale."

"I do, if you will tell me. Come, lie with me."

They lay entwined atop the blankets, she close to his side, her lips just a breath from his ear.

"Tell me," she urged once more. "I may be able to help you reach Deirdre, woman to woman."

He laid one hand on the soft flesh beneath her breasts, narrowed his eyes, and thought back to the night in question.

"I was asleep," he began like a man in a dream. "My mother woke me, calling my name and weeping— she, who never wept easily. Her tears fell all the while she told me what they had done, Gregor Avrie and his two young sons. They had walked into my da's library where he sat reading, wounded him mortally, and then hauled him out onto the stones of the courtyard to finish him. She saw it all and hid herself. When Gregor sent men to search the house, she knew what they were after. She reached me first and implored me to flee. I wanted to take Deirdre with me, but we could not find her, and the wolves were on the hunt.

"By then, our household guard had roused and engaged Avrie's men. 'Twas the distraction we needed. My ma and I crept to the courtyard, where I took my da's torc still with his blood upon it, and his sword. My ma sent me away by a route known to no one but the family and promised to send Deirdre after."

Jeannie's hand crept to his chest, a gesture of comfort. But comfort lay well beyond his reach. "I made my way out and waited for Deirdre at the head of the glen. She never came, and I had vowed to my mother I would go. I know now the Avries must have seized Deirdre even before coming after me. Clever of them, really, for they knew with me dead she represented the best claim on the land.

"I still remember how my mother looked when I parted from her, weeping and begging me to go, that I might come back some day and regain what was rightfully ours. I did not know 'twould be the last time I ever saw her."

"What happened to her?" Jeannie whispered.

"For years I did not know. I only learned later from a family friend in Fort William that she had died." He paused and swallowed painfully. "I have had plenty of time to wonder about it since, and to be certain I never should have left that night. I should have stayed and battled to protect her—to protect both of them—and the glen."

"You were but a lad."

"Old enough. I could ha' taken up leadership of the household guard, fought the Avries and their hirelings back. I might at least have saved Deirdre."

"How, if they had already seized her?"

He shook his head. "I swear I did suppose her dead all this while—oh, perhaps not that night, but long since. All these years, for her to live so. I should be slain for permitting it."

"You did the only thing you could," Jeannie comforted, "came back when you were able, and regained the glen."

Finnan turned his face to her. "Did I? Then why am I on the run? And they hold her still."

"She must know you are here, must have heard them speak of you. She will know you have come for her."

"She will scarcely be able to imagine the man I have become," Finnan said bitterly. Sometimes he barely recognized himself. "And I am sure I will not know her."

"You will. She has the look of you. She appeared steady, and strong."

"And has Stuart fathered his brats on her?" he wondered aloud.

"Aggie has never spoken of seeing children in the house, not in any of her visits."

"'Tis a blessing." Possibly the only one.

"Anything I can do for you," Jeannie vowed, "you need only ask." She followed the words with a kiss upon the corner of his mouth and then another square upon his lips. He felt her devotion pour into him and knew to his soul this was what he had awaited. He could—should—break her now, consider Geordie well avenged, walk away and never look back.

Or he could love her first.

His hand slid from her belly upward to cup one naked breast. He knew the depth and intensity of the fire that burned within her, knew exactly what it took to fan it. He brushed his thumb across her nipple, and she caught her breath.

She whispered into his mouth, "I would do anything you ask, Finnan. You know that."

"I do, Jeannie."

"Let me show you." Her body glided over his, silken skin making a delicious friction, even as she began to worship him with her mouth. Hot kisses, followed by the ministrations of her tongue, trailed downward. Finnan knew he must remain in control, but his desire rose as helplessly and unpreventably as his manhood. Aye, and he must savor this—every motion—as justice, when he laid his final blow.

No sword needed for this—his only weapons lay between his legs and in his cruelty.

This will be the last time, he told himself even as she took him into her mouth, as he threw her on her back and suckled her deeply, as he entered her with a rush of hunger that set them both afire.

And after—after, when she lay still quivering in his arms, when her fingers that just could not seem to get enough whispered over him, when he knew he owned her body and soul, he said, "And so, Jeannie, do you regret giving yourself to me?"

"Regret?" she repeated, as if she knew not the meaning of the word. She reached up and kissed him softly, with such tenderness Finnan's heart nearly quailed within him. "How can I regret anything that has happened between us? You must know how I feel for you."

He dragged his fingers through her hair and drew her head back so he could gaze into her eyes in the dim light; he needed to witness her pain. "And how do you feel for me, Jeannie?"

Her lips quivered, as if she could barely find the words, before she spoke. "I love you, Finnan. My heart is yours."

"Is it so? Have you given it to me? Do I hold it in my hands?"

"You do."

He caused his voice to harden. "And how does it feel, Jeannie?"

"What?"

His fingers tensed. "How does it feel to present your heart and everything you are—all your hopes and needs—to someone on a plate, only to learn he does not care?"

"I—" He felt shock spear through her, felt pain replace it as the barb went deep into her most tender flesh. "I do not understand."

"Och, I think you do—I believe that, at last, you understand completely. For I do not want you, Jeannie. I do not love you. I ha' been using you all this while. And now you know how Geordie felt—you feel what he felt—when you refused the gift of his heart."

He could not look into her eyes after all. He moved swiftly, violently, and got out of the bed while still she lay there unmoving like a woman struck to death. He donned his clothing, and she did not speak, did not stir. And she never called him back when he went out into the night.

Chapter Thirty-One

Finnan MacAllister stared into the pouring rain and told himself he should feel some measure of satisfaction. From the time he received Geordie's final letter he had planned revenge against the scheming lowland wench who hurt him. Now he had that revenge in kind; the thing was over and done.

He needed it over and done so he could turn his eyes to the other matters that beset him: Rescuing Deirdre. Settling the Avries for good. Getting on with his life.

His life? What was left of it? Aye, well, there was this glen—place of his devotion, loyalty, and heart. But there seemed something wrong with his heart now. Ever since he left Jeannie MacWherter lying in the dark it had struggled to beat in his chest.

And why did his flesh still ache for her touch? That was over now. He had paid his debt to Geordie, the obligations of duty and brotherhood fulfilled.

It did not help his peace of mind that young Danny remained so persistently happy. Indeed, ever since Finnan had stalked from Rowan Cottage and met up with him at dawn, Danny had done nothing but prate about his Aggie. He went on about her even now, when the two of them crouched beneath a granite overhang trying to remain hidden and keep from the wet.

"I tell you, Master Finnan, I never thought any

woman would want me. Me—with but the one arm. Yet when she came walking out to me last night, I could not mistake. A man does not mistake, does he, when a lass gives him her heart?"

Finnan grunted and cursed inwardly. Aggie had still been with Danny when Finnan came upon them in the half-dark. The lass had dressed swiftly and run off home, but not before Finnan saw her give Danny the kind of kiss that would have warmed him to his toes. And from what Danny had hinted, they had ample time before that to consummate their feelings.

"A priceless gift, a woman's heart," Danny went on, staring like Finnan into the rain with a faraway look in his eyes.

"Anyone's heart," Finnan asserted, trying to justify himself. How did Jeannie fare now? What had she done after he left? Stayed in the bed and wept? Hauled herself up on her dignity? Become angry? Cursed his name?

Had he destroyed her as he intended?

Aye, and now he must stop thinking of her. He must focus on Deirdre.

Danny said softly, "We ha' pledged ourselves to one another. And you ken, Master Finnan, what that means. You and Master Geordie taught me what it is to make a vow and keep it."

Aye, right, Finnan thought savagely—that was all he had done. Then why did he feel as if his own heart had been torn out by the roots?

"She is the one for me," Danny went on devoutly.

Finnan said, with no wish to be cruel, "Are you certain, lad? 'Tis not just your cock talking, is it?" Danny had been with few women, and Finnan understood the lure of the flesh, the gods help him.

Danny turned bright gray-blue eyes on him. "Nay, though I do say 'tis a miracle she would accept me, maimed as I am. Damaged. But when she took the clothing from me, she did no' seem to see that." His voice lowered, became devout. "Master Finnan, she kissed me—even where my arm used to be."

"You are no' damaged, lad," Finnan said. "For your heart is whole, despite all you ha' suffered." Unlike Finnan's. He saw now, indeed, he was the one maimed. "And," he added, "your Aggie sounds a good, generous woman."

"She is that. I never hoped to meet anyone like her. But now, Master Finnan, we need to get through all this trouble."

"Aye, lad, so we do."

****

"What is it, mistress? Are you unwell?" Aggie posed the query softly as Jeannie stood at the cottage window staring out blindly at the rain. The rage that had possessed her when Finnan MacAllister walked out on her—the helpless, blinding fury—had abandoned her slowly, passed off like numbness from a stunted limb, leaving a well of hurt so deep she feared to sound it. Black and wide and merciless it yawned inside her, full of darkness that threatened to rise up on its own and overwhelm her.

He had done this deliberately, and in the most hurtful way he could imagine. She had been over it a thousand times, lying in the bed last night after he left, had recounted and remembered every word and every deed they had shared since she met him at the pool. She had relived it all, cast in the new light he provided, and

227

saw what he had done: lured her, led her, used her—all for revenge. Not one single kiss had been true.

Yes, and what a cruel and vicious man he proved to be. Her father used to say nothing could match a highlander for vengeance. Now she knew it to be true. For none of this had been about any feelings Finnan MacAllister possessed toward her, save hate. It had all been about Geordie.

Her heart quivered inside her chest, proving it still sought to beat, and pounded pain through her in another wave. If she had caused Geordie MacWherter to feel like this with aught she had said, done, or refused him, then she deserved some pain. But she did not deserve having her heart torn out still bleeding, for she had not meant to hurt Geordie.

Never meant him any harm.

And Geordie had been a grown man who made his own choices, took his own chances.

As had she. No one had forced her to take Finnan MacAllister to her bed. No one had compelled her to bare her body—and her soul—to him, no one had implored her to kneel at his feet. That did not make this hurt any less.

And that must be the lesson Finnan wanted to teach. Her father's scholarly mind, that had instructed her so long, made her regard that fairly even now. Finnan believed she had hurt Geordie deliberately, had used and denied him. She had not. And looking back on it, she could not be certain Geordie MacWherter was a grown man inside. A part of him had seemed ever the lost child.

Those letters—the ones he had written to his friend most likely when in a whisky haze—Jeannie would give much to know just what they said, not that it mattered now. She was destroyed completely. Did it truly matter whether Finnan MacAllister had justification?

"Mistress? You have taken nothing to eat today. Let me make you some tea."

Perhaps the Avries would find him, corner him, put an end to his life—an end to his strength, grace, and beauty. For she found him beautiful yet. The remnants of her heart—poor quivering shreds—did.

He could not run forever.

And why did that thought cause her more pain?

"Come, sit down." Aggie coaxed Jeannie to the bench and crouched down beside her. "What has happened? Did you and Master Finnan quarrel last night?"

Jeannie shook her head. They had not quarreled, no. He had loved her quite well, let her taste him everywhere—for the last time—and then shattered her world.

"Is it that you are worried for him? The situation is dire, yes. I am worried for Danny, as well, and for the life of me cannot see how it might come right. But there must be something we can do to help. I will go to Avrie House as soon as this rain lets up, see what I can learn. No one knows we have taken sides in this quarrel. At the very least, we can get information to them."

Aggie got to her feet and bustled about making the tea. Jeannie felt sure she would not be able to drink any, but when Aggie brought the mug she reached out and snagged her maid's wrist, stared into her eyes.

"His sister," she said.

"Eh?" Aggie looked startled.

"MacAllister's sister is there at Avrie House. Listen to me. You must find a way to speak with her, let her know her brother wishes to meet with her, rescue her. Perhaps she can work from within even as he works from without. She may have knowledge that will help."

"You think so?" Aggie asked thoughtfully. "Does she want rescuing?"

"She was forced to wed Stuart Avrie long ago. Finnan will not rest until he frees her."

"But how am I to win a word with her, and she a lady of the house? I go there only to visit her servants. Indeed, mistress, I have not laid eyes on the woman."

"I have, the day I saw the Dowager. You will find a way, Aggie, clever girl that you are. Perhaps we can prevent further bloodshed." For despite all Finnan MacAllister had done to her, despite the pain inside and how angry she should be, Jeannie felt something for him besides rage and hurt. She did not want to see him hunted and trapped, seized and slain.

She pictured him so, lying in his own blood, arms flung wide, hair spread around his head, all the wicked light flown from his eyes. Her poor, abused heart stuttered again in her chest. No, not that—anything but that.

Because she loved him. Heaven help her! Even though she knew she should despise him, and despite all his cruelty, she loved him still.

Chapter Thirty-Two

"Mistress Avrie agreed to come and see you," Aggie announced grandly. She shed her shawl and tried to smooth her hair, disordered by the wind. Bright flags of color flew in her cheeks, and her eyes shone with victory. "I managed to steal a word with her in the end. You would have been so proud of me."

"I am proud of you," Jeannie said even as her stomach roiled beneath another wave of emotion. For the past two nights she had not slept nor, in truth, taken more than a sip or two of tea—not since Finnan walked out of her life. Foolish woman that she was, she kept listening for him to return. Despite all her lectures to herself, she kept hoping he would change his mind, reconsider—realize he had genuine feelings for her after all.

Was this how Geordie had felt? She had to push that thought away from her, she could not handle it on top of the bitter suspicion that, no, Finnan would not return: his work with her was done.

Wicked highlander that he was.

She should have known better from the first, known he was not for her. But he had woven his trap so well, and she had tumbled right in.

Now she tried to focus on the matter at hand. Perhaps she could still help him, or rather help ease the dire situation in the glen, even if he did not deserve it.

"When will Mistress Avrie come?"

"She could not say. She is kept close, watched often. She said she must wait until her husband is away. But I believe she will come. She was near in tears when I mentioned her brother."

"Yes?"

"I had only a few stolen minutes with her, mind, there in the parlor where she sat alone. But she said she has feared for him being hunted like an animal, and she seemed ever so grateful we are helping him."

"Come, Aggie, and tell me all about how you accomplished this miracle."

Aggie sat with her on the bench like the friend she had in truth become. "I did not think I would manage it at first. When I visit Dorcas and Marie we always sit in the kitchen, you understand. Indeed, I never even knew Mistress Avrie was there all this while. But then at the end, and just when I despaired, Dorcas mentioned her—you know, in that sly way she has."

"What did she say?"

Aggie's enthusiasm dropped a notch. "That the Dowager's grandsons were getting very close to snaring their quarry, and she could not imagine what his sister might say when they slew him. It seems they almost had him the other night and wounded him full sore. But that does not seem right, does it, mistress? For were he hurt, he would surely come here for you to tend."

Jeannie's gaze dropped to her hands. "He will not come here again."

"Why ever not? The two of you did quarrel. I knew it!"

Jeannie twisted her hands into a tortured tangle. "It seems Laird MacAllister's feelings were never in earnest. He only wanted to repay me for what he considers my ill treatment of Geordie, in Dumfries."

"Oh, sweet mercy!" Aggie reached out and covered Jeannie's hands with her own. "Never say it is so. That beast! And yet still you seek to aid him? He could not be more wrong about you, and I would love to give him a right earful. I will, if I get the chance. Does he have any idea how things were in Dumfries, how hard our backs were to the wall? You would not be the first woman to wed a man she did not love in order to save herself. And Master Geordie—he did not seem to mind."

"He did mind, though. He wrote Finnan letters complaining of me."

"Whilst in his cups, no doubt," Aggie denounced indignantly. "It is what some men do when drunk, go crying like babes. At least you were honest with him. Would it have been better for you to lie to him about your feelings?"

"I no longer know, Aggie. My feelings are all burnt away." Almost all, save for the relentless, sickening ache. "You must understand, though, I cannot stand by and see him killed."

"Yes, well, I could cheerfully see him so, for what he's done to you. I will be cursed if I want to help him now."

Jeannie raised her gaze to her friend's. "Tell me of his sister."

"Well, as I say, Dorcas mentioned her, wondered what she would do when her husband or his brother hauled her brother in and spilled his blood all over the stones of the courtyard at Avrie House. I made like I was curious to see her—was she aught like that devil everyone hunted—and Marie said she was about to take the woman her tea in the parlor, if I wanted to have a wee peek.

"And so it proved. I stood behind the door when Marie carried in the tray. She is very like him to look at," Aggie added judiciously. "You could not mistake them for aught but kin."

"No."

"And I made an excuse to leave soon after, but I did not go by my usual way. Instead I crept round through the garden to where those doors of their sitting room open out. I told myself, were she still there in that room, then it was meant to be. She was."

"That was wonderfully brave of you, Aggie."

"It was. I told her I was in touch with someone helping her brother, who wanted to meet with her. I wish I had not, now."

Jeannie experienced a twinge of disquiet. She had, indeed, endangered both herself and Aggie. For now someone at Avrie House knew of her involvement with the hunted man.

All for the sake of someone who hated her.

She must believe she could trust Finnan's sister, but how completely under her husband's thumb might Deirdre Avrie be? What if Stuart questioned her and learned about this meeting? He would come straight to Jeannie's door.

"How did she seem? What is her manner?" If Deirdre Avrie proved too downtrodden, she might not be able to help Finnan.

"Difficult to say. She had a great deal of composure—like hard iron beneath her beauty. Despite that, the mention of her brother did seem to affect her."

"She will help him. She must." Jeannie squeezed Aggie's hands. For surely, like Jeannie, Finnan's sister could not bear to see him dead.

****

"So you are the woman who is helping my brother. I saw you once at Avrie House."

Deirdre Avrie stood framed in the doorway of Rowan Cottage looking so like her brother it nearly took Jeannie's breath away. Jeannie reached out, towed her in, and hurriedly scanned the path behind her.

"You are certain you were not followed?"

"I was not. But I cannot be away long. It is far too dangerous. Where is Finnan?" Deirdre's eyes reached behind Jeannie as if she thought to find him.

"Not here."

"But he has been here? You have been aiding him?" Deirdre's eyes examined Jeannie closely. The exact shape and color of Finnan's, they were fringed with darker lashes. Her auburn hair, like his also, had been disciplined and confined in a knot at the nape of her neck. On her, his proud nose managed to look feminine, her oval face beautiful. She wore a grand dress of dark green that proved however her husband might misuse her he at least saw her well clothed.

"Come, sit." Jeannie pulled at Deirdre's hand. "We do not have long."

"I dare not stay," Deirdre said. "This place could too easily become a trap."

"Where are your husband and his brother now?"

"I am not sure. They scour the glen for Finnan. Trent rode out with a troop of men this morning, headed north. Stuart left me not long since. But tell me how you come to know my brother."

"I was married briefly to his close friend, to whom he bequeathed this cottage."

"Married, briefly?"

"I am a widow now."

"Ah. Not a bad thing to be." Something flared in Deirdre's eyes. "Though I do imagine some women must care for the men to whom they are shackled."

Gently, Jeannie said, "I understand you were forced to wed Stuart Avrie."

"Aye—forced to speak the words at knife point. I was but a lass of fifteen then. I learned much from my husband since—almost nothing of mercy."

"I am sorry," Jeannie told her. "But surely if you help Finnan defeat him, you will then be free."

"And how might my brother defeat my husband? He is alone and at bay—injured, so they say. Dun Mhor lies half ruined. How can this end well?"

"I thought you might know of some weakness Finnan might exploit, that you might work from within on his behalf."

"You think I would not, if I could? It has pained me, hearing how they pursue him and knowing there is little I can do."

"How many men has your husband left in his service?"

She shook her head. "I cannot quite say. I know Stuart rues each my brother has slain—but 'twould not take much to overpower Finnan now. The only way I see out of it is for my vile husband to die and his brother with him."

"And," Jeannie asked, greatly daring, "would you help Finnan accomplish even that?"

"Of course," Deirdre said without hesitation. "But

just as I would love to see Finnan, 'tis impossible. I am naught but another weapon in my husband's hands."

"There must be a way. If I arrange a meeting—" But that would mean seeing Finnan MacAllister again, and Jeannie did not know if her heart—her soul—could withstand it.

Light flared in Deidre's eyes. "I would be most grateful if you could arrange a meeting place—here perhaps, or somewhere else in the glen."

"If I did, would you be able to slip away once more?"

Deirdre shook her head again. "I hope so, but I cannot promise. I am watched." Her lips twisted in a grimace. "And I would not wish to bring more harm down upon him."

"We will need to be very careful then."

"Aye. When you ha' arranged something, send word to Avrie House by your little maid. I will do my best to get away."

Deirdre made to rise then, hesitated, and gave Jeannie another searching glance. "Do you love him, my brother?"

Not something Jeannie wanted to contemplate. She knew she still cared far too much, but surely her softer, more tender feelings had all been killed the moment he stalked from her bedroom. She examined the shreds of her heart and honesty caused her to say, "Yes."

"You are a good woman."

Your brother does not think so. Those words nearly crept from Jeannie also, but she held them back. Aggie was right about this woman—something in her repelled confidences: the iron she had developed, no doubt, in order to endure her life.

No matter. So long as she helped Finnan, all might still come right for him.

And, quite clearly, Jeannie was past saving.

Chapter Thirty-Three

"Let us go back to Rowan Cottage, Master Finnan," Danny begged. "These wounds of yours need tending, far more care than I can manage here."

Desperate, sore, and near run to exhaustion, Finnan MacAllister shook his head. Not that, not Rowan Cottage—he could never return. There existed no refuge anywhere for him now.

For he had burnt that bridge, had he not? Sent it up in howling flames. He remembered again how still Jeannie had lain when he delivered his killing blow— indeed, like a woman slain—how her naked limbs, the sweet curves of the body he had just loved shone dim white in the quiet of her bedroom, unmoving.

She might at least have given him the satisfaction of some reaction—anger, grief. He—Geordie— deserved that. Instead he could not get over the notion that he had left her killed.

And he wanted to go back. Oh aye, he did—he told himself he wanted to see how she fared, savor the pain in her eyes, feel her hatred. For surely she hated him now as only a spurned woman could hate. Trouble was he did not quite believe that was all he wanted.

He had grown accustomed to Jeannie MacWherter during his campaign to destroy her, to the look in those wide blue eyes, the way intelligence or rueful laughter lit them. He had grown used to the warmth of her flesh and the taste of her lips. He told himself he ached for those, nothing more.

Yet ache he did.

Were he honest, he would admit nothing had gone right since he broke Jeannie's heart. He'd had an unfortunate encounter with Trent Avrie's men in which he took a deep wound to his shoulder that hampered him yet. He had barely escaped with his life and had not been able to stop and rest since. Harried continually, he and Danny had been all up and down the glen.

At least Danny seemed to have conquered his fever, Finnan reflected, and regained strength even as Finnan lost his. He had to admit it: he could not recall when he had been lower in body or spirit.

"Never mind. Just pack the wound with that yarrow," he told Danny now, brusquely.

They had paused high on a slope at the north end of the glen. From here Finnan could watch for signs of pursuit. Yet he knew they could not remain up among the boulders long—it would be too easy to be spotted in turn.

Somehow he would have to find the strength to move on.

He grunted in pain as Danny began to pack his shoulder, the lad's hand moving as gently as possible. He dragged his thoughts away from Rowan Cottage once again.

"We should move south, Master Finnan," Danny said, precisely as if he had heard Finnan's thoughts. "I am that sure Aggie and her mistress would not mind helping us again."

"Too dangerous."

"There is that hidey hole they ha' not yet

discovered, above the ford. You could rest there and get some sleep."

Finnan had not been able to sleep, nor snatch even a moment's peace.

Danny looked Finnan in the eye. "I ache to see her," he confessed. "Aggie, I mean. That last time when I lay with her—"

Indeed, Danny and Aggie had still been together when Finnan stormed back up the hill, leaving Jeannie slain.

"'Tis risky, that," he said, gritting his teeth around the pain as Danny pressed the bandage on. The cloth, dirty, would likely do him little good. Everything they owned was filthy.

He wondered how long he could go on like this. He had lost everything...except the glen; that remained his yet. He had always believed it enough to sustain him in the face of any hardship. What if he had believed wrong?

Ah, he had given Jeannie a damaging stroke from the blade of vengeance, aye, but it seemed to have cut both ways and injured him, as well.

"Worth taking the chance, I think," Danny went on. "Mistress MacWherter will at least give us food, and perhaps shelter."

"You are to ask nothing from her."

"Eh?"

"Nothing, lad, do you understand?"

Their gazes met. Danny's turned puzzled and then determined. "What happened that night when you came and collected me in such a hurry? Did you quarrel?"

"Nay."

"Have you broken it off? I ken fine the two of you

were…"

"Aye, broken it off. Drop it now."

Danny whistled a breath between his teeth. "She will forgive you, no doubt, and help you yet, if she sees you in this state. She is a good woman."

"You canna' say that. You know naught about her."

"Aggie says she is loyal, kind, and generous."

"Aggie does not know her either, or else she lies."

Danny stiffened. "Aggie would never lie to me."

So the lad had given his heart as well as his seed—the fool. Memory caught Finnan unawares as he relived the glorious act of losing himself inside Jeannie's heat, giving her all of himself. But nay, he must resolve to forget.

Savagely he said, "You do no' ken what she did to our Geordie in Dumfries. Leave it, lad—I ha' paid her in kind."

Danny frowned. "I know more than you might think. Aggie likes to talk, and most of all when we were cozy after. She has said much about how hard life was for them in Dumfries. 'Twas marriage to Geordie or the streets."

"And did she need to toss his love back at him? Could she no' have been more kind and generous?"

Danny looked shocked. "But we canna' choose where we love, can we, Master Finnan?"

Finnan said nothing, struggling against the pain inside.

"Come, Master, up and lean on my good shoulder. Let us move before the hounds are at our heels again."

****

"He is up on the hillside and will not come to your

door." Danny said the words apologetically and refused to meet Jeannie's eyes. "I left him sleeping or senseless—I could not tell which. He took a terrible bad wound a day and a half ago. 'Tis dirty, and it hampers him much."

Jeannie gazed away past the lad's head and tried to ignore how his words made her feel. Perhaps her heart still functioned after all, for she felt it twist in her chest.

"In truth," Danny went on, "I only came to beg some food and clean bandaging. We have naught."

"I wish you could stay," Aggie told him, heartfelt. She had kissed Danny soundly when he appeared, and her face shone with gladness. "Of course we shall give you whatever we have. Right, mistress?"

For an instant, Jeannie did not reply. She could easily turn Danny away; she owed Finnan MacAllister nothing. Or she could walk up that hillside as she wished and find him, lay eyes on him, even touch him again. For despite all her anger and pain, and the numbness when both burned away, she did want to see him, even just once. The truth of that upset her almost as much as what had come before, but the honesty in her heart would not let her deny it.

She fought a silent war within herself. She did not deserve what he had done to her. She had never intended to break Geordie's heart, but she could never convince Finnan of that. He thought the worst of her. Best to leave all connections severed as they were, to let it be done.

"Give Danny whatever you like," she told Aggie flatly and looked at the lad. "It is fortunate you have come. Will you give your master a message for me?"

Danny nodded cautiously. What did he know? Had

Finnan gloated to him about her humiliation? No matter, she had little enough dignity left to lose.

"I have been in touch with his sister. She wishes to meet with him in the hope he may rescue her from her plight. Do you think he would be willing to take her and leave the glen?" Save himself, leave off the warring and the vengeance.

This time Danny shook his head. "Who knows? Anger burns hot in him. But he might leave for a time, if only to keep her safe."

"Then you and I must decide on a meeting place." She drew a breath and fought the nearly overwhelming desire to go up that hillside. "I will take word to her, and you take word to him."

And then, it would be done.

Chapter Thirty-Four

Finnan struggled desperately to clear the buzzing from his head and gather his senses. Just below him lay Jeannie's cottage, quiet in the drowsy heat of afternoon. He narrowed his eyes and searched for signs of movement but saw none. Had Deirdre already arrived?

His heart clenched at the prospect of seeing her again. He pictured her still as the young girl he had left behind that night so long ago: slim, long-legged, and full of mischief. Ten years and much hard living separated that lass and the woman he now went to meet.

He remembered again that night his father died, his ma waking him to the dim radiance of a taper, tears streaming down her face and terror in her eyes. "You must take your sister and go." But they had been unable to find Deirdre, and in a panic his mother bade him leave without her.

Finnan had hoped for a time that Deirdre must have fled to the hills, had perhaps seen what befell their father and flown. A wild thing back then, she had spent as much time off and away as he. In his heart he had feared her captured, or dead. Now he knew the truth.

But none of that truly mattered now. His ma and da were long gone, just like the girl his sister had been. The woman he went to meet must be a virtual stranger.

Upon that thought he saw Danny slip from the cottage and sweep the surrounding area with a searching gaze. He came up the slope toward Finnan at a half jog. Finnan, ever cautious, remained under cover until Danny reached him, perspiring and breathless.

"Well?" Finnan asked, barely able to contain himself. He could hardly believe Jeannie had arranged this meeting on his behalf, given what he had done to her. Would he see her also, in his sister's company? And why had she endangered herself this way to assist him? Was it possible some of the kindness he had seen in those blue eyes had been genuine?

"There is a place just south of here your sister used to call 'the castle.' Aggie says your sister awaits you there now."

The castle. In truth, it was no more than a ruined dwelling of tumbled ancient stones. "She used to play there, did Deirdre." His heart rose for the first time in days.

"She bids you go alone. But, Master Finnan, I will follow along on the heights and keep watch."

"Good lad." Finnan clasped Danny's shoulder. "And Mistress MacWherter?" The words slipped out before he could halt them. "How does she fare?"

Danny hesitated and then said, "Glad, I think, that she could help to arrange this. Best go, Master Finnan. And have a care."

****

Finnan felt stronger as he slipped down the shoulder of the glen. Here, beyond the ford, the burn widened to a loch that met the sea, and there stood the heap of stones, some still piled atop one another but leaning perilously. The scene looked impossibly peaceful; bees hummed in the gorse, and only the bracken moved, tossed by a gentle breeze. His glen seemed very bonny and devoid of danger.

Then he saw her. She stepped out from beneath the stone arch into the sunlight, which caught her hair in a blaze of red and, just like that, he knew her. His heart clenched again in his chest, and the intervening years seemed to melt away. He remembered...

The two of them barely a year apart in age, sharing laughter and silliness, climbing trees and teasing one another, planning mad midnight escapades and adventures, back when life had been good, when he had felt safe.

Now he only felt safe with a sword in his hand.

Or in Jeannie MacWherter's arms.

He beat that thought back hastily and started down the slope, nearly all his exhaustion chased by a wave of gladness. His heartbeat pounded in his ears, and his step felt light.

He had not gone far when Deirdre turned and saw him. Her head came up like that of a pony scenting home, and he hurried faster. He could not yet read the expression on her face, but when he drew near enough she called softly, "Finnan!"

"Deirdre." By all the gods! His throat tightened, and sudden tears blurred his vision. He flew down the last stretch of the slope, already reaching for her hands.

Before he grasped them he could see the changes, and that she little resembled that wild girl after all. For she now bore the years and composure of a woman. Nearly as tall as he, she stood slim and steady, with a warlike light in those eyes so much like his own.

But her hands reached for his eagerly, seized and clasped them hard. And her lips, blood red in her pale face, twisted into a smile before she said, "Brother! I scarcely dared hope you would come."

"It grieves me that you would doubt me, Sister. Are you safe and well?"

"I am." The light in her eyes flared brighter. "You are not."

At those words, men poured from the stone archway of the ruined building, out of the inner darkness. For one bare instant Finnan did not comprehend it. In that moment his sister's hands tightened on his cruelly, preventing him from stepping back and drawing his sword. As swiftly as that he lost his chance: men surrounded him, all with their weapons at the ready.

And, his fair hair gleaming like a cap of gold, Stuart Avrie stalked to his wife's side. He pointed his blade at Finnan's throat. "Go on, MacAllister, put up a fight. I would love an excuse to spit you where you stand."

Finnan barely heeded the words; he stared still at his sister, trying to accept the truth. She had trapped him, betrayed him. And the look he saw now in her eyes proved it all: bright anger, victorious gladness.

And hate.

****

"Mistress, mistress! Master Finnan has been taken. He is in the Avries' hands."

Danny stopped, stared into Jeannie's face, and fought for breath before he concluded, "'Twas all a trap. His sister has betrayed him."

The blood drained from Jeannie's face, and she swayed where she stood. "No," she whispered.

Danny nodded frantically. "He is captured and hauled away by Stuart Avrie and his men. North they went, in the direction of Avrie House. I did not know what to do. I fear I should have done something."

Aggie hurried forward and seized the agitated lad's arm. "How many men were there?"

"I did not count. Five, six—"

"So many? Then what could you have done?"

"She betrayed him?" Jeannie's heart beat hard and sickening in her breast. "How could she?"

"I do no' ken," Danny fairly wept. "But I was watching all the while from cover. I saw her walk out from the pile o' stones to meet him. All appeared quiet. He went to her, and they clasped hands. Then Avrie's men just came pouring out." Danny gulped, and his eyes reached for Jeannie's. "They will kill him, mistress. Then ownership of all these lands will pass to his sister. They must kill him."

Danny was right. Deirdre's heart—traitorous heart—must have turned. Or perhaps she was so afraid of her husband, so securely under his thumb, she would do whatever he ordered. She had not appeared to be a woman whose spirit was broken, but she had lived a long time under the Avries' sway.

"And I led him to it," she said bitterly. "I arranged the meeting." Her knees almost failed her, and she swayed perilously.

If he lived, he would never forgive her.

Fool, she chastised herself. He would not forgive her in any case. He hated her for Geordie's sake, and he had chosen hate over any softer feeling. Now he would have another reason, one of his own. Had she truly hoped that by reuniting him with his sister she might go some distance toward making him see her differently? Perhaps that had been in the back of her mind. Which made her a piteous creature, still seeking the regard of a man who had hurt her so. But, God knew, she could not help herself.

No matter now—for all hope was gone.

No, not all hope. Finnan MacAllister still lived. And if his sister acted under duress, Jeannie might yet persuade her to haul up her courage and act according to her loyalty and the dictates of her heart.

****

"Ah well, Brother, is this not a fond reunion? And but ten short years too late."

With difficulty, Finnan raised his head from the place where he lay and looked at the woman who had walked into the room. His sister Deirdre she must be, aye, but she bore only physical resemblance to the lass he had known. A sharp, cruel smile curved her lips, and her steps rang on the flagged floor of the room that had once been their father's library. Confidence enfolded her like a cloak.

He knew then this was no cowed maid. She must be full partners with her husband in this evil endeavor.

He closed his eyes on a rush of pain far fiercer than that which pulled at his shoulder. Pegged out and secured hand and foot to iron shackles driven between the stones of the floor, he believed he would die here in the place his father had loved, now gutted by fire and partly open to the sky. For Avrie and his men had dragged him not back to Avrie House, but to Dun Mhor.

Open sky soared above him, the sunlight in his eyes shifting to the west. He supposed it fitting that he should end up here, where his father had received his death wound, his blood flowing onto these same stones.

"Deirdre," he said, only that, for his sorrow half choked him.

"Aye, Brother dearie?" She paced with deliberate steps beside his head and gazed down at him. Such hate flared in her eyes that for an instant he thought she meant to kick him, and he braced himself for the pain.

"Do you know me, Finnan? I confess I would not have recognized you. All those nasty scars and pictures on your skin. Whatever would Ma say? What would she think of her bonny boy now?"

"Or her daughter," he grated.

"Ah, but in the end she cared far less for me than for you. She proved that, did she not, the night Da died? When she thought she could save but one of us, she ran to you."

Again Finnan craned his neck, trying to see her face where she stood above him, a dark silhouette against the dying sun.

"She only came to me because she believed our enemies would slaughter me in order to gain control of the glen. 'Twas no preference."

"But"—Deirdre's voice, clear and strident, overrode his words—"they did not hurry to slaughter you, did they? Instead they came to my chamber, a troop of men, terrifying in the dark, and dragged me from my bed and away."

Finnan narrowed his eyes against the glare and wondered what he heard in her voice besides anger. Hard to tell, with that brittle cruelty overlying all.

"We tried to find you as soon as Ma roused me, Deirdre. We both did."

"I believe you, darling brother—truly I do. 'Tis what happened after that sticks in my craw. For what did you do when you failed to find me?" She bent toward him, leaned down, and her face swam into view. "You saved yourself. You buggered off away out of the glen and left me in their hands." He saw it then, the bright desire for vengeance in her eyes. "'Tis for that, my dearest brother, you will now pay."

Chapter Thirty-Five

"Well, Wife, and if you are done reuniting with your brother, I think we had best finish this." Stuart Avrie walked slowly into the chamber, his expression guarded, and took up a place at Deirdre's side. Aye, Finnan thought, and the man came armed for the job with sword and dirk thrust through his belt, both of which glittered in the dying light.

And so his life would end on a blade after all, following his wandering and fighting, all the battles and struggles. He once more raised his eyes to the sky. At least he would die in this place he loved more than his own existence.

He moved his gaze from that beloved sky to his sister's face. Her hair shone in a halo of red, and that of the man beside her in gold.

"Ah, no, Husband. I have only begun to pay my beloved brother as he deserves."

Pay as he deserves. Finnan heard an echo of his own words, his own sentiments, in hers. He had lost the past ten years of his life to the need for vengeance in one form or another. It seemed Deirdre had, as well. Aye, so, and they were far too alike.

That hard knowledge seemed to settle beneath his breastbone like a rock.

Deirdre stepped closer, reached out with one foot, and caressed Finnan's cheek with her toe. Finnan could

253

feel the waves of hate coming off her and knew this gesture for the precursor to pain. He stiffened in an effort to prepare himself but, again, the foot did not strike.

Instead, Deirdre slanted a look at her husband. "Surely you will not deny me my satisfaction? Have I ever denied you yours?"

Stuart Avrie stepped forward also. His arm snaked around Deirdre's waist in a gesture of pure possession, and he drew her against his side. Finnan's jaw clenched as he watched the man's hand stroke her hip and move lower. For an instant he was sure he would vomit; somehow he choked back the sickness.

"Satisfaction," Stuart echoed, "or revenge?"

Deirdre smiled, and again Finnan saw himself in her face. "They are one," she purred.

Finnan closed his eyes because, suddenly, he did not want to behold that sharp avarice in a face so like his own. He had never denied himself that sort of satisfaction—not against Gregor Avrie, not against Jeannie MacWherter.

Jeannie. A vision of her swam into his mind: golden hair spilling down across her shoulders, bodice unfastened, and desire in those wide, blue eyes.

Desire...or was that love?

Nay, Jeannie had never really loved him, though he had invited that emotion in hopes he might wound her more deeply. It had been mere lust they shared. He doubted her capable of actual love.

And he? Of what tender emotions was he capable? He had loved his father and mother, been bonded deeply with Geordie. He had loved this woman who now stood here wrapped in hate.

He opened his eyes to find her crouched down beside him. She peered into his face. "Give me the lend of your dirk, Husband," she requested and reached back a hand. "I would busy myself a while repaying him."

Stuart extracted his knife from the loop at his hip. "Better to end it, Wife. Until he dies, you do not own the land."

"I know that very well." She slanted a look at Stuart. "Only promise me when the time comes he will die by my hand."

Stuart grunted. "I care not how, so long as he dies."

"Leave that to me."

Somewhat to Finnan's surprise, Stuart went out. Finnan gazed into his sister's eyes.

"Well, now." She settled herself on the stones beside him, the dirk in her hands. "Do you know how long I have waited for this? Dreamed of it?"

"Ten years."

"Aye, since I was fifteen. Fifteen, Brother. That was my age when they took me that night. Would you like to hear a story before you die? Shall I tell you the tale of all that befell me?"

"Much befell both of us."

"And there speaks my matchless brother, selfish to the bone. Will you think of no one else, even when you stare death in the face?"

Finnan closed his eyes on another wave of despair. "Tell me."

"They came at me out of the dark whilst I lay sound asleep. Suddenly they were just there, in my chamber, five men. Not Gregor Avrie, no—he and Trent were busy killing Da. But he sent Stuart. 'Twas the first time he touched me, that night.

"They bundled me out of the room so swiftly I barely had time to comprehend what was happening. He covered my mouth so I could not scream. But I could hear mother wailing out there in the courtyard when she discovered Father dead. I thought she would come for me then, and save me. Or you would."

"I lay asleep, Deirdre, and did not know. It would have been too late, anyway—from what you say, Stuart had already been sent to seize you even before they slew Da. That must have been their plan all the while, to secure you before they came for me. There is no way I could have reached you in time."

"Perhaps so. Still, you might have caught me up, had you tried. Oh, aye, Brother, I have been over and over it in my mind. Despair does that to a lass. She relives. She even hopes for a while that her brother will rescue her."

"We searched everywhere for you, as I say. You were nowhere to be found."

"So you went blithely off and saved your own skin."

"Nay—"

"Never fear, Brother. Gregor Avrie arriving with a stout troop of hired men did put our household guard to the rout, and you could not best them all that night. I will give you that. But let me ask you this." She leaned toward him, the dirk balanced in her fingers, her gaze accusing. "After that night, did I cease to exist? Did the thought of me in their hands, awaiting succor, never touch you?"

"To be sure, it did." Finnan's throat, tight and dry, almost prohibited speech.

"Yet, somehow, you never returned nor risked

yourself for me."

"I thought you dead like Da. I was but a lad, and buried under the weight of my own pain."

"Ah, so 'tis all about Finnan—again."

Finnan searched her face and flinched at what he saw there. "I did inquire after you. For years I did. I asked Da's friend in Fort William to search out word of you. There was none. I did not know—"

"That I was wife to Stuart Avrie? But I was, from that very night. They dragged me away to a priest, and let Stuart pluck me, too."

"By all that is holy, I am sorry, Deirdre!"

A curious smile curved her lips. "My husband and I came to terms eventually, just as soon as my anger hardened and it became evident he and I wanted the same thing. He is no' so bad when you get used to him." She widened her eyes deliberately. "And a braw man between the blankets once he got me broke in."

Again Finnan felt his stomach heave. He closed his eyes in an effort to shut the images away, but found he could not.

"I did no' forget you, Dee. 'Tis why I battled so hard to come back. 'Tis why I slew that bastard Gregor Avrie."

"Aye." She nodded solemnly. "For revenge—the same thing that drives me now. Look at me, Brother. Look at me!"

Finnan obeyed, straining at his bonds. He gazed into his sister's face and saw his own determined hate.

"You," she said almost lightly, "live for revenge against the Avries, and I for revenge against you. Are we not alike? Now I need only decide how best to take my price from you—in pain."

Chapter Thirty-Six

"We cannot leave him in their hands." Danny, who spoke the words, sounded every bit as desperate as Jeannie felt. "He would not leave me, were our places reversed."

"Yes, love," Aggie told him and reached out to touch his shoulder. "But we must think carefully and not just go rushing in. We are but three alone, and the Avries have many men."

Jeannie could hear the terror in Aggie's voice. Aggie feared Danny might throw his life away for Finnan's sake; she loved the lad just as Jeannie loved...

She caught herself up fiercely and slammed the door on that thought. Now was no time to contemplate her tangled feelings. Better, far better, to try and deny them.

For who could love such a man as Finnan MacAllister? What fool? Truly, if she could dismiss that lithe body, the clever hands, the hot mouth, what was left? For those attributes spoke only of lust, and though powerful, Jeannie could not say that would last.

But love? That required caring for the man within—he who had destroyed her—with his ironic humor, quick, agile mind, and the warmth that made him care for those sworn to him. Finnan MacAllister: when he loved he loved hard, and when he hated he hated completely.

He hated her. A practical woman at heart, she could not deny it. From the moment he knew her identity, he had planned every move, every smile, to wound her as deeply as he could. Surely that was enough to make her put aside any soft feelings she still had for him.

She groaned inwardly. What had Geordie written in those letters? She would give much to know, but knowing would not change the present situation.

And now, if she ascribed to the penchant for revenge that seemed to possess this place, she need do nothing save fold her hands, sit back, and wait for Finnan to get what he deserved. Yet she did not think the sickness in her belly would let her, nor the pounding of her wounded heart, nor the look in Danny's eyes.

Through wooden lips she said, "What is to be done? How can we suppose to help him?" The Avries would kill him, she had no doubt; it had been their one aim these many days. They must kill him, so ownership of the glen would pass to Deirdre.

He might already be dead. Why would they wait? Why not make sure of their quarry once they had it in their hands?

Jeannie's heart seized at that thought, and she experienced a rush of pain that far exceeded any Finnan had brought her. His changeable brightness gone from the world... There would be no reason for her to continue on.

"I should go." Aggie, pale of cheek, drew herself up with resolve. "To be sure, I am the only one who can. Dorcas will think I have come looking for gossip. I can get inside Avrie House."

Danny exchanged an agonized look with Jeannie

259

over Aggie's head. "But the Avries now know your mistress is in league with Master Finnan. Will they not suspect you, as well?"

Aggie tossed her head. "No matter; I am of little importance. And I might be able to discover a way——"

"There is no way," Jeannie whispered. "I cannot believe she betrayed him—her own brother."

"Aye, so," said Danny, clearly torn. "But we must try. I cannot just leave him there."

"I will go," Aggie said again. "Give me a kiss for luck, lad—lest I never see you again."

The kiss Danny bestowed was long and lingering. Aggie caressed his cheek then and looked into his eyes.

"I am that glad I met you, Daniel MacPhee— whatever may come next. I am glad I carry you in my heart."

Danny kissed Aggie's hand tenderly, and foolish tears flooded Jeannie's eyes. She saw her little maid brace herself with resolve.

"You must come along and keep watch, both of you—but stay hidden until I bring you word what I discover."

And Danny said, "Just try and leave me behind."

****

"He is no' there." Aggie, cheeks now flushed red as apples, struggled up the rise to the place where Danny and Jeannie waited in concealment. "No one is there save the Dowager and her servants. Dorcas thinks they are all at Dun Mhor."

"But"—Jeannie struggled with it—"Dun Mhor was put to flame."

"Damaged, but not burnt down," said Danny, bringing to mind what Finnan had told Jeannie. "Most of it still stands, if gutted. That place will be full of meaning to them—the seat of MacAllister power. They must hold him there."

"Alive?" Jeannie turned her eyes on Aggie. "Did Dorcas know that?"

Aggie shrugged and shook her head.

"Aye, well," Danny breathed, "we must go there, see—"

"Wait." An idea, or the ghost of one, whispered into Jeannie's mind. "We cannot go running off will-he, nil-he. We need something with which to bargain."

Danny lifted his empty hand. "What?"

"Have you a weapon?"

"Just my dirk. But—"

Jeannie asked Aggie, "How many guards remain at Avrie House?" Please God they had all gone with their vile masters to Dun Mhor.

"I saw only one at the front of the house and a pair on horseback riding away northward. Why?"

"Because, as I see it, we have only one bargaining chip—and she is there, below."

****

"Well, my friend—you have got yourself into a real bind this time, right enough."

Every muscle in Finnan's body leaped painfully when he heard the voice so close beside him, and he opened his eyes wide in disbelief. How much time had passed since Deirdre left him? Not as long as it seemed. The agony of his flesh stretched the time; the agony in his mind obliterated it. Now, surely, madness nibbled at him, for this presence could not be as it seemed.

He turned his head on a sickening rush of mingled horror and gladness and looked at the man who sat on the floor at his shoulder.

"Geordie MacWherter—big as life and twice as ugly." Did he really actually speak the words? His lips moved, but he did not think any sound came.

But Geordie heard. He directed a sorrowful look at Finnan from those hazel eyes and shook his head ruefully. "Look at you, just—pinned to the stones and awaiting death. We ha' been in many a hard place in our time, lad, but none, I am thinking, as bad as this."

"You may be right." Finnan's heart lurched again as he admitted it. "But how come you here? You are—"

"Dead, aye, right enough." Geordie gave Finnan another look. Finnan had forgotten how expressive Geordie's hazel gaze could be, or that his friend could speak many sentences with but a glance. "But should you be so surprised to see me? Did you no' tell my wee wife you had spoken with my shade?" Geordie spread his broad hands, palms upward. "Well, now 'tis true."

"I am that glad to see you, despite everything."

"And I, you. You became a habit with me, Finnan, lad, like wearing an old coat through the sunshine and rain. But you ken the thoughts in your head have power. Think them hard enough, and they will come true. 'Tis why I am here, because you made it so. You maun be careful what you think."

"I ken that fine."

"Aye, to be sure, you have always been like a wizard, mumbling those prayers and believing in the magic everywhere." Geordie leaned closer and widened his eyes. "The magic is true, lad. But it must be invoked with a grateful heart. And hate kills it, sure. The trout told you that."

So it had.

Finnan's lips twisted in an ironic snarl. "A bit late for me now, Geordie, do you not think? Wounded—bested—I do not have long."

"Bested? When ha' we ever been bested?"

Finnan gave his friend a grave look. "When you were in Dumfries, it seems. Why did you not call on me? I would have come."

"Would you?"

"I hope you know it!"

"But you had your own quest that led you through every hardship and back here again—you were well caught in the fight for this place. How could I call you away?"

"Because you are my friend, my brother."

Now Geordie smiled. "Aye," he said softly, "aye. Is it not a strange thing, Finn? We traveled so long together, yet we stayed so different. For you always thirsted after revenge, and I after love."

"Jeannie," Finnan said, and the emotions inside him tangled impossibly: regret, aye, and desire even now. "I paid her right well, Geordie, for what she did to you."

Again Geordie shook his head. "Aye, you waged a right war against her, did you not? But Finn, lad, 'twas all for naught, for she did nothing to me. Have you no' been listening? I did it all to myself: I it was who put the rise and set of the sun on how she felt for me, when she could not choose how to feel. I let her decide my worthiness—when all the while 'twas a decision I made back at Culloden that weighed on me. How many good men died because of us, Finn? When I tried to sleep, they would walk through my mind. Even the drink did not chase them, no matter how much I took."

Laura Strickland

Realization speared through Finnan like a bolt of pain. "It was never about Jeannie, then. 'Twas about Culloden. But we made up for what we did that day. In the end, our hearts remained highland, and true."

"Is that what you told yourself? Well, but, Finn, that did not bring back the men we slew at the outset. 'Twas they who haunted me. Sometimes they would sit down next to me in the tavern as I sit with you now, and speak of their wives and children."

"We were mercenaries, Geordie. Hired swords!"

"Aye, and turned coat—twice." Geordie leaned still closer. Finnan could see the flecks of brown in his eyes and follow the curl of the grouse tattooed on his cheek. "Listen to the trout, lad. Choose peace. Choose Jeannie."

"No time." Finnan swallowed hard. "I am going to die."

"Ah, and where is the Finnan I know? When have you ever thought it too late for anything? How many times, lad, did you keep me going on a march with the promise of a dram or a rest at the end of some ill-fated campaign? Aye, and now you truly have something for which to live."

"What is that? Deirdre means to kill me. My own wee sister, Geordie!"

"Aye, for she has chosen hate. There is another path for you, Finn. Listen to me, lad, if ever you have done. I wanted Jeannie to love me, aye. What man would not? But 'tis you she loves."

Finnan closed his eyes on a terrible rush of pain. "Loved. No more, Geordie. I ha' destroyed all that, if ever it was true."

"If you think so, then you do not know the woman

264

she is. Her heart may be hard won—the gods know I could not claim it. But once won, 'tis bestowed for good and all. She loves you, Finn. She loves you yet. And you love her. You need to admit it."

"I have lost everyone I loved. My da and my mother. You. And now Deirdre. 'Tis safer not to love."

"Safer, aye, maybe. But I can tell you, for I know—in the end 'tis the one thing that matters and worth the fight, if ever anything was." Geordie gave Finnan the smile that had, for so many long and weary miles, traveled at his side. "I promise you, 'tis the one thing that can save you now."

Chapter Thirty-Seven

Morning light broke over the glen in a delicate wave of radiance. What a morning, Jeannie MacWherter thought, to decide the outcome of her life. For after the agony of the night just past, it seemed apparent her future rested all on one question.

Did Finnan MacAllister still live?

It did not matter so much if he never saw her for the woman she was, that she might never kiss him again, or even that they would not be together at any time during that future. Her heart could continue to beat so long as Finnan lived somewhere in this world.

What difference if this scheme on which they embarked proved entirely mad? What, if she must sacrifice her own life? She knew she would trade her existence for his.

Because fight it as she might, she loved him.

Very well, then, she told the mystical, bright morning. Have it your way. I am a fool of a woman. I love the man who hates me.

Yes, and she found some small comfort in admitting it.

"Come ye out!" Danny shouted at the empty, singed doorway of Dun Mhor. "Or she dies!"

The Dowager Avrie jerked in Jeannie's hands. There had been considerable discussion among the three of them—Danny, Aggie and Jeannie—as to how they must play out this gamble. A one-armed man could not hold a woman, even a frail, old woman, prisoner and keep a dirk at her throat. And yes, the Dowager Avrie was frail; Jeannie could feel the woman's bones beneath her clothing, fragile as those of a bird. For Jeannie did service as captor while Danny employed his dirk.

She could not feel the Dowager breathing; it crossed her mind the woman might yet pass away in her hands and cost them their sole chance to bargain.

Jeannie heard fear in Danny's voice, and a corresponding kick of terror tore through her gut. Aggie, standing at Jeannie's back, went armed with a knife stolen from the kitchen of Avrie House, where they had snatched the Dowager at dawn. Jeannie dared not so much as glance at her.

People began spewing from the blackened doorway of Dun Mhor. The scene seemed to shimmer in the clear morning light: first came two men at arms, then a confusing knot of other figures, two with heads of glossy dark gold. Another had a flaming auburn mane.

Deirdre. Jeannie let out a breath she had not realized she held. The Dowager Avrie stiffened at the sight of her grandsons, and Danny, very close to Jeannie's side, pressed the blade tighter against the old woman's throat.

"Ask," Jeannie bade Danny. "Ask if he lives."

Instead, Danny called, "We have a captive, as you can see, and wish to trade."

"Grandmother!" called one of the Avries—Trent, Jeannie thought.

Stuart Avrie stepped forward from the small throng, and Deirdre with him. Jeannie tried desperately to count heads in order to weigh their chances. Seven people she could see; no doubt others lurked, unseen. Avrie would send men—probably guards—to surround them.

No matter. Right now Jeannie needed to know only whether Finnan still occupied her world.

Stuart and Deirdre conferred hastily, heads together, and Jeannie felt a flare of satisfaction. They had not expected this. Their quarry caught, they believed themselves in an unassailable position.

"Send out your prisoner," Danny called, "and we will release ours. Quickly now—'twould be the easiest thing in the world to kill her."

"Do not listen to him, Stuart," the Dowager cried in a surprisingly strong voice. "I am ready to die so you may legally claim what we are owed."

Desperate sweat broke out all over Jeannie's body. She increased her hold on the old woman—one arm across the bony torso, one hand clutching the woman's wrists—and felt the Dowager tremble.

"Does he live yet?" she called, and Danny twitched violently. He had made Jeannie promise to let him do all the negotiating. The promise had not endured in the face of her fear.

"Ah, so it is the dutiful widow," Stuart said cuttingly. "What is your stake in all of this? What will you gain by dying here today?"

"His freedom."

Shockingly, Deirdre Avrie began to laugh. Her mirth tumbled into the morning, brittle and far too bright. "Ah, so my brother's charm works still! Foolish woman, do you not know Finnan's interest has only ever centered around himself? He merely projects an aura of genuine worth. My father believed in it—aye, and my mother also. And now you? Have you bought into his lies, as well?"

"He owns my loyalty," Jeannie answered. And her heart.

"Ah, and so the three of you—ragged remnants of his adoring many—come here, do you, to succor him?" A terrible smile twisted Deirdre's lips. "How very touching."

"Just haul him out here," Danny sounded shaken, "and let this be done."

"Done?" Stuart Avrie rejoined. "This will not be done until the blood of the bastard in there"—he jerked his head at the ruin at his back—"wets these stones."

Jeannie nearly fell down, so great was her relief. He lived. They had not slain him during the endless, terrible night.

"Do no' be a fool, man," Danny called to Stuart. "Do you want to see your grandmother dead?"

Again Stuart and Deirdre conferred. Jeannie adjusted her grip on her captive; the old woman turned her head and looked into Jeannie's face.

"There is something you do not know," she said in a low voice. "My grandsons' cause is just. They have a right to this place, as much right as Finnan MacAllister." She gave a tight smile, and her eyes grew frenetic. "My son Gregor, you see, was no Avrie but a MacAllister born. Finnan's grandfather and I were lovers. Och, do no' look so shocked. 'Twas never that weak milksop wife of his he loved, but me. And he promised Gregor would have a fair share of all he owned. He lied, but Gregor's sons will have it now, even if it costs my life."

Cousins. They were all cousins. Jeannie's throat went dry, making it difficult to speak. "Then convince them to let Finnan go and talk it out amongst you. They have no choice but to make this exchange."

Stuart and Deirdre seemed to arrive at the same conclusion. Concern marked Stuart's handsome face; Deirdre's looked dark with anger. Trent stepped up, arguing hard in his brother's ear. Jeannie's poor, abused heart rose on a wave of genuine hope. Of course they would not take a chance with the old woman's life. They could do nothing but release Finnan. She need only find a means to get him safe away, after.

"Very well," Stuart called, and the Dowager Avrie jerked again, violently, in Jeannie's hands.

"Nay, Grandson—do not! Fight, fight for the land, for what is yours by birthright. Fight to the end and avenge your father!"

Without warning, the old woman leaped forward, tearing herself from Jeannie's grip and into the blade Danny held against her throat. It happened so swiftly Jeannie could barely react; before she grasped what happened, the Dowager's warm blood streamed down over her hands.

Someone screamed; it took Jeannie an instant to realize the sound came from Aggie. The Dowager sagged in Jeannie's arms even as the life passed from her frail body. The onlookers bellowed—all but Deirdre, who smiled the sort of smile that might grace the countenance of the devil's wife.

The bright morning wavered around Jeannie. She released the Dowager's corpse, which slid into a heap at her feet. For an instant she feared she must tumble down also, impaled on the sharp blade of despair.

Only one sound broke the horrified silence. "Seize them," Deirdre said.

****

"I have to thank you, Mistress MacWherter. My inestimable brother will be glad to see you."

Deirdre Avrie spoke the words in a purr that carried the bite of an adder. She lounged, all confidence, in one of the chairs pushed back from the table of what had once been the dining hall of Dun Mhor. This room appeared only partially gutted by the fire that had heavily damaged the other chambers Jeannie had seen. Part of the ceiling lay open to the sky, and the delicate sunlight filtered in.

It lent a reddish halo to Deirdre's hair and swirled dust motes before Jeannie's eyes. Stuart Avrie, who held Jeannie captive, had both her arms pinned hard behind her back. So far he had not spoken. Was he in shock over what had just happened outside?

Jeannie's mind stuttered over it: Danny had fought valiantly and was now wounded, he, Jeannie, and Aggie all prisoners. Their rescue plan lay in shreds.

She sagged in Stuart's grasp and almost fell down. Without pity, he hauled her up again.

Deirdre leaned toward Jeannie; the smile she had employed outside once more twisted her features. "Do you not wish to know why I should thank you, Mistress MacWherter?"

Jeannie shook her head, too sick to speak.

"But I will tell you anyway: I have not been able to break my brother, not all this night past."

Jeannie's throat closed abruptly even as her stomach heaved. Terrible images flooded her mind and paralyzed her tongue.

"But now you have presented the weapon I need. The question is, how best to use you? Tell me, have you slept with him? Have you had him in your bed?"

Jeannie's throat spasmed, and Deirdre laughed. "You need not answer, I can see it in your eyes. I suppose he thinks he owns you, like everything else in this place. Interesting."

Somehow Jeannie fought through the terror and sickness to say, "He does not care for me. It is as you said outside—he cares only for himself."

"Oh, there can be no question he does no' love you. You have that right—he loves no one but the grand Finnan MacAllister. But he will fight to preserve whatever he believes belongs to him."

Jeannie spoke again through wooden lips. "That night—so long ago, when your father died—Finnan did not want to leave you. He agonized over it."

Deirdre laughed again, a shrill sound. "Stuart, husband mine, only hear her defend him!"

Stuart grunted in response. Jeannie could feel emotions streaming from him, though she could not identify them.

"He had years—*years*—in which he might have tried to rescue me, though after the first few I would have refused to leave this new family of mine. Fine and fierce they are, and know how to hate."

"Let Danny and Aggie go," Jeannie urged. "They are of little value to you. I will persuade Finnan. Only let me see him."

"Oh, you shall see him, right enough. And we just may let your two companions go. What do you say, Husband? The man is sore injured, after all, and the maid useless. We might show some mercy."

Stuart grunted again, and Deirdre said, "Mistress MacWherter, I might even let you go, once you have served your purpose. But that all depends, does it not, on whether my brother is willing to sacrifice himself for you?"

Chapter Thirty-Eight

Finnan stirred painfully in his bonds when he heard the sound of approaching footsteps. Geordie had left him at some point during the night, when Deirdre returned with her blade, but Finnan sensed he had not retreated far and would be there when Finnan released his hold on this life and slipped into the next.

And what would follow then? Would the two of them—he and Geordie—inhabit some warriors' afterlife consisting of endless battles and wandering? Would there be no peace?

Peace, the trout had whispered in his ear, back in the pool. Aye, but he had chosen revenge. If he could do it all over again…

Ah, and what would he do different? Refuse to avenge his father? Find a way to rescue his sister? Call off his campaign of revenge against Jeannie MacWherter?

Jeannie. A bright image of her flowed into his mind, and his poor heart bounded. If only he might see her one more time.

But he knew he would be granted no such miracle. The stone floor stretched cold at his back, and the bright sky yawned above, mocking him. He had prayed to that sky all night, each time Deirdre employed her blade, driven by the pain not in his flesh but his heart.

And now, when he heard those footsteps, he lacked

the strength to lift his head. How much more could his sister hurt him?

The door of his prison, singed and half burned away, swung open upon three figures: Stuart Avrie, Deirdre, and—

Finnan lost what breath remained in his body. *Nay, nay, nay—*

With a violent shove, Stuart tossed her into the room, her loosed hair a golden flood of brightness, to land on the flagged floor beside him.

"A gift for you, Brother," Deirdre called almost gaily. "Is it not generous of me? I will even afford you some time together, during which you can decide which of you will die first." The two of them, Deirdre and Stuart Avrie, went out and the door of the prison banged shut behind them.

Finnan's heart sank within him, so hard and fast it felt like a mortal injury. During the hours just past, he had not believed he could feel any more desperate. This one moment proved him wrong.

Jeannie had landed hard on the stones and slid. She lifted her head, and he gazed into the blue of her eyes, now darkened by pain.

"Nay," he said again, aloud this time. Her cheek, scraped against the stone, showed a livid abrasion. Her left arm had received similar treatment. The front of her dress was soaked in blood, as were her hands and forearms.

Finnan gasped and choked out, "What ha' they done to you?" If they had harmed her because of him…

He could not bear it.

Jeannie, his Jeannie, warm, sweet, and so welcoming beneath him. So loving…

Aye, and when had he given her his heart, this poor, stunted thing that even now took up a double rhythm, struggling to beat not only for him but for her? Geordie had been right: Finnan loved her; by all the gods, he always had. And so long as she lived, he must keep on living also.

For one blinding, wondrous moment nothing else mattered, not what had happened in the past nor whether they had a future together, just that she was with him now, his whole world beside him.

As if she heard his thoughts, her gaze kindled; she took light from what she saw in his eyes.

"Oh, Finnan, Finnan, thank God."

On hands and knees, she crawled the short distance to reach him. He felt her hands touch his chest, careful for his wounds, saw tears flood her eyes. She should be angry with him—he knew that full well. He had hurt her in the worst way possible and by the most deliberate means he could find. But in her eyes he saw only love; in her touch he felt nothing else. Humility swamped him in a staggering wave. He did not deserve this woman's heart. But gratitude followed the humility, deep and strong, for he could see he possessed it yet.

"What have they done to you?" she sobbed.

"Never mind that." He could scarcely reply, his throat tight with emotion. "Jeannie, forgive me. Forgive me if you can. I know full well I ha' not earned your forgiveness, just as I never earned your love. Not one thing has happened to me since I left your door that I did not deserve for how I used you. I know it. I know it full well." He closed his eyes against one single rush of desire, to impart how he loved her. For he knew they had only moments, and those rushing like sand through the fingers of the gods.

She touched his face, the slightest brush of love, and his heart nearly burst within him. He opened his eyes, and they gazed at one another long.

Perhaps he did not need to tell her, after all. Perhaps the bond that had formed between them at some point even while he sought to hurt her—magical, unpreventable bond—let her feel everything that lay in his unworthy heart. She deserved better, far better. She deserved someone like Geordie, who understood softness, kindness, and the wisdom of choosing love. But he knew until his last breath she had his heart instead, a ragged, damaged gift, but hers completely.

She smiled, wobbly and trembling, through her tears. "Tell me I belong to you," she bade him. "It is all I need to hear."

"Like my breath," he vowed to her, "like my heartbeat. Like everything I am or ever will be."

"Then nothing can part us—not hard words or old anger." Her lips trembled again. "Not death."

"By all that is holy, Jeannie, I am sorry I brought this upon you—"

He got no further because she leaned forward then and covered his mouth with her own.

And what did he sense in that kiss? Her fear, aye, but also her certainty, and enough love to tear down the walls of this prison.

He knew then he had received an answer to his night-long prayers, far better than he deserved. He knew that in the midst of hatred, his heart had found peace.

Her lips left his, touched again very gently, and lingered. Her sweetness lifted and strengthened him.

She raised her head once more, and her light flooded upon him.

"I love you, Finnan MacAllister."

"I love you, Jeannie MacWherter. Faith, I did not know what love was until you came into my life."

"Well, then." The light that embraced him strengthened and united them. "I am complete."

"Are you?" His lips twisted. "'Twould have been far better, love, had I admitted it before all this trouble came upon us. Where is Danny?"

The gladness in her eyes dimmed. "Caught, him and Aggie both. We made a bid to rescue you with the Dowager Avrie as captive. We failed."

"That blood all over you"—his gaze caressed her, as his hands could not—"it is not your own?"

"The Dowager's. We meant to exchange her for your freedom, Finnan. But she sacrificed herself, threw herself against Danny's blade." Darkness flickered in Jeannie's eyes. "How well do you know her, Finnan?"

"I knew her all my life."

"And did you know that she and your grandfather were lovers? That Gregor Avrie was his son, rather than her husband's?" Jeannie licked her lips fretfully. "I think she may have been behind much of this trouble, Finnan. She believed Gregor entitled to an inheritance; I suspect she drove the men of her family to chase it."

Surprise curled through Finnan, battering his already strained emotions. "That means the night he came to Dun Mhor"—the night Finnan's world had fallen apart—"he slew his own half-brother." Finnan's anger stirred again. "And then wed his son to his half-niece." And he, Finnan, had killed his own half-uncle, upon his return to the glen. Ah, the sorrow that had come from all the twisted desire, greed, and hate!

And no way out of it, now. But he had to find a way out of it, for the sake of this woman at his side.

"Jeannie, see if you can free me. We have not much time." Deirdre's cruel version of mercy would not extend long.

"How?" Desperately, she eyed the manacles that bound him. "It needs a key, Finnan."

"See can you loosen the pegs from between the stones." He had worked at just that during the brief intervals he had been alone, between Deirdre's terrible visits, without success. But now he had much more for which to live.

Willingly she slid over the cold stone to reach his wrists. He heard the jangle of the chain as she pulled at it. "The hasps are pounded in tight."

Aye, and surely Stuart Avrie would never have left Jeannie here if she had a hope of freeing him. He had rarely felt so helpless or, were he honest, so frightened—for Jeannie, if not himself.

"I ken so, but try," he urged.

She did. She grunted and pulled with all her might, using her slender body as leverage. Finnan helped as best he might by pulling at the shackle, and felt the skin at his wrist tear, but to no avail.

She sat back on her heels and shook her head. Tears choked her voice when she said, "It is tight."

Finnan thought desperately. "Do you think you can scale a wall and get out?"

She tipped her head up and examined the place. The shelving that had once housed books had burned and fallen away from the stone wall; most of the ceiling gaped open.

"Leave you, you mean?" Her gaze returned to his and locked on. Blood oozed slowly from her scraped cheek, but courage fairly illuminated her. Never had she looked so beautiful. "I will not."

"Please, Jeannie, lass. For she will use you to hurt me." Of all things, he could not bear to witness that.

"These walls are too high. And they will have men keeping watch outside."

Aye, Deirdre would be canny, for she played a game with him. She wanted to see what he would do, whether he would sacrifice himself for Jeannie. He would, in an instant. But if he could not trust Deirdre and her husband, what would that serve?

"Listen to me, Jeannie. This was my Da's room, the very place where he received his mortal wound. He always kept weapons about him. There must be something we can use." He sent his thoughts reaching back over the years. "Go to the fireplace," he told her, his voice a rasp. "Quickly now, before they come. There is a stone on the right hand—six down from the coat of arms. See?"

She scrambled up onto her feet, swayed where she stood. She crossed to the far wall, and he lost sight of her. "Where?"

"There is a loose stone. Draw it out. My father kept a cache of weapons."

"I do not see—ah." He heard her fumble. "It is too hard to pull out, Finnan. I do not think I can."

"You must."

Did she have strength enough? Not the kind required to move the stone, nay, but to use what she might find within. When they came, would she fight to save herself? He could hope for no more.

But he understood now what had prompted his mother's actions on the night his father died. She had sent Finnan off, leaving her beloved daughter behind, because she knew she could go on if at least one of her children remained living. Finnan felt that way for Jeannie, now. So long as she drew breath, saw the sky over her head, beheld beauty...

"It has come loose," she said with a new note in her voice. "There are weapons within."

Chapter Thirty-Nine

"Tell me all the Dowager Avrie said to you," Finnan demanded tersely, "before she died."

"I already have," Jeannie replied with false calm. Finnan could hear so much in her voice now—all the emotions that filled her heart, varied as the colors of this glen he loved. He heard fear and longing and determination like iron.

She sat curled on the stones above his head, working furiously with his father's dirk to loosen the mortar around the shackle that secured his left wrist to the floor. How much time did they have? Surely Deirdre would not leave them together long, unmolested. She and her husband would soon come. Sweat broke out all over his body at the very thought.

"Why did she tell this thing to you?"

Jeannie's attack against the mortar never ceased: *ding, ding, ding.* Would they hear her beyond the scorched doorway?

"She wanted to destroy my hope they would trade her for you. She wished me to know she believed in her cause—that her son and grandsons claimed full right to this place. She seemed to think the blood gifted the claim."

"So it does." Finnan's voice wavered in his own ears. Blood was blood, his own father had taught him that. And what value legitimacy? Could he say the heart had no right to choose? His lips twisted. Feuding was an old game in the highlands, but not usually among blood kin.

Softly, Jeannie went on, "She said your grandfather had promised Gregor a share, but when he died there was no bequest."

So the vassals had remained vassals, and ire had soured the old woman's heart. Finnan could understand that. "Stuart, Trent, and I are cousins," he mused. "As are Stuart and Deirdre. Aye, well, cousins wed often enough in the highlands." It explained why Gregor had thrown off the bonds of loyalty, so many centuries strong.

He found it difficult but not impossible to imagine the Dowager capable of the kind of passion he and Jeannie shared. Yet if he had learned anything these many days past, he had learned that love came as it would, and could not be gainsaid.

He looked at the woman huddled on the floor and felt his heart struggle within his breast. Whatever happened to them—however terrible—he knew at least the love would endure.

Upon the thought, he heard the sound he had been dreading all the while, that of approaching footsteps.

"Jeannie, Jeannie, they come." He implored, "Kiss me one last time."

She complied and bent to him, her lips warm and tender.

"And," he pressed then, "promise to follow as I lead."

"That, my love, I can pledge to do—always."

****

Jeannie's heart beat in sickening thuds as she heard

her captors approach. How long had she and Finnan been here together? She could only guess, but the sun had moved over to the west, creating a pool of shadows on one side of the room. She secreted the dirk in her waistband at the small of her back and shoved the second weapon she had taken from the hidey hole—a longer, bone-handled knife—up her sleeve. Then she stumbled to her feet and backed away from Finnan.

She could barely look at him, for the wounds he bore. Wrists and ankles seeped blood where he had fought the shackles. The older wounds at his shoulder and down his arm had broken open, and many new cuts had been laid.

At the same time, she could not keep her gaze from him. For she knew each glance might be her last.

He loved her. Her laboring heart struggled and bounded in her breast. One miracle, at least, had occurred: the hatred he felt for her on Geordie's behalf had transmuted into this unbreakable bond. Might they not expect yet another such miracle?

The scorched and flame-darkened door opened, and Jeannie prepared herself for what she expected to see: both Avrie brothers and a troop of their men, set on murder. But she saw only Deirdre Avrie with a knife in her hand.

Tall and straight as a spear, Deirdre moved into the room and closed the door behind her.

"Well, Brother? Have you decided how you will die?"

Finnan reared up and met his sister's gaze. "Have you come to kill me by your own hand? Is your hatred so very bright?"

Deirdre had no chance to answer. The door opened

again, and Stuart Avrie stepped in. He, too, came armed, still wearing his sword and, no doubt, with a dirk secreted somewhere about him. His face wore an expression of cautious consternation.

"Wife…" he began.

Deirdre shook her head as if she knew already what he meant to say.

"There has been pain enough," he told her. "Let it be done."

She answered, without ever taking her gaze from her brother, "Aye, so it will be, this day. But first he will suffer. I want him to choose. He must make an impossible choice, even as I did."

Stuart Avrie drew a breath, and his gaze moved over her, considering. "We are so close to having all we ha' ever wanted."

She did turn her head then and look at him. "All *you* ha' ever wanted," she corrected. "Take the glen, Husband. I want only his heart."

Abruptly she switched her gaze to Jeannie, who felt its touch like the bite of cold iron. "Only, I think it no longer lies within his body."

The breath scraped in Finnan's throat as he drew a ragged breath. "Let her go," he said. "She has no part in this."

"Oh, but I think she does." Deirdre's smile looked sharp as the blade in her hand. "Hard to believe my brother could care for anyone—actually experience love—and feel it true. But I suspect 'tis so. He will do anything to save her, Husband. He will seek to save her, as he never did me."

Finnan did not attempt to argue it, merely stared at his sister in mute agony. His chest rose in another convulsive breath. "Only let her go, and I will do anything you ask, die any way you choose."

"Och, you will do whatever I ask, Brother. Remember how it was when I entertained you with my blade all last night? How much better if I give her the same treatment? Cut her face, so 'tis not so pretty. Slice through that white flesh."

"Deirdre," Stuart said, an objection, and she rounded on him, displaying sudden fury.

"You shall not deny me this! Call your brother—the two of you will hold her down while I let her blood. See what he offers us then."

"I offer it now!" Finnan bellowed. "You want my signature on some paper? Bring it. You want my heart bleeding on this floor, Deirdre? Take it. But first you will set her free."

Jeannie's emotions rose like a wild conflagration, like unstoppable flame, and she turned her gaze on the man who arched against the stones. All the strength and loyalty ever he had harbored, and for the sake of which he had fought, was now hers alone. He gifted it to her on the strength of his love, far more than she had ever hoped to gain. Ten years had he battled, so hard had he struggled. This glen meant all to him, yet he laid it—and his life—at her feet.

"Get your paper," Deirdre told her husband. "Call your brother."

"We will no' need Trent to finish this." Stuart drew a paper from inside his vest. Carefully, he circled Finnan as he might a maddened dog on a chain.

"Let her go first," Finnan said again. He did not so much as glance at Jeannie, but nodded at the sheet in Stuart's hand. "And you will need to unbind me if you want my hand on that."

"You will give over all ownership of the glen?" Stuart pressed. "You surrender it to me and mine?"

"So long as you guarantee Mistress MacWherter's safety."

Stuart grunted and slanted a look at his wife. She said nothing, but avid light filled her eyes.

Jeannie had seen Finnan harbor that same light, and fear twisted her gut.

"No," she said, only that, but it snared Deirdre's attention. The woman clutched the knife—the same with which she had cut her brother?—and circled behind Jeannie.

"Go ahead, Husband, unfasten his right hand— bring the ink and let him sign. If he makes one wrong move, she will die."

For answer, Stuart dug into the pouch at his belt and produced pen and ink. He fumbled with those and the sheet of paper, laid them all at Finnan's shoulder. Then he caught up a key that hung on a chain round his neck—that to the shackles, as Jeannie saw.

Her poor, beleaguered heart rose. Dared she hope they might escape this with their lives? Once Avrie had his paper, surely there remained no reason to kill them. He would have full claim to the glen. Yet she could feel Deirdre close behind her, bristling with menace.

Stuart went down on one knee and used the key on the iron at Finnan's right wrist. As soon as it came free, Finnan gave a mighty bellow—Jeannie's name—and heaved his body upward.

All his remaining strength lay in the movement, and it tore the shackle on his other wrist—that on which Jeannie had worked so diligently—from the ancient mortar between the stones. As he rose he swung the chain, still attached to the shackle, in a wide arc that took Stuart Avrie in the side of his face. At the same moment, Jeannie leaped forward out of Deirdre's reach.

"Finnan!" she cried, drew the long knife from her sleeve, and placed it in his waiting hand.

That left her unarmed save for the dirk at the small of her back. She spun to face Deirdre, already looming above her, knife at the ready, and a wild look in her eyes.

All her life Jeannie had lived a civilized existence. The most vicious aspects of Dumfries were its gossip and alehouses; her greatest fears had been want and uncertainty. Now she faced danger at its most primal in the form of Deirdre Avrie with a stained blade in her hand.

Would she rise or fall? Stand or flee? Jeannie spared a thought, if not a glance, for the man on the floor behind her who, from the sound of it, was engaged in a battle of his own. Then she looked deep inside herself. She drew the dirk from her back and leaped at Deirdre Avrie.

Chapter Forty

Finnan ached to know what happened behind him. He could hear that his sister and Jeannie confronted one another, and he knew Deirdre had that wicked, sharp knife in her hands. But he dared not steal so much as a glance over his shoulder, for he found himself in an unholy, unequal battle of his own.

Stuart Avrie had no time to draw his sword or call for his guards once Jeannie passed the long knife into Finnan's grasp. But Stuart, looming over Finnan, had the power of superior position. And Finnan, in a weakened condition and with his ankles still shackled, could not rise to fight.

If he did not overcome Stuart swiftly, Jeannie might well die.

That thought gave him strength. He looped the chain that dangled from his wrist around Stuart's neck and pulled rather than thrust away. Stuart, his face already bloody where the end of the chain had caught him, fell atop Finnan, his weight a crushing blow, and they thrashed together like wrestlers. Finnan grunted, desperate to find room enough to employ the knife.

Stuart, fit and strong, drove his head into Finnan's chest. Finnan fell back, and his skull hit the stones of the floor. For an instant, blackness swam behind his vision. The sounds behind him— unseen and terrifying—gave him the impetus he needed to tighten the chain around Stuart's throat and press the point of the knife beneath the man's ear.

"Call off your wife," he grated. "Call her off, or you die."

Stuart stared into Finnan's eyes, and Finnan experienced a thrill of recognition. Many long years had hatred ruled his life, the need to avenge his father and regain ownership of this beloved place. It had formed and perhaps even warped the man he was. But now he knew Stuart for kin, and to his own surprise did not want to let his blood.

"Deirdre!" Stuart hollered.

But the ugly sounds of two women struggling failed to cease.

****

Jeannie's skin stung in half a score of places where Deirdre had slapped, clawed, or caught her with the edge of her blade. Facing Finnan's sister felt like being snared by one of the sudden, violent highland storms from which there was no escape. Jeannie knew herself badly overmatched; she had not the nature nor the recklessness needed to prevail. Her small dirk seemed inadequate against the longer blade in Deirdre's hand, and fear for Finnan drove her, rather than hatred such as her opponent held.

Hatred and madness.

For she did not doubt she faced a madwoman. And she knew, too, that the rational, civilized woman from Dumfries did not lie far beneath her own surface.

She whirled and tried to stay out of Deirdre's reach as the blade struck out again. Her skirts tangled about her legs, and she very nearly stumbled. She knew without doubt if she fell she would die.

"Deirdre!" Stuart Avrie bellowed. Deirdre's only response was a flicker of her eyes. She never looked away from Jeannie.

How long could Jeannie last? She asked herself the question. How long before the others in the house—Trent Avrie, the guards and hirelings—heard the sounds of confrontation and came running?

She turned again, foundering, as Deirdre lunged, stepped back, and barely caught herself. A terrible smile spread across Deirdre's face, and the light in her eyes intensified.

She thought she had won.

"Deirdre!" This time Finnan called out. "Look at your husband. I ha' finished it!"

Deirdre spun, the stained blade held before her. Jeannie allowed herself to look at Finnan for the first time.

Ankles still shackled to the floor, he crouched above the body of Stuart Avrie.

Deirdre gave a cry; the dreadful, stained blade dropped from her hand. She fell to the floor and then crawled across the stones—much as Jeannie had earlier—to her husband. When she reached him, she covered his body with her own and went as still as he.

She loves him after all, Jeannie thought in amazement. Despite how she had come to be his wife, despite the supposed hatred and desire for revenge that existed between them, they had bonded on some deep level.

She is not so different from me.

Jeannie raised her eyes to the face of the man she loved—her heart, her reason for drawing breath. Emotions shadowed and brightened his features as he looked at his sister, not the least of them tenderness.

"Here, Deirdre." He reached out torn and bloody hands to capture his sister and lift her head. "He is no' dead. Do you hear me? No' dead—you have him yet. Deirdre, lass, let this madness be done. I am sorry for all you ha' suffered and all I did not do to save you. But in the midst of it you have found your heart." He glanced at Jeannie. "As have I."

Deirdre said nothing. She turned her eyes back to her husband, marked his closed eyes, the blood on his face, the shallow rise and fall of his chest.

"Lass," Finnan said, "we are all of one blood, and there is enough room here for each of us. Forgive me?"

Chapter Forty-One

The gloaming came down softly, light hanging long in the western sky, with air soft and kind as a blessing. The stones of the garden wall, firm behind Jeannie's back, still retained the warmth of the day, and not far off the burn, tumbling over the stones of the ford, sang a song wild and sweet.

Not as sweet, though, as what Jeannie could feel emanating from the man beside her.

In the east, away over the hills, the first star appeared in the sky. Jeannie made a fervent wish on it and, as if he heard, Finnan's fingers tightened on hers.

Almost, she did not want to speak and break the spell, so wide and deep. She did not care if she ever emerged from this place where she rested, one in which Finnan MacAllister loved her and nothing in their world could change.

Yet things must be said. So many of them crowded Jeannie's mind she did not know how to begin.

Finnan spoke before she could. "This is gey peaceful. You know that first day when we met, I was lying in that pool trying to learn some wisdom from a trout."

"Eh?" Jeannie turned her head and looked at him. The hazy twilight blurred his features and nearly erased the new wounds he wore.

Finnan MacAllister, as she knew, bore wounds in

plenty. But her eyes could see nothing but perfection.

He gave her the smile she loved, the one that turned her bones to water.

"They will speak to you, you ken, if you lie very still and keep the proper frame of mind."

"Still, and naked?"

The gathered light glinted in his eyes. "That too. The trout did speak to me. He urged me to choose peace."

"An uphill battle on the part of the trout."

"Aye, so. I did not imagine such an elusive thing would ever be available to me. I did not know then I needed only choose love over all else. You taught me that, and far more bonny than any trout."

He leaned toward her, cupped her cheek and very gently laid his lips on hers. Jeannie's heart leaped and sped helplessly, as it would forever when she touched this man.

"It needs only for you to forgive me," he whispered then.

"I already have." Surely he had sensed that, back in the library at Dun Mhor.

"Aye, but I find it hard to reconcile how any woman, be she angel or otherwise, could put aside what I ha' done. Jeannie, I tore your heart out—I hurt you the worst way I could, and on purpose. I chose hate and vengeance even over what I felt for you."

"But you chose love in the end, over everything— even your hate for the Avries." Now she kissed him so softly their lips barely made contact. "Just tell me one thing: is it over? Can we believe Deirdre's heart is truly altered?"

"Nay."

She started. "No?"

"Yet I think we can believe Stuart's is. He, as much as I, wishes an end to the killing and strife. I slew his father, even as his father slew mine. What good will it do to keep that battle alive?" Finnan's fingers caressed Jeannie's face softly. "I suspect he was driven to the worst of his actions by two women—his grandmother and his wife. Like me, he knows we are of one blood. Our families lived here in harmony for centuries. Why not again?"

"But Deirdre?"

"It shook her, thinking she had lost Stuart. It seems she is very like me after all, and I know how I felt, thinking I might lose you."

Again his lips brushed hers softly, the merest whisper of sensation.

Third time is the charm, Jeannie thought fervently. *Only let the spell hold and last all our lives*. For this man carried as many charms about him as battle wounds.

"Will you be able to forgive her? She took a knife to you in hatred."

"Nay, not in hatred: in hurt and fear. If I cannot forgive her, Jeannie, how can I forgive myself? I carried that same bloody banner so long. And it almost cost me everything."

Jeannie drew a breath that seemed to fill her whole body, gazed into his eyes, and said, "I would have suffered far more to win you, Finnan MacAllister. Just promise me one more thing: there will be no more lies or deception between us."

He raised her hand to his lips. "I do so promise."

"Then finish telling me of Culloden."

"Ah." He froze with her fingers caught in his. "Does it matter, Jeannie? Could you not find it in your heart to love a turncoat?"

"Were you a turncoat?"

"In truth I was—twice." He lifted his head and stared away into the rising stars. "At the time of the battle, Geordie and I were in the pay of a chief called Colin Campbell of Ballinore. He had been busy gathering men, you see. We neither knew nor cared why—we seldom did. 'Twas all about the pay, for me. I needed the silver to win my way back here and claim my birthright.

"'Twas not until we mustered and moved out Geordie and I tumbled to the truth—in this battle we stood on the opposite side from men of our own blood and kind. Their fight should have been our own. But Jeannie, you ha' to understand we had gone where sent and killed as bidden for so long. One more battle, I told myself. No different from all the rest. Yet, once the fighting started, it was different."

He narrowed his eyes on the gathering darkness, as if watching over again what had been. "Geordie and I found ourselves stationed on the left flank, facing Kilmarnock's Footguards—Scotsmen all, Scotsmen like us—many of them lads no older than Danny.

"When the battle turned—nay, even before—the Prince, that symbol of right and wrong, of honor and bravery, was persuaded to withdraw and save himself while braver men fought on and died."

Bitterness stole into Finnan's voice. "The connection between myself and Geordie, then, was wide and deep. We had been fighting together a long while, had each other's backs so long we rarely needed to use words to speak. We knew at the same moment we had taken our fill of that battle. When Kilmarnock's began to fall back, we turned and fought with them—defended as many of our fellow countrymen as we could."

He stopped speaking as if what he saw in his mind proved too terrible to relate.

"We survived," he concluded then, in wonder, "even as so many did not. We fought hard, and eventually fell back through a river of Scottish blood. But, Jeannie, I have come to see that Geordie did no' survive, not truly. He was broken that day, struck to his heart. The wound festered and took many years to kill him."

Jeannie said nothing, though she knew it for truth. She had witnessed Geordie's final death throes in Dumfries, whence he had fled in an effort to outdistance a past not even whisky could eradicate.

"He used to talk about it, before we parted." Finnan merely whispered the words. "They dogged him—the men we might have saved during that battle, had we fought shoulder to shoulder with them from the start."

"I never really knew him," Jeannie realized aloud. "I did not meet the man you knew—your brother-at-arms—only the man suffering that mortal wound."

"I should have been there for him." Finnan closed his eyes in pain. "I should have stood with him, had his back as I had done countless times before. Instead I was chasing my hate here, and he fought—and lost—that final battle alone."

It was time, Jeannie thought, for this man she loved so well to give up his fighting, to stop battling conflicts of the past.

"We can change none of that now," she told him. "We can only take what we are given and carry on. Look at me, Finnan."

He opened his eyes and gazed into hers. She felt the strength of him then, firm and steady despite every wound, felt the depth of his love. Joy lifted her heart.

Softly, she said, "Aggie and Danny mean to marry. It seems a fine idea, does it not?"

Light ignited in his eyes. "It needs no priest, Jeannie, to make me yours. I need only swear it on all these things I love—the stones of this place, the water and sky, the fire in my heart."

Jeannie clasped both his hands in hers. "I give myself to you, Finnan MacAllister, all the love I can hold, every day for the rest of my life. And I take you in kind."

One corner of his mouth quirked upwards. "Scars and all?"

"Scars and all," she assured him.

His gaze turned suddenly serious. "Aye, and I give myself to you, Jeannie, with all I possess. And I promise for your sake to lay down my sword at last. As the trout bade me, I will become a new man—one who chooses peace."

Hands still in his, Jeannie leaned closer in the twilight, near enough to catch the flame of devotion in Finnan's eyes. "Not too much changed, I hope," she told him. "For I confess I still desire the man I saw arise from the pool that first afternoon. Will you keep at least some of your wicked highland ways?"

"Only let me show you," Finnan said. And he did.

A word about the author...

Born and raised in Western New York, Laura Strickland has pursued lifelong interests in lore, legend, magic, and music, all reflected in her writing. Though her imagination frequently takes her to far-off places, she is usually happiest at home not far from Lake Ontario with her husband and her "fur" child, a rescue dog.

Author of Scottish romance *Devil Black* as well as The Guardians of Sherwood Trilogy consisting of *Daughter of Sherwood*, *Champion of Sherwood* and *Lord of Sherwood*, she also enjoys writing Victorian-era Steampunk. Her latest release, *Dead Handsome*, is a Steampunk romance set in 1880 Buffalo, with a sequel following. In addition, she has penned two Christmas novellas: *The Tenth Suitor* and *Mrs. Claus and the Viking Ship*, all published by The Wild Rose Press, Inc.

Thank you for purchasing
this publication of The Wild Rose Press, Inc.

If you enjoyed the story, we would appreciate your
letting others know by leaving a review.

For other wonderful stories,
please visit our on-line bookstore at
www.thewildrosepress.com.

For questions or more information
contact us at
info@thewildrosepress.com.

The Wild Rose Press, Inc.
www.thewildrosepress.com

Stay current with The Wild Rose Press, Inc.

Like us on Facebook

https://www.facebook.com/TheWildRosePress

And Follow us on Twitter
https://twitter.com/WildRosePress

www.ingramcontent.com/pod-product-compliance
Lightning Source LLC
Chambersburg PA
CBHW051520260626
47170CB00003B/714